W9-CEV-636

OCT - - 2011

SMITH-ENNISMORE-LAKEFIELD
PUBLIC LIBRARY

THE SAVAGE BREED

**Center Point
Large Print**

**This Large Print Book carries the
Seal of Approval of N.A.V.H.**

THE SAVAGE BREED

RANDY DENMON

CENTER POINT PUBLISHING
THORNDIKE, MAINE

This Center Point Large Print edition
is published in the year 2010 by arrangement with
Kensington Publishing Corp.

Copyright © 2009 by Randy Denmon.

All rights reserved.

This novel is a work of fiction. Names, characters,
places, and incidents are either the product of the
author's imagination, or are used fictitiously. Any
resemblance to actual persons, living or dead,
or events is entirely coincidental.

The text of this Large Print edition is unabridged.
In other aspects, this book may vary
from the original edition.
Printed in the United States of America
on permanent paper.
Set in 16-point Times New Roman type.

ISBN: 978-1-60285-684-4

Library of Congress Cataloging-in-Publication Data

Denmon, Randy.
  The savage breed / Randy Denmon. -- Center Point large print ed.
    p. cm.
  ISBN 978-1-60285-684-4 (library binding : alk. paper)
  1. Ranchers--Fiction. 2. Texas Rangers--Fiction. 3. Mexican War, 1846-1848--Fiction.
  4. Large type books. I. Title.
PS3604.E5857S28 2010
  813'.6--dc22
2009039441

*A*ll new states are invested, more or less, by a class of noisy, second-rate men who are always in favor of rash and extreme measures. But Texas was absolutely over-run by such men.

—SAM HOUSTON

Prologue

Presidio del Norte, Republic of Texas,
April 1846

Travis Ross sat on the porch of the dusty, adobe office, where he usually spent his early evenings, swaying tranquilly in his rocking chair. His right leg crossed over his left, and he played with one of his spurs as he looked out over the mesa at a marvelous rainbow on the horizon. The sun was at his back. And the checkerboard of green and granite, dotted with colorful cacti, yuccas, wildflowers, and sage, gently danced with the late afternoon breeze. Above, a quarter moon rose against the clear, blue sky, and the high-pitched howl of a far-off coyote drifted over the landscape.

Travis loved the evenings. And this one was as beautiful and serene as any he had witnessed. He sucked in a deep breath and picked up his jug of whiskey. His temperament was disgruntled, as it had been for almost as long as he could remember. The day had been long and boring, like all the days for months. He felt as if something was dying inside. He had been in this world for forty years now, the last few the unhappiest. He sensed he was going nowhere; he had nothing to keep his mind occupied, as if he were only waiting around to die in this land so far from anywhere.

He stared out at the brown Chisos Mountains—only a tangled, mysterious mass of lava outcroppings—falling away in the distance and hovering like a raised oasis in the throes of the desolate Chihuahuan Desert. The peaceful mountains put him in a reflective mood, let him sort through his memories and think back to more blissful times. The sound of leather boots on the wood plank floor behind him broke him from his thoughts.

"Those fence posts aren't going to unload themselves," his longtime partner, Chase McAlister, scoffed in a loud, irritated voice from the doorway behind the porch.

Travis did not nuisance himself with turning to look at Chase, but did glance down at the ramshackle horse wagon loaded with pine posts in front of the porch. "If you thought I was going to unload 'em while you were in there taking a nap, maybe it's getting time for you to take up the rocking chair."

"Wasn't taking no damned nap—paying the bills, doing some paperwork. This is a business, if you haven't forgotten," Chase countered. "Ranchin's a tough job."

"I don't know if those posts will ever get unloaded," Travis said lazily. "You done run all the Mexicans off—worked 'em to the bone. Sent 'em all back across the river. It's bad when life is better in Mexico than it is at the M&R Ranch. It's only my gambling and cardplaying prowess that enables us to eat around here. I've got Hancho in there so indebted, he can't afford to quit cooking for us. You ought to be grateful for that."

"I'm going to run Hancho off if he keeps letting those chickens run loose around here—stinks the place up and makes us look like a roughshod outfit. You, too, if you don't start doing something."

Travis lifted his jug to his mouth and took a big swig. "You promise? I'll make you a deal: you can have my half of the riches we've made here."

"You ain't supposed to be drinking during working hours. You're supposed to be working."

"I *am* working. On the lookout for Indians. You know, those red-skinned heathens that gave you that big scar on your chest. Don't know what we're going to do when the Mexicans close that fort across the river. Besides, I need a drink every now and then. Ain't seen a white woman in months."

"I guess this is my folly. Thinking I could come down here and christen a ranch with the biggest loafer in Texas."

"Hell, no, it's my fault. I was dumb enough to sign on. Sounded romantic, sitting around the bar in San Antone. Maybe you're right. I should give up whiskey."

Travis heard the footsteps again. They got closer to the front of the porch. He slowly turned to look at the tall, rugged, powerful figure, resting his broad shoulders against one of the porch columns. Chase McAlister was a month short of forty. His brown hair was departing and his skin looked wind weathered and tan. He had a square jaw—a brawny, confident face. But overall, his appearance was youthful, contrasting with his alert hazel eyes; they told of age and wisdom. And he carried a strange swagger of vanity and virtue. Most knew he had the character and stomach to back it up. Travis looked at Chase's knee-high leather boots, leading up to his brown cotton trousers, topped with a leather waist holster holding a Colt five-shot revolver—above the pistol, a neat, white, button-down shirt. Travis's partner was his opposite—someone content to be alone.

"We got company coming." Travis picked up his jug again and nodded to the dirt trail leading up to the ranch house, an unsightly scar on the pristine landscape. A few stems of dust stood above the mesa, a quarter mile distant. Just as he spoke, Travis discerned a horse bouncing through the illusion of the belated sun.

"Hell, if my vision's not failing me, I believe that's Chester Woods," Chase said in a matter-a-fact way.

Travis squinted, but the light buzz from his jug precluded good focus. "Chester? What the hell's he doing way out here?" Travis sluggishly got to his feet with interest. Guests were rare at the M&R, and his spirits perked at the thought of a new sparring partner, someone other than Chase. He might even be able to get up a card game, one that might actually require the use of his brain.

Travis put his right hand above his eyes as the tall sorrel trotted up to the porch, kicking up a small dust storm. He looked at the rider, who pulled back on his reins, bringing his horse to a sliding stop in front of the porch. Atop the horse and awash in dirt, Chester was only a body clad in trousers, topped with a white shirt and hat. "I'll be damned," Travis said. "The Texas Rangers finally got here. You're too late. We already run off all the Comanches."

Chester wiped the earth from his brown eyes and young, unshaven face before removing the hat from his sandy blond head. With a subtle smirk, he looked around briefly at the three run-down shacks that made up the M&R headquarters. "About like I figured. You're not cut out for hard labor, Travis." He turned and nodded his head to Chase. "Captain McAlister."

"You probably won't be here long. Unfortunately, we don't have a fine hotel or brothel in town." Travis stepped forward and grabbed the horse's reins. "But we do have a cook."

"What brings you out here?" Chase said in a deep, serious voice.

"Colonel Walker sent me. General Taylor has authorized him to raise four regiments of Rangers —for the war. Speck he'll be moving south before long."

"Colonel Walker?" Chase replied.

"Yeah, now that we're part of the army, he's a colonel. Hell, they made me a lieutenant," Chester answered as he dismounted. "He thought you boys might be tired of living the honest life . . . I suspect you'd both be elected company captains or better. That is, if you're interested in mustering on."

"Can't speak for Chase, but my fighting days are over. You know that. Ten years was enough; I've seen enough killing for one lifetime," Travis said, extending a hand and helping Chester up on the porch.

"What about Tony Flores? Any truth to the rumor that he's taken up arms for the Mexicans?" Chase asked, again in a sincere voice.

"Yes, sir," Chester answered. "He's signed on to fight with Rayo."

"Rayo," Chase said, lifting his eyebrows and looking at Travis.

"I guess every man's got to pacify his own soul," Travis added. "It would be difficult for me to take up arms against men I've fought with under any circumstances. And it's about time Señor Rayo gave up fighting."

"War's coming," Chester said. "You can't run from it. The Mexican army will be here some-time. You'll have to fight them one way or the other. Or fight the Indians if they leave. I guess you could sit around here raising stock for Little

Face . . . wait for him and his braves to come get your horses *and* your scalps."

Chase groaned and mumbled. His eyes narrowed. "Don't you worry. I'm going kill that Injun one day."

Travis laughed. He patted Chester on the back. "Enough of this talk of war and scalps." He handed Chester the jug and reached over to rub the top of Chase's almost bare head. "You know how it stirs up Captain McAlister. He doesn't have any hair to give. Let's go inside and have a drink. You can tell me what all the boys are up to."

"To tell you the truth," Chester admitted, slapping his hat against his legs in an attempt to extract some dust, "I thought you two would be eager to get back across the border. See some people you haven't seen in a few years. Finish any unfinished business you might have, especially you, Travis."

Travis turned to look down at the crystal-clear Rio Grande, then across the river to the enigmatic, gorgeous arroyos leading off to the sunset. What waited in that land he had not entered in a decade? What inner demons lurked just over the horizon that he wanted to service? His enemies were there: the evil bandit Paco Medina and the cunning Comanche Little Face—both had evaded him for years. Also, the woman he loved and longed for was there. Would he ever go back across that river? He had given up the gun to pacify his soul. He would have to take it back up to go. Was he prepared to do that? He had been thinking it over, struggling with the decision for months.

"Lot of old scores to settle over there," Chester continued. "Bunch of Mexicans betrayed Texas during the revolution. Thought you might want to be around when we get there . . . might have some things to settle down there."

Travis sighed deeply. His stomach lurched, and he felt his skin grow cold as he turned to Chase. The two exchanged silent stares for a few moments before strolling inside.

PART ONE

Chapter 1

Travis nonchalantly strode up to the sturdy, stucco walls of the governor's palace. It was a cool, fall evening, perfect for the annual celebration of independence. Loitering outside the handsome residence, a couple dozen *patróns* talked in their best outfits— men in light, white jackets, ladies in their finest evening dresses, priests in their black cassocks, soldiers in their gaudy uniforms. Atop the white ramparts, guarding the building on all sides, colorful red, green, and white regalia, illuminated by a score of burning torches, fluttered with the soft breeze and made the residence stand out dramatically against the dingy and dull backdrop of the town.

Travis tipped his hat to several people he recognized as he entered the house, which was so full of gaiety, the chattering and gossip filled his ears before he crossed the threshold. Two young soldiers, clad in meticulous uniforms, stood at attention at the entrance. Travis paused at a large mirror in the foyer to scrutinize his dress and tidy his disposition. He removed his hat and spent a few minutes admiring himself—his youthful, thirty-year-old face; his long, combed brown hair; his blue eyes; and his tall, lean figure all made up his

17

affable, optimistic appearance. He adjusted his beige coat and pulled up his matching slacks until their position passed his inspection. Travis certainly enjoyed advertising his easy, comfortable nature.

He finally brushed his thin mustache a few times and turned to inspect the large ballroom. The floor was full, alive with the motion and noise of bodies, ladies' hand fans, and servants. Behind the crowd, a five-piece military band strummed patriotic songs. A short mestizo man, dressed in a nice white jacket and carrying a tray of drinks, offered Travis a glass of wine that he accepted.

As Travis scanned the ballroom for familiar faces, he caught sight of the woman in the crowd. Her green eyes stood out against her pure white skin and long yellow hair. She turned and made eye contact, eyes wide and round, penetrating, even from across the room. She moved elegantly toward him, emerging from the crowd. Travis noticed her long, fine lines and well-proportioned hips, cloaked with a long, proper skirt containing a slight slit that occasionally exposed a supple lower leg with her easy stride.

As the woman moved closer, her face gained life, and with it, more attractiveness—sumptuous female perfection. Her lashes were long, dark, and full of life. She returned Travis's stare with a spunky smile, causing Travis to bashfully turn away. But he continued to feel the weight of her stare. He could sense her getting closer. He looked back around to find himself face to face with her. Her collar was tall and stiff, signifying something proper, he thought. And her mannerisms were dignified. She stepped closer with polite correctness and extended a silent hand.

Travis returned the gesture, quietly appreciating the lovely woman for a few moments.

"I could not help but notice you admiring me from afar," the woman finally said in perfect English. "Thought I'd introduce myself. My name is Mercedes Rayo."

"You're as beautiful a female specimen as I've seen in these parts," Travis said self-assuredly. He politely bowed. "I'm—"

"Lieutenant Travis Ross . . . the famous Indian fighter. And I'm sure you've seen many women much more beautiful than I."

Travis recoiled from his bow and took a sip of wine. "Well, I must confess. Your candor complements your looks."

Mercedes giggled and her eyes danced with amusement.

"Your laugh is wholesome and unabashed," he said, "a slip of etiquette, but very enticing . . . I hate crowded places. Too noisy in here. You want to go out to the veranda?"

Mercedes nodded, and Travis led her a few paces to a door. Outside lay the idyllic and star-filled Texas night. Travis lit a cigarette while Mercedes sat down in a chair, folding and smoothing her dress over her thighs. "Your English is excellent," he said. "Where are you from?"

"Coahuila. A proud Mexican. And you?"

"England, but I grew up on the Sabine River." Travis paused, thinking as he ashed his cigarette into one of the immaculate flower beds abutting the patio. "Are you daughter of Javier Rayo?"

"I am."

"Then you're a very wealthy woman."

"Yes. That is if you measure wealth in only tangible things, such as land."

"What are you doing here?"

"I've been on the east coast with my aunt. I'm on my way to my father's ranch in Laredo."

"A proud Mexican. That's rare around here. What do you think of all the talk of war?"

"There's no talk in my family. We're Mexican through and through. My father fought in the War of Independence. Mexico has rewarded him well. I just wish all the problems would go away . . . and I could meet a handsome, dashing Ranger who would sweep me off my feet." Mercedes grinned mischievously and rolled her eyes.

Travis stood speechless, staring at the woman like a man does when he thinks he might be looking at the right woman for the very first time. This one oozed a sort of smoldering passion that intrigued him. He turned and walked to a colonnade. He rested his shoulder on the stucco column and looked out from the palace to the limestone walls of the Alamo fortress, a quarter mile across the San Antonio River, its white face illuminated by lanterns. He turned to look at the other imposing structures of the town: the San Fernando Church and the Bexar Customs Exchange, an imposing monolith of stone, four stories tall. In the distance, he saw the other Spanish missions, all imposing edifices with tall spires and bell towers, marvelously lit and standing commandingly over the mass of rickety adobe shacks.

"It's beautiful, isn't it?" Mercedes said, walking up beside him.

"Yes." Travis turned away from the town to look at Mercedes.

She brushed her hair back and held her head up to face the cool breeze.

"Does a few minutes on the patio with a handsome, dashing Ranger get your temperature up and juices flowing?"

Mercedes bowed her head, trying to hide a laugh.

"These parties aren't really for me," he said. "You want to go for a walk along the river?"

"I don't know. That might be a tad much. I only just met you. I don't know if I'm ready for that —might overheat. Especially if you're as chivalrous and quick-witted as the local papers make you out to be."

"Most of that is exaggerated, but not all of it." Travis laughed, reaching out and grabbing Mercedes's willing hand. He then stepped off into the darkness of the night.

Chapter 2

January 1836

Travis sat up in bed, shivering, and pulled the wool blanket up to his neck. A cold winter wind heaved at the wooden door, rattling its rusty bolt as the firm gusts whistled through the diminutive adobe house, fraught with cracks. He wiped the sleep out of his foggy eyes and looked over at a small cast-iron stove beside the bed. Mercedes was stoking a fire, only a quilt over her firm body.

"Come back to bed," Travis mumbled. "I'll go fetch some more firewood."

"I'd love to, but I have to get up and get going. I have to go to Mass with my family today," Mercedes replied, continuing to stir the fire. She looked over her shoulder and smiled at Travis. "I must ask for forgiveness for all my transgressions with you."

"I've got to go see your father today myself. And then I have to go back to San Antonio." Travis looked out the window at the gloomy, uninviting day, aglow with thick, white clouds whose bright glare stung his eyes.

"Do you have to go so soon?" Mercedes turned and kissed Travis on the lips before slowly crawling back into the warm bed. "Do you want me to draw you a bath?"

"No."

"All this war talk scares me. I worry about you and my family. What will happen? Can't we just go to Saltillo? There's no war there. I'm sure my father could ensure you get a good post with the Regulares."

"It's not that simple, love. I'm a Texan. If Texas declares independence, I'll be with Texas. After all, I *am* a Texas Ranger. And if I went to Mexico, I would be disgraced. I could never be a Regulare; they might force me to take up arms against the Rangers and Texans. I could never do that."

"Why is all this happening? And you're not a Texan, you're a Mexican."

"I was once an American, like most Texans. We came here while Mexico was a republic. Now it's not. Santa Anna rules. The Anglos, myself included, will never tolerate that, or being forced to conform to Catholicism, or put up with these Mexican soldiers trampling on our rights, or any more of his tyrannical rules."

Mercedes put her soft hand on Travis's chest and began to gently massage his ribs. She looked up at Travis, a few silent tears forming in her deep, piercing eyes. "I am scared. I may never see you again. I cannot accept the thought of you fighting my family—or of something happening to you."

Travis took in a deep breath and looked down at Mercedes's long, feminine fingers stroking his chest. "There's nothing I can do about it. Santa

Anna shouldn't have invaded Texas. But don't worry so much. This all may turn out to be nothing. And if there is a fight, it will be against Santa Anna. Texans and Mexicans don't want to fight each other.Texas has no animosity toward Mexicans—only the current Mexican government, which most Mexicans hate anyway."

Travis grabbed Mercedes's hand, and the two made eye contact. He sensed that his words carried little solace for her, and he reached over and ran his hands through her hair a few times, almost feeling the anxiety in her warm, tense scalp. "Don't worry. I'll never do anything to harm you. The sooner this is over, the sooner we can get married."

Mercedes sniffled a few times, and wiped a tear from her faultless, pale cheek with the palm of her hand. She started to murmur a reply, but a loud bang on the door startled the two.

Travis's heart skipped a beat as he sat up alertly, reaching over for his revolver, hanging holstered on the bedpost. "Who is it?" he yelled.

"It's just me," a muffled voice said through the door.

"Well, come in," Travis said, relaxing and leaning back in bed as he watched the door open and Chase, bundled in a long overcoat, casually come into the room. "I wasn't expecting you for a few more days."

"Your week-long siesta's over. Major Williamson is rallying the company in San Antonio the day after tomorrow," Chase said bluntly. He removed his hat briefly and held it to his chest in deference to the young lady, then squatted by the stove to warm his hands. "You ready to go?"

"Don't I look ready?" Travis answered, reaching over to the small table beside the bed and picking up his brass pocket watch. "I guess I don't have any choice. Let me say my good-byes to the well-heeled señorita, and I'll meet you at the old mission in an hour."

"Make it thirty minutes," Chase said, and stood. He walked over to the bed and put the back of his hand on the cheek of the still-troubled Mercedes. "Too damn cold out there to hang around an hour . . . where in the hell did you ever find a beautiful, blond Mexican out here in the middle of nowhere? Much less get her to crawl in bed with you. She must have bad eyes."

"Aw, I don't know. Found her on the trail some-where. Not sure she's worth all the trouble. But her eyes are fine." Travis stirred Mercedes's hair playfully.

Chase smiled and looked down at Mercedes. "Don't worry. I won't let him get into any trouble that he can't get out of. We'd both probably feel a lot better if you'd go back to Mexico where you'll be safe."

"Go on and get out of here," Travis retorted loudly. "I need to get started. You know how difficult it is for women to say good-bye to me."

Mercedes laughed, but tears again filled her glorious eyes. "Get him out of here before he keeps misbehaving and I banish him for good," she said.

An hour later, Travis rode within sight of the small Agustin Mission, just outside of the almost deserted pueblo of Laredo. Ahead, beyond the town, lay the harsh chaparral and brush country of the Rio Grande Plain, destitute of water and fit for only meager cattle grazing and bands of outlaws, scorpions, and tarantulas. The scorpions and tarantulas caused as much fear in Travis's mind as the shrewdest bandit; nightmares of these creepy creatures crawling in his bedroll had prevented him from having a peaceful night under the stars for years.

As his short, stocky, black and tan paint mustang dodged the thorn scrub and mesquite, Travis stared into the distance. It would be a hard and fast trip to San Antonio, which entailed traversing one of the most hostile and foreboding landscapes on the continent. Since the onset of strife between Texas and Mexico, the strip of land lying between the Nueces and Rio Grande Rivers had become totally devoid of law and citizens—save for a few isolated ranches.

As he adjusted his buckskin jacket and chaps, essential for riding the prickly plain, Travis finally saw Chase, visible atop his horse, at the mission's gate. Travis's mount clopped over a small wooden bridge, then loped toward Chase, who was loading his Colt. He had removed the revolver's cylinder and was currently placing percussion caps into the chamber's bored holes as he packed the powder charges and balls into place.

"Day after tomorrow—that will be a long, tough haul," Travis said, removing a hanky from his pocket and polishing the shiny, two-inch Ranger badge affixed to his jacket.

Chase reinserted the cylinder into the pistol and sniffed the pure, cold desert air. "Traversing the brush with an idler like you won't be easy, but we'll make it." He handed Travis half a loaf of hardened bread and lit a cigarette. "She's too young and good-looking for you."

"Women don't ever get too young for us. We just get too old for them. I guess I'm aging with grace." Travis grabbed a nine-inch knife, which had been secured to his waist, and cut the bread into a few mouth-sized chunks. He looked over at Chase's horse, an antsy, long-legged bay mare, laden with two large water skins, two straw foliage sacks, and a mix of other weapons and supplies. Travis removed one of the water skins and a haversack filled with jerked beef, and secured them to his mount to lessen Chase's load. "I guess we better get on with it. Let's go see Rayo on the way out of town. We might make the Nueces by nightfall. We'll be lucky if we don't have to shoot a bandit or an Injun between here and there. Hope you loaded a couple of spare drums." Travis spurred his mustang and trotted off, leading Chase.

It was only a casual ten-minute ride to the Hacienda de Rayo del Norte, and the two Rangers approached the ranch's headquarters via a half-mile dirt drive sided by aged cottonwoods. Two expensive carriages and a few well-groomed horses were parked outside the grand, square limestone structure dominating the countryside.

Travis and Chase dismounted and looked around at the hacienda, a tidy arrangement of courtyards, corrals, and well-constructed buildings. A half dozen men loitered on the grounds: a few desperadoes, cattle hands, and two Lipan Indians, decorated with feathers and paint. Travis looked up atop a twenty-foot flagpole to see a Mexican flag fluttering, a rarity in these parts. "How many of the Mexican landowners are falling in line with the rebellion?"

"About half. Each half is more stirred up about the other than either is about the Texans." Chase paused and smiled. "Got a regular blood feud going on. It probably won't be settled any time soon."

Sided by Chase, Travis entered the house, passing through the spacious entrance hall. The fifty-year-old Javier Rayo stood in his large, plush living room sipping a glass of cognac from fine crystal. To the casual eye, he looked the part of a *haciendado*—short, wiry, and proud, with jet-black hair and skin browned from exposure. He was covered with ostentatious and colorful aristocratic riding clothes, apt for a horse parade but hardly fitting for trudging the backcountry.

"Good morning, Señor Rayo," Travis said, politely stopping at the far side of the room. He looked up briefly at the portraits of three generations of Rayos adorning the walls, the bronze Spaniards all eying him.

"Would you like a drink? Good French brandy," Rayo said in accented English. He walked toward the two Rangers.

"No. I won't be drinking for a while . . . From the looks of things, I guess you've taken sides." Travis looked at Rayo's midnight eyes; as always, they were intense, rowdy, brash, and outgoing.

"I've not only taken sides, I intend to take up the fight against these treasonable rebels," Rayo continued, stopping in front of Travis and squaring his shoulders.

Travis stood quietly for a few seconds before speaking. "I'm sorry that you've come to that decision. It's the wrong one. I wish you would side up with us. Texas could use good men like you. The cause is just. And I hope we can still be friends." Travis extended a hand. "But if that's your decision, I won't pester you further."

Rayo accepted Travis's hand cordially and offered a handshake to Chase. "I actually wanted to make you two an offer . . . to fight for Mexico. Your skills are exemplary. Mexico would like to keep you in her service. Of course, you would never be asked to take up a fight against Texans, but we need tough men to suppress some of the other areas of the country that have revolted against Mexico City." Rayo paused and thought solemnly for a few moments. "You could be greatly rewarded—maybe a land grant. You two could have a good life, a lot better than trolling these dusty trails protecting your scalps."

Travis listened to the words, not at all wanting to hear them. He faced the Mexican jefe with an outward show of indifference. But in fact, deep inside, he had spent months struggling internally with this, flipping and flopping back and forth. Would he fight for what he believed in or join the Mexican army? Technically, he currently served at the pleasure of the Mexican government. But he had finally decided he had only one choice, the only one he could live with. But he was sacrificing much. And he knew Rayo had an ace in the hole, his alluring, almost entrancing daughter. Could he ever really tell her no or say good-bye to her?

"No, I've made my mind up. I'm with the Anglos," Travis answered, and looked at Chase, who nodded in agreement.

"Can I get you boys anything before you go: food, water, fresh horses?" Rayo said.

"I think we've got what we need," Travis answered as a set of footsteps caught his attention. He turned to look. "Good morning, Francisco."

"My son will ride with me," Rayo proudly said,

putting his arm around the young man as he approached.

Travis gazed at Francisco, only twenty years of age. He was in tailored riding clothes, similar to his father's, with a red bandana around his neck. Francisco was a good-looking lad, with black hair and pale skin. Travis often thought he looked like Spanish royalty, like an aristocrat, whatever that meant. And Francisco acted the part, his manner refined, charming, and gregarious. It was not hard for Travis to imagine that many a young lady was easily wooed by his well-kept appearance. In fact, Travis had always been fond of Francisco, thinking the young man reminded him of himself in his youth—or at least his own image of himself. "How are you, my amigo?"

"Well, and you?"

Travis took a deep breath, for the first time he felt himself getting jittery around these men whom he might soon be fighting. He felt that way especially about Francisco, who had so much to lose. He liked him so much. Did the young Mexican have any idea what might be ahead?

"It is good to see you." Travis extended his hand anew to Rayo, then to Francisco. "So long, my fine friends. I sure hope, and I pray to God, that I don't see you two anytime soon, especially through a gun sight."

"I hope not," Rayo said, lifting up his glass of brandy. "But if we do, it won't be personal."

Chapter 3

The dusty, thorny prairie was shaded a stunning gold the next morning when Travis and his partner recommenced their journey north. The two had enjoyed a short but uneventful night, encamped in a heavy thicket on the banks of the Nueces. The sky had cleared, and the new day held the promise of cherished warmth. As Travis followed Chase down the little-used but well-defined trail, the morning sun showed the scenery getting greener, and acacias, oaks, and buffalo grass began to supplant the sage and cacti.

Not an hour into the ride, Chase tightened his reins, bringing his mare to a slow stop.

"What's up?" Travis inquired, pulling up next to Chase, who nodded his head toward a small cloud of dust rising from the earth a mile up the trail. Travis strained his eyes at the wide panorama, currently stretching from flat plain to rolling hills. A few winks of silver in the brown blur told him the riders, whoever they were, were well armed. "Mexicans?"

"I doubt it. They haven't crossed the Los Olmos River yet. And I've never seen a Comanche or Apache stir up that much dust."

While Chase spoke, Travis thought he heard a few gunshots in the distance; any noise carried for miles in this country. He looked at Chase, studying his reaction. The two had a bond carved from many battles. They were friends, but Travis trusted Chase like no other, and knew his moods and thoughts like the back of his own hand. Chase's look of worry infused Travis with cold concern.

"Whoever it is, they're in one hell of a hurry south. Let's ride up on one of these hills and investigate." Chase slapped his horse on the neck with his hat, and the mare reared sideways before racing headlong off into a thicket.

Only a minute later, Travis topped a small hill and made a running dismount. He removed his field glasses from his saddle and rested his eyes and elbows on the back of his horse.

"Hell, that's Texas Rangers chasing somebody," Chase suggested, also studying the posse in a similar position.

"Whoever they're chasing is ducking into the river," Travis added. Through his binoculars, the men in question were only faint images. But Rangers were easy to spot, with their red shirts, white hats, and familiar repeating pistols.

"Let's go give 'em a hand." Chase put his glasses back in a saddlebag and quickly remounted.

Ten minutes later, Travis led Chase, angling through the brush to the dusty north bank of the Nueces River. The gunfire had subsided. Ahead, down the riverbank a hundred or so yards, he saw the lawmen, circling on horseback, trying to pick up a track. He cupped his mouth with a hand and yelled, "Lieutenant Travis Ross! We're coming in. Don't shoot."

In the small opening, the three Rangers came into view, and Travis knew two of them: Chester Woods and Tony Flores, seasoned veterans. Flores had mestizo blood, all 120 pounds of him: tiny, dark, and humble, but with a heart as big as a wagon wheel and fortitude envied by the entire Ranger contingent. Both men had been under Chase's or Travis's command during the first Ranger engagements with the Comanches around the Brazos.

"They hit the river back a piece and then moved east," Chase said. "Who were they?"

"Bandits," Chester answered. "Robbed a store in Cotulla. Killed an old man for two horses and six dollars."

Travis turned in his saddle, looking out at the lonely land and giving the backdrop a weary inspection. It was still mid-morning, the day barely holding its cool nip. He rode over and shook Chester's hand, then Tony's. "Good to see you, Sergeant Flores. What you boys doing way down here?"

"Looking for you two. There's been a change of plans. Got orders from Major Bob Williamson himself," Chester said, boasting. "I quote: Get their sorry asses over to Goliad with all haste. Report to Colonel Fannin there. And no dabbling in watering holes and gambling houses—there's a fight coming."

Travis and Chase laughed.

"I can see Bob's never been to south Texas," Travis added. "But if we win this war, I may open up a gambling and sinning establishment. You sure need one after crossing this depressing bush." Travis turned to the third Ranger, a young, freckle-faced, whiskerless man—almost a boy—with clean clothes and a new pistol. "Who's the pup?"

"This here is Private James Fitzmorris—just signed on," Chester replied.

Travis followed Chase over to the young man, and the two formally introduced themselves.

"James," Travis said, "I'm glad you gave your body to the cause. We need it. But what they didn't tell you is that when you sign on with this bunch, you're giving your soul to the Devil."

Chase and Tony snickered, and Travis turned to see both men's smiles stretching to their ears.

"Well, if the good Major Williamson says we better get to Goliad, we better get going. We'll follow the river east. Might find these bandits and administer some justice," Travis continued, gently kicking his heels against his pony.

Mid-afternoon found Travis and the Rangers lying on their stomachs, inspecting a deep ravine cradling the Nueces River. The Texas sun was at their backs, illuminating the flat, white rocks, the maroon dirt, the yellow foliage, and the clear, indigo river trickling peacefully along. Travis was studying three men camped at a bend in the river, almost a quarter mile downstream. The Texans had tracked the outlaws to here, almost twenty miles from the Laredo trail.

"That one standing is Rubio Medina," Chase whispered, continuing to look through his field glasses.

"You sure?" Travis said in a low voice, looking at the suspect in question, a short, skinny, dark-skinned man wearing a bright green shirt. From this distance, few details were discernible, but Travis had learned over the years that his partner was rarely wrong, his vision acclaimed to be the best south of the Brazos River. "How can you tell?"

"I just can. The way he moves. Nobody else wears a big black and red sombrero. That's his two brothers with him."

"Really," Travis said with interest, moving his glasses from the man standing to the other two bandits, lying under the shade of a small oak. "You think one of those is Paco?"

"He ain't got but two brothers," Chase answered.

"You know these thieves?" Tony said softly.

"Wretched lot of outlaws—horse thieves, murderers, marauders," Travis answered. "One of those two under the tree is the chief *federale* for Coahuila. They do most of their plundering on the border or south of it. Likely up here because the arrival of the Mexican army has put them out of business down there."

"He's a thief *and* he's the state police?" Chester asked. "No wonder the Mexicans are revolting."

"Rubio's the bad one—mean as a snake," Chase continued. "They call him Diablo. Would rather cut your throat than look at you. Paco's just as crooked, but he lets Rubio do most of the dirty work—covers for him most of the time. Don't know the other brother, but with blood like that, he can't be a saint."

"What happened to the other three? We were tracking six," Chester asked.

"Probably branched off to camp somewhere else. Mexican bandits usually break their campsites up into several locations," Travis mumbled, scanning as far as the eye reached for anything unusual.

"I'm going to shoot that son of a bitch right now," Chase said with a calm voice. "Rubio's got a bounty on his head. We'll just leave him right there for the coyotes and move on."

"You can't hit him from here," Travis retorted.

"Yeah, I can," Chase answered. "Tony, go get me that Kentucky long rifle and ammo pouch off my horse."

"You're just going to stir them up like a bunch of pissed-off fire ants," Travis said, turning to look back at the river and the tiny image of the men in the distance. "Mexicans get worked up over family. You'll probably rile 'em up even if you miss."

"I'm not going to miss. They'll never know what hit him. We'll move out of here quietly and on to

Goliad. I've been wanting a chance to shoot this bastard for several years—not going to pass up the chance. Besides, if I kill him, especially with this shot, word will get back to Goliad before we do. I'll ride in there like a hero with all my admirers."

"If you miss, you'll be the laughingstock of the bar at Johnny's tomorrow night," Travis answered.

Chase grabbed the fifty-inch, nine-pound, maple-stock rifle from Tony and opened the small leather ammo pouch. He sat the rifle on the ground, butt first, and removed a wooden powder horn from the ammo bag. He carefully poured the fine black powder into the barrel, measuring the quantity meticulously as he slowly tapped the horn with his forefinger. He then removed a cotton patch and sphere-shaped, fifty-caliber ball from the pouch. He placed the patch on the end of the barrel and the slug in his mouth, wetting it nicely before placing it on the patch. With his thumb, he gently pushed the slug down the barrel, then removed the long, steel ramrod, stored below the stock, and rammed the slug to the base of the barrel, smoothly seating it against the powder with several light strokes.

Travis smiled at the other Rangers as he watched Chase take up a comfortable position on the bank, chest and elbows on the dirt. Chase made a small bench out of some rocks and rested the rifle, decorated with ornate brass, on the rocks. He cocked the rifle's hammer and secured a tiny percussion cap to its tip.

"Get your pistols ready, boys. We may have a fight on our hands," Travis murmured softly.

Chase pulled the curved silver plate of the butt securely to his shoulder and adjusted the double-set trigger, allowing the front trigger to collapse with a hair's touch. He licked his finger and held it high to check the wind, more show than anything else, before putting his cheek to the stock.

Travis looked back at the creek. Rubio was still standing, glaring in the late-day sun. Travis and the other Rangers got deathly still. Travis felt his stomach move with apprehension and anticipation. A few seconds passed slowly. He heard the metallic click of the hammer fall, a small pop, and an instant fizzle before the earsplitting eruption. Travis trained his eyes on Rubio—maybe a second's delay. The man tumbled backward. The hush held for a few more seconds before some screaming drifted up from the river.

Travis raised his glasses. The two men in the shade were scurrying for the cover of thicker brush, up the riverbank. He looked at Chase, who wore a big smile. "What a shot," said Travis. "I'll be forced to hear about this for years. Let's get out of here. We'll be lucky if any of us ride into Goliad by tomorrow."

Chase stood up and dusted his pants. "You mean like the old bandit you gunned down up on the Brazos? You've exaggerated and retold that story so much, it's nothing but a fable now."

On Chase's words, the five Rangers promptly mounted and struck out from the river, storming into the sage. The group rode hard for a half hour before they heeled atop the pinnacle of a hill, spelling their horses and allowing an inspection of the ground below.

"Our horses are pretty near spent for now. And we need to find some water," Chase said, breathing heavily.

Travis looked at the horses, their coats dripping wet and spotted with salt lines. He patted his paint's wet neck. The group was all staring into the valley below and the approaching cloud of unsettled dust. "They're on our tail. Ground's not fit for covering our tracks, and I don't think we're going to outrun them. We're going to have to fight." As he spoke, Travis pulled his Colt five-shot revolver from its holster. He checked to make sure it was fully loaded, then slowly spun the cylinder a few times to check its freedom, the action producing several eerie clicks. He held up the pistol, muzzle pointing skyward.

"Shouldn't be difficult," Chase said. "We'll split up. I'll take Chester and Private Fitzmorris with me. You and Tony will break off and double back behind this hill at a place where you won't kick up much dust. We'll drive on, making a big dust storm, and then find a place for good defense. That will suck them in, and you and Tony will come in from behind. We'll get them from two directions."

"All right," Travis agreed, spurring his mount and settling in his saddle. "But don't go more than a half mile or so. On this ground, it's unlikely we'll be able to stay behind them very long without being noticed. We'll wait till we hear some shooting before we come in, to make sure you've got their attention."

Travis had a worried look. From the shelter of a small grove of oaks, he and Tony watched the bandits' trail, only a sand sprinkle moving above the rampant shrubs. Three black birds chirped in the trees, the only sound other than a wispy wind cutting across the plain. The two had managed to fall in behind the outlaws without being detected. But Travis was now watching the bandits divide into two groups, one flanking off to their right.

"Didn't plan on this," Travis said, still on horseback. "One of those groups is going to get ambushed, but the other will flank around and get Chase and Chester from the rear or come in behind us. Pretty good idea, but rare for these bandits. Either way, it complicates things."

"Looks like it's all five of them," Tony added, looking down at the tracks below his horse. "What you want to do?"

Travis slowly rode out of the grove. "When the shooting starts, we'll charge in. But on a flank, hopefully on some high ground with cover that can be easily defended. Get both bunches."

No sooner had Travis gotten the words out of his mouth than the firing commenced. The shots unequivocally delineated Chase's location; the Rangers' novel Colts fired much faster than the flintlock revolvers common south of the border, also producing a much crisper and more distinctive *bang*. At a slow trot, Travis led Tony to a rock-strewn ravine, a hundred yards left of the firing, which had reached a crescendo. Also heard among the gunshots were a few shouts in English and Spanish. Travis looked at the ditch, figuring Chase and the Rangers were using it for the ambush. He put a finger over his lips as he stepped down from his stirrups, motioning Tony to do likewise.

Travis hunched low, pistol at the ready, and scurried through the brush, weaving around the cacti and cat-claw. He finally squatted behind a horse-sized boulder where the ravine bank dropped off sharply, wiping a dab of perspiration from his brow with a sleeve. Tony joined him. Beyond the boulder, in the ravine, shots danced off the rocks on each side of the dry creek bed and bullets zinged through the foliage. Travis eased up to steal a peek at the action. As he did, he heard a shriek, a loud scream in English. He could see that one of the bandits had crossed the draw and taken up a position in an elevated rock garden, commanding a good view of Chase's position, fifty paces down the ravine. The labyrinth of stones was a patchwork of distorted dark colors, shade, and sun. Travis knelt back behind the cover and pointed. "There's one over here. Sounds like he's already shot somebody. Circle around and fill those rocks with bullets from the rear. When that flushes him out, I'll shoot him."

Travis patted Tony on the shoulder, and the young mestizo Ranger disappeared into the deep gorge. Travis followed, pausing in the shadow-draped ravine. He looked up at the opposite bank, where he planned to make his assault. The area was exposed; certainly he'd be in harm's way. He counted the seconds, trying to speculate how long it would take Tony to get in position, not wanting to crawl into the open before he could shoot. He counted to ten as his heart moved up into his throat. All the commotion had kept his nerves calm, but only a few seconds of inactivity had gotten them going.

Travis searched the opposite bank for cover, any-thing—a small draw, a stub of vegetation, a rock. He ducked behind a little pear cactus, not much cover, and peered over the bank at the rock promontory. Fortunately for him, Tony simultaneously began to pepper the boulder complex. Travis scrambled over the loose rock, finally standing. He saw a head appear from the maze of stones. He drew a bead. It was a fifty-yard head shot. Without confidence, he charged onward. The bandit had turned his head, haphazardly firing a few shots behind him. Travis stopped at twenty yards. He put the side of the man's head in his sights, paused his breathing, and pulled the trigger. His gun spoke only once, and the bandit fell from sight.

"I got him!" Travis yelled and dashed forward, leaping over a few rocks. The bandit lay on the ground in a death spasm, blood gushing from his head. Just for insurance, Travis put another shot in the man's chest as his heart rate slowed. He turned his attention back to the ravine and the other gun battle; he had blocked it out during his assault. The shooting had stopped. He gave the area a diligent inspection: no movement or noise at all.

Travis exhaled a deep breath as he reached over and grabbed the bandit's boot, dragging him a few paces to where the late-day sun illuminated his face. He put his foot on the outlaw's greasy black mane, turning his face up. As he did, he heard a few footsteps pattering on the dirt behind him. His skin tingled and instinctively, he whirled around, pistol fully extended.

Paco was standing, flat-footed, on the bank of the ravine. The sinking sun amplified the Mexican's cold, sly, killer eyes, filled with rage and locked on Travis, who cast his own harsh, unwavering stare on the Mexican *federale*.

Travis squinted his eyes, stared through his sights over the muzzle of Paco's revolver, and sighted on his chest.

The part-time bandit wore shiny black leather and a gold necklace. His hair was raven black, with a rare streak of blond over his left ear. He had an inch-long scar under one eye and a long, stringlike beard that fell down to his neck. A white sombrero hung over his back.

"You killed my brother. Now it's time for you to die," Paco said calmly but with unmistakable earnestness.

"The scourge of the earth," Travis answered, feeling a drop of cool sweat run down his back. He tried to lock his vision on Paco. He attempted to focus his whole body, everything, on the man's chest, being sure not to get distracted by his eyes, his awful expression. "I'm not going anywhere. Take your best shot. You'll be in hell in five minutes anyway." As Travis spoke, as delicately as he could, he held his pistol tightly, squeezing his trigger, slowly increasing the pressure while continuing to badger the bandit. "I'm fixin' to do the Mexican people a—"

At last, there was a crack and the recoil. Paco hunched over, snarling, cursing, and dropping his pistol. He grabbed his bleeding right forearm. Instead of striking the chest, Travis's bullet had punctured the bandit's arm. As Paco regained his composure, he dove to the ground, reaching for his pistol with his good arm.

Travis slowly cocked the hammer of his Colt as he watched the Mexican squirm on the ground. Instead of putting a second slug in the *federale*'s back, he could not resist firing a shot that intentionally missed by a few inches. He enjoyed watching the bloody bandit flinch in fear. With gratification filling his soul, Travis quickly cocked the Colt again. But this time, the chamber of his trusty sidearm jammed.

"Shit," Travis mumbled to himself, working the cylinder with his free hand for a few seconds before dashing to cover.

Paco looked up and fired two shots with his off hand. Both ricocheted off the rocks. "I'm going to kill you, Ross," he grunted, and laughed, struggling to his knees.

"Where you at, Tony?" Travis yelled as he crouched low, trying to free his jammed revolver.

"Hold on, I'm coming," a muffled voice responded. "Had to go back across this creek to get there."

Travis peeked over the boulder to see Paco getting to his feet. As he did, Travis heard gunshots, demented hollering, and horses rustling through the brush. Shortly, the horses broke from the cover to his left, carrying more bandits. From the depths of the ravine, Tony also appeared, instantly spraying Paco with three bullets that missed their mark.

Paco fired another reckless, vain shot at Travis, then turned to look behind him. Travis also looked. Chase and Chester, still out of shooting range, were making their way toward the skirmish. Paco stomped an embittered foot and stumbled toward the horses, clutching his wound in pain. One of the bandits raced forward, hoisted Paco onto his horse, and reared around, dashing back for the brush. Paco turned while atop the horse and took a final shot at Travis as the bandits disappeared.

Dazed and almost spent, Travis collapsed, falling to his buttocks, his tension abating. He reached up and mopped his now-saturated face with his sleeve—a calm now settling over the bloodstained turf. As he leaned his back against the cool rocks, he heard Chase and Chester stumble on the scene.

"Ya'll get 'em?" he heard Chase ask Tony.

"One," Tony replied softly.

"They got Fitzmorris. He's dead," Chase said, walking over and standing above Travis.

"I shot Paco in the arm," Travis grunted with eyes still closed, thinking how stupid and unprofessional he had been by firing that teasing shot at Paco. Would he one day regret that? How much torment and suffering would the *federale* dish out to innocents in the future? He had let his emotions impede his job—a powerful disappointment.

"You think we should go after them?" Chase said.

"They've got a wounded man," Travis sighed. "We could probably get them in a day or so. But we probably better move on. We've got more important business. Fannin is expecting us. We'll get Paco another day."

Chapter 4

Travis looked out at Goliad, then at Fort Defiance, now partially in flames. The morning was only a few hours old and still foggy, but the large, gloomy fires of the fort's stock and provisions warmed his cheeks. He turned to the interesting little town on a rugged, almost treeless, ivory sandstone escarpment above the San Antonio River, rippling clear over a rock bed. Between the numerous gullies, a dozen white stone buildings and twice that many wood shacks, all square and flat-roofed, were stacked up the side of the terrace like steps. Across the river lay the ruins of the huge Spanish mission, Espiritu Santo. The glare from all the shining stone caused Travis to squint his eyes.

It had been a month since he had arrived here —not a pleasurable month. Only a week earlier, the fort had received word that the Alamo had fallen, with all its defenders slain in its defense. Since then, refugees and soldiers had been flocking to the little town, now garrisoned with almost five hundred soldiers. But now, they had been ordered to leave, to move east to Victoria, then on to Gonzales to rendezvous with the other Texas forces, now under the command of a new general, a Tennessean named Sam Houston.

The orders to depart had just come down, and the little village buzzed with activity and panic, troops hurrying to load up personal items and citizens ambling around trying decide their best course. Travis shook his head and looked at the fort, guarded on three approaches by a bend in the river. It was a daunting obstacle, much more so than the Alamo. And the Texans had spent the past few months shoring up its defenses. The fort was almost four acres, surrounded by a seven-foot-thick stone fence that also protruded down to the water to allow access during a siege. Its corners housed fortresses and watchtowers. Outside, deep trenches had been dug around the fence. Inside the grounds were ten pieces of four-pound artillery, all now spiked and sitting atop the flat roof of the fort's church or centered in the grounds. The troops and wagons sat lined up outside the fort, the wagons overloaded with powder, water, personal belongings, and several cannons. Lounging around the wagons were four hundred volunteers from New Orleans and Mobile, known as the Grays because of their distinctive wool, coal-colored uniforms.

Travis reached over and picked up a young, dirty-faced girl, not six years in age, cradling a worn-out doll and wandering through the fort and the chaos aimlessly in search of a parent. He hoisted the girl up, coddling her in his arms and bouncing her gently. He brushed her hair. Her skin was smooth and tinted, eyes a deep blue—innocent, beautiful, but filled with fear and amazement at the surroundings. "Where's your mama?"

"Me and Tony are going on to Victoria, ahead of the column," Chase blared, walking up behind Travis. "What you got there?"

Travis turned around and handed the girl to Chase. "What?"

"What's your name?" Chase whispered playfully, wiggling the girl's nose before turning his eyes to Travis. "I managed to secure you a cushy job, escorting the Grays to Victoria."

"She's not very talkative," Travis said, and looked at Tony. "What time are you two leaving?"

"Now," Chase said, putting the girl down and holding her by the wrist.

Travis turned back to the dreadful fort; the soaring flames and mass hysteria gave the town an air of doom that spilled over him. Where were they headed? Nothing was more vulnerable than a slow train on the prairie. It made him feel uneasy, uncertain of the situation—too many unknowns. "I guess I'll catch up with you two in Victoria. Don't know why we're leaving. There's not a better place in Texas for defense. Much rather be behind these walls than get caught out in the open. Take her down to the town hall for me on your way out of town."

Chase reached down, grabbed the girl, and handed her up to Tony, who had just saddled up. He then looked at the train of wagons, twenty in number. "We'll see you down the trail. Keep 'em moving. Probably take you three days to get to Victoria."

• • •

It was mid-morning before the five hundred soldiers and the wagon train got moving. Spring was showing itself, the day warming ahead of the common March breeze that would come. The primitive trail to Victoria was nothing more than a worn plot on the prairie strewn with rocks. The overloaded wagons, pulled by mules and oxen, were not making good time, maybe a mile and a half an hour. And in the first two hours alone, two wagons lost wheels and were left on the trail.

Travis rode alone at the front of the line, picking his way along the path, trying to avoid rough spots on the trail while keeping a good eye out for anything unusual ahead and on the flanks. The country was enchanting, uncultivated, and spotted with a countless succession of little meadows and light forests full of life, harboring numerous herds of cattle and some whitetail.

By mid-afternoon, the slow-moving column, a half mile in length, had come to a vast prairie, ten miles of flat grassland in every direction. Travis inspected the open area suspiciously. The day had warmed considerably; the mules and oxen were now all but done in by the heavy loads. The animals moved at a snail's pace, one laboring step at a time. Travis rode ahead about halfway across the plain, and heeled his mount atop a small knoll projecting a dozen feet above the land. He took a drink from his canteen, and turned to look back at the line of marching men and vehicles kicking up a cloud of dust visible for ten miles. He looked back ahead. His heart skipped a beat as he saw some movement, only a mosaic of color against the olive backdrop. He reached for his glasses. It was a group of horses, at least a hundred. He steadied his eyes, identifying the bright colors of the Mexican cavalry uniforms: beige, red, and royal blue.

Without thought, he spurred his mount and raced back to the column. An officer rode out to meet him. Travis never broke stride as he continued to gallop to the rear of the line. "Mexican cavalry ahead, at least a company," Travis yelled as he passed the officer, who swung in behind him. Travis finally rode up to another good lookout point midway back along the column. As his horse settled, he saw the horses, another line of cavalry, this one larger, a half mile behind the column hovering at the edge of the prairie. He turned to the officer, who had removed the hat from his head and folded it under his arm. "Two lines of cavalry, three or four hundred. They've got us boxed in. Looks like they plan to attack us here."

The slight officer, in his late twenties with black hair, an unshaven face, and shifting gray eyes, looked at the prairie. "This is the worst place for defense, open terrain, no water."

"Captain Moses," Travis moaned, looking ahead, his mind racing. "I've crossed this prairie twenty times. About two miles ahead is a little creek with good banks and water. I suggest making for it. The group in front of us is smaller. Probably have to fight your way there, but it will be a good place for defense. There's five hundred of us. We can hold out from there. If we have to stand here and face this cavalry, it will be costly. That's Urrea's cavalry. He's the most capable commander the Mexicans have. His troops are the best." As Travis spoke, he looked at the long line of men; three more horses were currently riding toward him. From the rear, more scouts were also racing forward.

"Two miles? Our animals are pretty near done now," the officer said. "Here comes Colonel Fannin."

Travis looked out at the scene. The Mexicans had surrounded the Texans, who had circled the wagons in a defensive position on the prairie. Despite the objections of his officers, Colonel Fannin had decided to stop in place and defend the column. A brief attempt to reach the cover of the river had been made, but the mules and oxen were too beat for a hasty dash.

The Mexicans, probably a thousand—several hundred cavalry augmented by infantry and a couple hundred Lipan Indians—formed a long line, 360 degrees around the Texans.

Over the distant sound of the Mexican bugle and the wild cries in Spanish, Travis saw the bodies and horses growing more numerous on the savanna, blocking the horizon in all directions. They were still several hundred yards away, out of firing range, but closing the gauntlet with a slow, steady step. Travis looked at the sun, still hanging four or five hours above the prairie. Energy raced up his spine like a jolt from the ground; darkness would not save them.

Travis turned to the Grays, most on a knee, positioned in a hundred-yard box around the wagons and animals. A few packed their Barker carbines; others held them upright, the butts against ground, bayonets fixed. The men's faces stood stern, indifferent, eyes roving. A single *boom* from a Texas cannon broke the quiet. The Mexican line parted briefly, a few riders unseated, and two soldiers fell, but the gap quickly filled. As the line got closer, the musket fire started slowly, at first random pops, but only seconds later, swirling into a constant stream. A dozen more Mexicans fell, but the fence of men, the line of flickering orange blasts, grew larger and nearer by the second.

Travis sucked in a deep breath and got to a knee, his Colt in his firing hand, the Mexicans still well out of his pistol's range. He looked around. The location was not ideal, but he felt confident. Although they were outnumbered at least two to one, he was sure the Grays were better men, and they had to hold out only until dark. They didn't have to take any ground, only hold their positions. And unlike the assaulters, their lives depended on winning—a hell of a motivation. The Mexican casualties were sure to be high. If the Grays could punish them enough, they would likely beat a retreat.

Travis turned to look at the friendly forces; the officers were brazenly moving up and down the line, encouraging the men, who continued to fire and reload. The smoke got thick, almost suffocating, burning the eyes and blinding. The officers urged the men forward, not in an assault, but a few feet out of the haze, where their aim was surer.

For the next hour, the Mexican line advanced and retreated with volley and counter-volley, each sequence sending scores of men to the earth but bringing the Mexicans closer—two steps forward, one back. The friendly cannons tore holes in the Mexican lines, but one by one, artillerymen fell, finally silencing the guns. Travis had begun firing, at least ten cylinders from his pistol, each shot carefully aimed. He was sure he had downed at least two horses and five men. As he continued to shoot, his hands got raw from disassembling and packing the Colt. The minutes passed without track.

Despite the wall of musketry and heavy losses, the Mexicans continued to steadfastly close in. The hour of work, sacrifice, and death brought them to within a hundred paces of the Grays, almost blocking out the sun and giving Travis a fit of claustrophobia. Then he heard the ominous bugle. The Mexicans charged forward, reaching the perimeter of the defensive circle. As they did, the scene turned to confusion, the musket roar the most constant and deafening of the day, the smoke interfering with vision and any sense of direction.

In the bleak smog and late-day sun, Travis continued to fire, and watched the fighting devolve into point-blank shots and bludgeoning knives or bayonets. The Grays unleashed everything, all their vigor, killing the Mexicans by the dozens, almost as if they were enjoying it. Over the shrills, Travis heard the Mexican bugle again, cascading through the smoke, urging the attackers on at the critical moment. He shot two more soldiers appearing out of the fog. The cries grew louder, more frequent. Over the fray, Travis heard a ball whiz by his ear, so close he felt a burn. He reached up and touched the ear, his hand returning full of blood. Then the bugle sounded again, the note long—the retreat.

Travis fell to his knees. The sounds of killing slowly subsided; the haze slowly cleared. The air was still; not a breath of wind moved the thick smoke. The sun was setting over the worn, soot-smelling turf, turning it a shade of orange. Around him, the exhausted earth lay maimed with bodies, friend and foe. Travis's mind slowed as he put a hand on his chest, almost checking to make sure he was still alive. He looked at the prairie, covered with hundreds of dead.

The Mexicans were now in full retreat, out of

firing range and at an ample trot. They surely would not attack again this day, he thought.

Travis stood and turned to the wagons. More than a hundred sun-scorched men were sprawled on the ground, the doctors now moving among the groans.

Travis felt no reprieve. He held a quick counsel with himself. Though they had beaten off the assault, they were still surrounded, trapped. Like his comrades, he was lathered with sweat and grit, his throat burning with thirst. He had finished off his canteen hours earlier. Without water, they were as good as dead. And without rescue, most of the injured would perish. The Mexicans used copper bullets, extremely deadly, spattering the flesh and leaving metal scattered through body.

He looked again at the Mexicans and the darkness beginning to envelope the savanna. It would be a long, frightful night, and they had traveled only six or seven miles on this protracted, vile day. Would tomorrow be worse?

The night was cloudy, but not completely dark. Somewhere overhead, the moon was out, tinting the clouds but giving no hint to its location. Travis stood, his reins in his hands. It was almost midnight. Around him, the wounded were suffering, begging for water to quench their terrible thirst, their moans filling the murky air. But more than three hundred men still remained at the ready, lying around the wagons, some sleeping, others keeping a watchful eye on the prairie.

A man appeared out of the darkness, only an image. He handed Travis a leather satchel. "Maybe you can get through. If you do, get this to Victoria. There may be some troops there. Find somebody. If we don't get some water or reinforcements, we'll all die."

Travis recognized the voice. It was Colonel Fannin. He put the pouch's strap over his shoulder. "Don't worry, sir. I understand the predicament. You won't see me back here. If I don't get through, it's because I'm dead or captured. Don't give me any cover. I'll have a better chance to sneak out, but if you hear firing, empty into their ranks. It may distract them."

Travis reached over to check the tightness of the girth strap on his horse, then put a foot in his stirrup and felt for his pommel, lifting himself into the saddle. He trotted to the edge of the lines, then quietly rode into the no-man's-land. In only seconds, he turned to look behind. There was only darkness. Ahead, the ground lay open; visibility was only a dozen paces. Travis sensed his horse's pace to make sure it was sturdy, and counted to himself. It was about a two-and-a-half-minute ride to cover the distance between the forces. At about a hundred seconds, he would charge into the darkness, putting his fate in God's hands. The night was silent; only his heart thumping rapidly, his horse's gentle steps, and the mumbling of his counting disturbed the quiet.

As his count approached the magic number, Travis leaned forward over his mount's neck, securing his boots in the stirrups. He tugged back on the reins and listened—nothing. He spurred the horse and stormed into the darkness. Ten seconds, then five more, he continued to goad the horse with his heels, the night still a peculiar quiet. Travis galloped on for another five minutes until his surroundings started to darken more. He jerked back on his reins. His horse was panting heavily. Overhead, a canopy of sparse trees blocked the sky. Travis dismounted and walked another thirty paces until he found the creek bank. Feeling his way, he led his mare down to the creek, where the horse plunged her mouth into the water. Travis filled two canteens and transferred the water to his dehydrated body. He instantly felt some of his strength return.

Travis slowly sat, leaning back against the cool, damp embankment. He looked at the other side of the shallow creek. Where was he going? He looked up. There were no stars to guide the way. He had learned many times, painstakingly, that the prairie could not be navigated without getting his bearings. He could mosey around all night, only to end up where he started—or worse, in the Mexican lines. He did notice that the clouds were on the move, probably coming up from the gulf. These moving clouds would lead him. But first he needed to let his horse rest a couple of hours, freshen up in case he had to make a running escape.

By daylight, Travis had traveled in an easterly direction another fifteen miles. The progress was slow. He had to dismount and lead his timid steed across a creek or draw every mile or so. With the blue of morning, his pace would increase. He might make Victoria in only a few hours, and he would have the rising sun to lead him. But daylight also brought other obstacles: he was visible for miles on the open grassland. Even more troublesome, he was riding directly into the sun, illuminating his horse's tack and all his metal like a lantern, the horizontal rays refracting, reflecting, and magnifying his movement for anybody ahead to see for miles.

An hour after daylight, Travis spotted a ranch house in a small meadow. He made a cautious approach, scanning the house carefully with his field glasses from more than a mile away before riding ahead. The large ranch house was deserted, and surrounded by unfinished earthworks. Travis's gut was full of hunger pangs, and his mount grew less hearty by the hour. As he arrived on the grounds, he made a beeline for a wood-planked barn beside the house, where he found stores of hay and oats. He left his horse to feed, and walked to the house. Inside, the rough prairie residence was in disorder, the residents surely having fled in recent days. Travis found some molded bread and a strip of dried meat that he quickly gobbled down.

After the thirty-minute respite, Travis was again in the saddle, riding off from the ranch. There was a nice wagon trail leading to the east, but he decided to veer off and ride parallel to the road a few hundred yards. But just as he entered the large meadow encompassing the ranch, he saw a dozen horses coming up the road. He smoothly pulled back on his reins, freezing in the saddle. His insides rumbled. Since he was looking into the sun, the images were difficult to see. He put a hand above his eyes. The bright red saddle blankets of the Mexican cavalry became visible. Travis looked around. The ground was open, but to his left, maybe a quarter mile away, was a wood line, probably a creek or dry gully. He heard the screams from down the road, announcing he was spotted. He spurred his mare so hard that she bellowed, and reared her around toward the tree line.

In less than a minute, he arrived at the cover. He urged his horse into the concealment of a deep, dry gully. In the ditch bottom, he saw only brown earth and scrub. He continued to push his mount and raced down the gulch. Clumps of thorny sage ripped at Travis's shirt and skin as he held on. The horse leaped over holes and bucked like a bronc as Travis watched the earth and brush rush by, bouncing in all directions. Over the commotion, he heard nothing. He came to a fork in the ditch and never slowed, charging down the right fork. A few hundred more paces, and the sage cleared and the trees overhead disappeared. Travis jerked back on his reins. He wanted to ride up the bank and peek into the prairie, but the sides were too steep.

He jumped off his horse, intending to crawl up and see if he had lost the cavalry. As he hit the ground, he heard the ghastly sounds, metallic clicks, one after another, like dominoes falling. He froze and looked up. On both banks, staring down on him, were four horses, their riders' pistols locked on his chest. A few more horses appeared, riding up to the ditch, their riders looking down at him under the brims of their hats. Travis felt a sense of doom come over him. He was breathing hard; a drop of cold sweat fell from his nose onto his mouth. He tasted the salinity.

Chapter 5

Day was ending. The long shadows of the iron bars covering the musty cell's lone window had made their way across the floor and were now disappearing, merging with the darkening stone floor. Travis sat on the ground, his back against the wall. On the other side of the cell, another man lay on the floor, sleeping. He was also a Texas soldier, a Red Rover, another volunteer unit from Alabama, who had been detained here two days earlier.

It had been a week since Travis's capture. He had been taken that day to this cell in La Vaca, a small settlement on Matagorda Bay. He was familiar with his quarters. The two-room jail in the ten-structure town had often been used by the Rangers to hold prisoners. But he had always looked at his current confinement area from the other side of the bars.

The day after his arrival, his guards, a pair of obstinate Mexican cavalrymen, had informed him that Colonel Fannin had surrendered his entire command the morning after his departure, about the time of his own submission. Travis had doubted the news, either not believing it or not wanting to believe it. But the arrival of his new cell mate two days earlier had confirmed the story. More than three hundred of the men who had fought so gallantly beside him on the prairie were now being held at Fort Defiance.

The Mexicans had managed to take the fort by way of defeating its defenders, not by storming the ramparts, but by capitulation on the open prairie —gross incompetence. The news tore at Travis. In less than a month, the two major bastions in west Texas had fallen to the Mexicans, one without a fight. The new Texas republic was getting off to a shaky start, one that might quell independence before it even got started. If there was one thing to take solace in, it was the fact that the Grays were being held by General Urrea. Travis knew him. He was one of most honorable officers in the Mexican army; his comrades would be treated like prisoners of war, unlike those at the Alamo.

Travis pulled out his watch. In only an hour, the room would get dark, staying black until the window again glowed with the first light of morning. The two guards showed themselves five or six times during the day, only poking their heads in to make sure their prisoners behaved. But usually just before dark, Travis would get his daily rations, a bucket of dirty brown water and maybe a slice of bread, or a bowl of broth. One day he had received half a watermelon, cut open days before. His throat was dry, and he ached for the water. He looked down at his midsection. He had already lost ten pounds this week.

As he rubbed his stomach, he heard the steps outside; then the door swung open. Agusto, the gruffer of his two jailers, barged into the little jail with the two buckets of water in hand. He set the buckets outside the thick cell bars and brushed his long, greasy, black mane. "No food tonight. But good news, at least for me. You two are going back to Goliad tomorrow, be with the rest of the traitors. I won't have to worry about your stinking asses anymore." Agusto turned around and stormed back out of the jail, his leather boots rattling against the floor.

Travis reached through the bars to secure the little tin cup in the bucket. He filled it with water. For the first time in a week, his spirits perked up. Compared to this cell, Fort Defiance would be heaven: friends to converse with, fresh air to breathe. Just the thought of the long ride, though surely shackled, brought a smile to his face. He turned up the cup of brown water and downed it.

Two pistol shots rang in Travis's ears, waking him from his light nap. He jumped to his feet and looked out the window, then back to his cellmate, still sleeping. Outside, Travis saw nothing, only the cool night air, the dirt street lit by moonlight. He heard a third shot. What was it? Were the Texans liberating the town? Was it a shoot-out at the little cantina down the street, or maybe a drunk Mexican taking aim at the moon? Travis wondered as he pressed his face against the bars, trying to get a wider view. He removed his watch. It was four in the morning. He strained his ears. The night was still, but he thought he heard some footsteps. Travis looked at the cell, its barricades sturdy. He hated being trapped, especially if gunplay was occurring outside. He felt more defenseless than he had all week. He looked outside again—nothing. The footsteps grew louder. A terrible thought crossed his mind: Someone coming to kill him. They had been warming up, checking the weapon.

The feet reached the door. Travis hugged the cool wall with his back as the grave sounds of the squeaking door filled his ears. He visualized Agusto, in a drunken stupor, barging in, filling the cell with haphazard shots, laughing, excitement filling his wicked soul. Travis slowly turned his head to the door. A man walked in with a quick pace. It was Tony Flores, his left arm bleeding badly. Travis exhaled a long breath. His sweaty body cooled.

Tony quickly walked to the door, inserting a hand-sized key into the lock. "Hurry up. Let's get out of here."

"Never been so glad to see you," Travis said. "I guess you and Chase got through to Victoria."

"Yes, we did. Never saw a Mexican," Tony answered.

"I've been wondering about you." Travis walked forward. As he did, he lightly kicked his cell mate. "Wake up. We've been set free."

"Who's that?" Tony said.

"One of the Reds. Been here a couple of days. What about my keepers?"

"Both in hell," Tony replied promptly. "I've got one spare horse." He reached down and slapped the man on the cheek; he was still lethargic, not comprehending what was happening. "Get up. Won't be long before the Mexicans show up. There's a few horses down at the prefect's station. You can ride out with us. No saddles, you'll have to go bareback. Get that rope off my saddle."

"Let me take a look at your arm," Travis said, walking out of the cell. He reached down and jerked the volunteer to his feet, then pushed him out the door. "Down the street on the right. We'll meet you there."

"We'll look at it later," Tony said, following Travis outside.

"You just decide to come get me? Or somebody order you here?" Travis asked, mounting up. He looked around at the town. All was still quiet; his cell mate disappearing down the street was the only movement. He had seen no one but his two guards all week; the town was deserted.

"No. It's terrible. Santa Anna has ordered all the captives killed. Everybody at Goliad, tomorrow."

"What?" Travis yelled in disbelief. "Word I got was Fannin surrendered on honorable terms. He and his men to be shipped back to New Orleans. There's a boat on the way."

"Santa Anna overruled Urrea. Massacre is to be tomorrow, Palm Sunday."

"Can't be. How do you know this?" Travis's tone got solemn.

"Little Rayo sent me a message. Met him in the sage. He told me you were here. The orders had just come down. Guess he didn't want to see you shot. I promised him I'd tell nobody." Tony finally looked up into Travis's eyes.

"We've got to get down there," said Travis. "Let somebody know. Do something about this."

"Too late. They'll probably be dead before we get there. I only heard about this tonight. Came straight here. Couldn't let you die like that. You took me into the corps. Taught me everything I know."

"Where's Chase?"

"Don't know. He took out for Goliad two days ago to try and get some information about the boys. Haven't seen or heard from him since. I'm worried he's been captured also."

Travis's heart sank. There was no joy in his rescue and little reason to be thankful to Tony, who had risked his life to save him, his arm now mangled and still bleeding. This could not be happening. Worse yet, he was getting spared. In a few hours, he would have been in front of a firing squad. A chill ran down his spine as he thought of his comrades and their fate. And what of Chase? What an awful way to die—no fight, no glory, only helplessly staring at death. His breath picked up. He fought an internal battle with himself to ride off into the darkness and make for Goliad.

"Let's go, Travis. Nothing you can do about it. You're alive. We'll get those bastards."

"Maybe you're right. But we're going to go look for Chase at the very minimum. If they've got him, they might be holding him somewhere like me."

"There's nothing but Mexicans south and west of here. It will be chancy."

"We'll go see Red Wolf. See what he knows."

"Who's Red Wolf?"

"An old Tonkawas chief, used to scout for us. They're allied with Texas. He hates Mexicans. He'll know what's going on. Stays over on Green Lake, about a two-hour ride. It's a good time to travel." Travis turned to look down the street. The Red loped up, bareback. "We're going to look for more captives. You can come or head out on your on."

"I'll stay with you. Not much chance out there alone." The volunteer looked at Tony. "Name's Jim. Jim Barker."

Tony shook his hand and introduced himself.

Travis turned and looked down the road behind him. It was creepy and dark, except for a smattering of starlight. He didn't envy the thought of descending the treacherous trail.

Chapter 6

It was thirty minutes after dawn when Travis and his companions arrived on the south bank of Green Lake. Travis looked out at the shining water, extending ten miles out. Around the lake, the land lay flat and big, salt grass and marshes, swept clean of trees by centuries of hurricanes. With the morning sun and early breeze, the grass fluttered, the only movement in the grim calm. Travis sniffed the salt in the air. He looked at a group of gargantuan whooping cranes, their white wings spanning seven feet. In the water, five or six loons trawled for crustaceans.

"It's fresh water," Travis said, and pointed. "Red Wolf's camp is just down the bank a little ways, about a mile, I think. Let me take a look at the bandage I made."

"It's fine,"Tony said.

"You got lucky, didn't get the bone," Travis said as he tidied the cotton cloth.

Tony, his eyes as big as silver dollars as he marveled at the strange land, goaded his horse in the direction Travis had pointed.

"Be on the lookout for alligators," Travis said with a grave tone.

"Alligators?" Tony pulled back on his reins.

"Yeah," Travis continued, trying to restrain a smile. "Giant lizards, twelve feet long. This area's full of them. They'll eat you. Swallow you whole."

Tony's eyes got bigger. The brave little Ranger looked down at the still-gray earth and the muddy, grass-covered bank. "You lead," he said in a timid voice.

Travis, seeing the concern on Tony's face, felt his insides relax a little for the first time in weeks. It always gladdened him and filled his soul with bliss when he could get his daring, intrepid comrades to fret over something trivial. With his most serious face, he reached over and grabbed Tony's pistol, holding it high and in the ready position. "Stay close. They feed in the early mornings. Quieter than a jaguar. All you'll hear is his big teeth clamping down on your neck. Your little tender ass won't be anything but a morsel."

In less than ten minutes, the three arrived at the Tonkawas camp, wood and bamboo huts on the lake's bank. The camp was alive. The twenty once-proud hunters and warriors were now preparing their little skiffs and nets for a day of fishing, while the tribe's women cooked tortillas on flat tin plates over four fires. As the soldiers emerged from the morning shade, they caught the camp's attention, and forty silent eyes fell on the three.

Travis moved a flat hand over his chest in a gesture of peace. "We're looking for Red Wolf."

One of the braves stood and pointed to one of the bamboo shacks.

"Sit tight," Travis said to Tony. Then he dismounted and slowly walked to the shack. He knocked on one of the poles and slowly entered the dark hut, lit by a small fire. Inside, Red Wolf sat, barely visible, on the ground as an old Indian woman rubbed some oil on his bare feet. "Times must be getting bad when the great chief can't get a young woman to rub his feet anymore."

Red Wolf turned and looked at Travis, then stood. "Young women are good for many things, but not the delicate job of foot rubbing. They have too much spirit. Only an older woman, who is not in a hurry, can do such things."

Travis extended a hand as Red Wolf came into view. The Indian was old, in his sixties. He wore baggy leather, a blanket draped around his neck, and his ears and wrists were adorned with beads. His skin was rough and red, his eyes narrow and dwarfed by his big nose. This and his clever hunting skills had earned him his name.

Red Wolf received the hand. "I thought the Mexicans got you."

"They did. But you know they couldn't keep me. I'm looking for Chase."

"I have not seen Chase. But the Mexicans have a camp up the river. I hear they have Texans there."

"Where?"

"Spring ford, past Carlos."

"What else you hear?"

"Nothing, except they have three hundred Texans at Goliad."

"How about guns? You have any guns you want to sell?"

"No, only one old flint pistol for settling squabbles—mostly over whiskey or women nowadays."

Travis put his hands on his hips as he stared at Red Wolf and thought silently for a few seconds. He offered a hand again. "I'd like to take some breakfast if that's all right. If these women can make your old feet feel good, I bet they can do wonders with flour. But we need to get going before the sun gets up. Thank you." Travis touched his heart with his right hand, patted Red Wolf on the shoulder, and walked out of the hut.

"What did you find out?" Tony whispered as Travis remounted.

Travis wheeled his horse around and spurred her out of the village. "Not much. Mexicans have a camp at the spring ford past Carlos. They have Texans there. We're going to go check it out. But first, we've got to get some weapons."

"Where we going to get guns out here?" Tony questioned as he and Jim rode up beside Travis.

"Carlos," Travis said. He turned in the saddle and handed each man a tortilla filled with a tasty fish mixture.

"That's a Mexican stronghold," Jim alleged around a mouthful of the breakfast.

"Yeah, I know." Travis took a sip from Tony's canteen. "But the madam there is an old girl-

73

friend of mine. Didn't really depart on good terms. But she's still got a soft spot for me. We'll hustle on. Be there before it gets good and light."

"This is crazy," Tony murmured. "I didn't bust you out of that jail to get all three of us killed."

"It's going to be all right," Travis answered, looking at a small wood house on the perimeter of the twenty buildings on the ranch, a hundred yards ahead. "That's where she lives. She runs the general store, keeps the officers supplied with girls. She's in tight with the Mexicans, probably making a fortune off of them. Let's get up there before it gets seeing light." Travis turned to inspect the other buildings. There were only three horses hitched up at the ranch's entrance. No lanterns were shining in any of the windows. "Doesn't look like there are any Mexicans here anyway. She's a spunky redhead from Georgia. Name's Doll Gibson. Her store has plenty of guns."

"But that camp is less than a mile away," Tony said.

"Come on." Travis lunged forward in the saddle, easing through the tall grass. He picked up a full trot and ten seconds later, swung off his horse at the back of the house. He shuffled up to the house's back door and banged on the single glass pane a few times. After waiting a few seconds without a response, he knocked again, this time harder and with more urgency.

"Who is it?" a hushed female voice finally said from inside as Tony and Jim arrived at the door.

"It's Travis, Travis Ross."

"Travis Ross, go away. I don't want to see you," the voice continued.

"Thought you said she had a soft spot for you," Tony said.

"Open up, Doll," Travis said, raising his voice a little, "before a damned Mexican lancer shoots me. You want that on your conscience?"

"Yeah, it might clear my conscience," Doll replied.

"I'm going to break this door down if you don't open it." Travis rapped the door two more times.

"All right," Doll answered, and the door opened.

Travis, with Tony and Jim on his heels, darted inside.

"Haven't seen you in two years," Doll mumbled from the darkness. "And you show up here like this with a couple of your dusty soldiers."

"That's because you ran off and left me," Travis replied in an astonished voice.

"After I caught your hand up Mary Stevens' skirt."

"I told you twenty times," Travis answered. "She slipped and fell. Cut herself on the upper hip. I was just tending to her; that's my job—to look after the people. If I had known you were going to run and leave me for that dumb undertaker, I guess I could have let her bleed to death, poor girl." As Travis spoke, the room and Doll slowly came into focus. He looked over at the short, fair-skinned woman in her nightclothes. Her green eyes locked on Travis, who walked forward and put a hand on her cheek. "You're more beautiful than I remember."

"Don't give me any of that," Doll said in a strong-willed voice, but she did not retreat from Travis's touch. "What do you want? And what are you doing here? Mexicans catch you, you'll be dead by noon."

"Need some guns, pistols."

"Don't have any pistols. Two old muskets."

"We'll take 'em. And some powder and balls."

Doll did not move as she continued to stare at Travis.

"Come on. Do it for me. I need it, and we need to get out of here."

Doll finally disappeared into another room, arriving a minute or so later with the two guns and a little leather sack. She handed the rifles to Travis. "You need anything else?"

"Maybe some of those buttermilk biscuits you used to make me in the mornings," Travis answered, and grabbed the guns.

"Come on, Travis, let's go," Tony interjected impatiently. "We're surrounded by Mexicans. We don't have time for you to flirt with your old girl-friends all morning."

"How many Mexicans at that camp?" Travis asked, making a quick inspection of the rifles.

"About twenty," Doll answered. "I don't guess you have any money, do you?"

Travis stepped forward and bent over to kiss Doll on the cheek. "Just a kiss for now. I owe you."

"You owe me for this!" Doll said in a high-pitched voice, recoiling from Travis. "You owe me for a bunch of stuff, you rascal!"

The sun sat halfway to its apex by the time Travis got his first look at the little Mexican camp, only ten tents under a few oaks on the western side of the roaring San Antonio River. Tony and Jim lay beside him, hidden behind a low ridge on the other side of the river. The country was open, flat plains for the most part, the marshes giving way to grassland and a few dunes.

Tony handed Travis his field glasses. "Pretty smart. Camp's in the open. That ford is the only place to cross the river for twenty miles during the spring rains. Nobody can sneak up on them or even cross the river without the Mexicans seeing them. Looks like Riveria's calvary."

Travis squinted his eyes and stared at the camp. He didn't believe what he was seeing. He checked again. It was Chase—amazing. What were the chances of them finding him in only a few hours? "I believe I see Chase."

"Where?" Tony asked.

"On the right. Hands tied behind his back, on a horse. They must be getting ready to move him." Travis slowly moved the glasses over the camp. He settled them on three horses, the only other ones saddled in the camp. "Markings on those blankets look like Riveria's. Chase must feel like he's important. The colonel himself is going to bring him in. Probably doesn't have any idea he's riding to his death." Travis handed the binoculars back to Tony.

"What you want to do?" Tony said, putting his eyes back against the glasses.

Travis looked at the open country, then back at the camp. "Hell, day's turning out pretty good for me. Twelve hours ago, I was a dead man. Now, I'm fixin' to kill the famous cavalry colonel, rescue the gallant Ranger, and I managed to get one of my old girlfriends misty-eyed about me in there somewhere." Despite his rhetoric, Travis's standard way of relieving tension, he was starting to feel desperate as he looked at Chase, helpless in the camp. If they did not get him, he would surely be dead by dark. Travis studied the two old muskets. He would have two shots, Tony five—one chance—Chase's life, and possibly the three of theirs, was on the line. And his foe was no regular soldier; Colonel Riveria's fame was earned by skill and cunning, not breeding.

"She didn't look that misty-eyed to me. But if you say so," Tony replied.

Travis scooted back down behind the ridge and sat quietly, thinking for a few minutes. "We can't do anything here. That would be suicide. We're going to have to hit them on the trail somewhere. They'll stop at the purple spring and water. We can ride faster than them. We'll get there first, lay in wait. There's a perfect ambush spot there."

"But this is the only place to cross the river," Tony added, crawling down beside Travis.

"We'll cross at the rope bridge." Travis picked up one of the muskets.

"It's a five-mile walk from there." Tony looked at Travis as though his mentor's words made no sense.

"We'll take the horses across the bridge."

"How're we going to do that?"

"Trust me," Travis said, looking at Jim, who had come down the hill. "Can you shoot?"

"I'm not bad."

Travis looked the man over circumspectly for a few moments. The Red was a steady, strong hand, with neutral eyes and a healthy build, but Travis didn't get a good feeling about his marksmanship. "I'll take both musket shots. You can load. There will be three of them. We'll wait here until we see them get ready to leave. As formal as they are, it will take fifteen minutes for them to leave the camp. That'll give us a little head start."

The little henequen rope bridge hung precariously over the river. It had only half-rotten wood boards, two feet wide, and hung suspended from two small ropes that spanned the river as it cut through a narrow, deep gorge. The wind had only just started to pick up, but the fragile, flimsy bridge was already swaying over the jostling water, forty feet below.

Travis dismounted and walked to the bank. The cool mist of the river washed up onto his face. He grabbed one of the ropes and tugged on it.

"We can cross," Tony said, still on horseback and inspecting the gorge. "But a branding iron wouldn't push our horses across that bridge. Probably a good thing. It won't hold them."

Travis pulled off his shirt. "We'll blindfold the horses. Lead them across. One at a time. The Indians do it all the time in the mountains."

"But the ground's not moving then," Tony countered.

Travis removed one of the muskets from his horse and handed it to Tony. He then draped his shirt over his horse's head, tying a knot below the chin to secure the mask. "I'll go first. If I don't make it, try to go get Chase on foot. Glad I got a mare. Horses are the opposite of humans. Females are less turbulent."

Travis grabbed his reins and pulled on his mare. With a few gentle words, he led her to the bridge. He put a foot on the wood planks to check the steps. The boards were solid, but wet and slippery. With his free hand, he held the rope rail, two feet above the boards, and started onto the bridge. To his relief, the horse followed as he slowly sauntered. It was a fifty-yard walk to the opposite bank. Travis tried not to look down at the bolder-strewn river below; a fall was certain to be fatal.

As he reached the center of the bridge, the mangle of rope and wood swayed more. The bridge dipped a foot; the ropes creaked and squeaked as the fiber tightened. The horse hawed. Travis paused, his hands almost trembling and the hair on his neck rising, and waited a few seconds as the swaying receded. He looked below. He was hanging in midair, the air cool and damp over the water.

Ahead, the slippery wood planks of the bridge led back up to the opposite bank. Travis took a deep breath, his legs wobbly, and recommenced his journey, turning to check his nervous mount's footing. If she spooked, she might lunge into the river and bring the bridge down. Travis grabbed the rope rail firmly. As he got closer to the bank, he hurried his steps until he finally landed on solid ground. He exhaled and wiped the sweat from his brow. He turned to Tony. "See, nothing to it."

• • •

The spring was quiet, the only sound the trickling of water over the purple rocks as it fell down to the crystal-clear, half-acre pool. The three soldiers had hidden their horses behind the granite outcropping, projecting fifteen feet above the plain, and taken up a position behind some boulders where they were looking a few feet down at the spring. They had chosen a group of rocks shaded from the sun in hopes it might conceal their position.

Travis picked up both muskets to check their loading and the placement of the percussion caps. He looked at four trails leading to the spring and pointed. "They'll come up that trail. I'll shoot Riveria first. Tony, then you open fire. We'll wait until they start to water, unless they get spooked. Then we'll open up."

"All right," Tony said, kneeling behind another set of rocks ten feet away.

Travis leaned both muskets against the rock face and looked at Jim, squatting beside him. The two had set out the reloading material and rods on the ground, ready to be used on short notice. Travis then looked at the spring. He had a terrible feeling inside as he surveyed the scene. Even with their camouflage and the element of surprise, rescuing Chase would be a daunting task. It was more than a hundred yards to where the horses would likely water. And if they didn't kill most of the party with the first barrage, the rocky hill around them could be easily surrounded. All this also assumed the Mexicans and Chase were coming. Travis and the others had been hiding in the rocks for twenty minutes without seeing a thing. Travis removed his watch from his pocket and checked the time. "If they're not here in fifteen minutes, they're not coming."

"I see them now," Tony said, carefully lowering himself for better concealment.

Travis looked out onto the plain. There was a small tendril of dust in the distance, still a half mile away, rising and moving sideways with the breeze. Travis also lowered himself and secured one of the muskets. "About five minutes."

Travis squatted and poked the rifle through a little slot in the rocks, cocking the hammer and setting the trigger. He maneuvered the musket until he found a position where both of his elbows were secure. The five minutes passed slowly, the four horses growing larger in his vision. Riveria led, Chase behind him, followed by two more soldiers.

As the horses neared the spring, the group stopped thirty yards short of it to briefly inspect the grounds. Travis heard a few muffled words. He put Riveria in his sights. The four horses moved forward, Travis continuing to cover Riveria with the barrel. The Mexican colonel was a slight man, just over five feet tall and weighing less than 110 pounds. Travis had learned over the years that it was much easier to kill a man on horse than on foot: he was exposed in the air, less likely to be moving quickly, and couldn't bob around randomly. Travis decided he would pull the trigger as Riveria's horse paused at the spring, just before he dismounted.

Travis watched the party approach the water, fear almost overcoming him. He was worried that they would be spotted and the Mexicans would tear off onto the safety of the open plain. He watched Riveria's face as the Mexican cautiously scanned the spring. Travis knew he had one shot. If the colonel fell, it would send the other two men into disarray. This might be Chase's last chance. If Travis failed, he possibly would never see Chase again. He steadied himself as he never had before. His fears drifted out of his mind, replaced with unemotional focus. He covered Riveria with the small sight, paused his breath, and squeezed the trigger. The shot pierced the silence. Riveria tumbled off his horse.

Jim handed Travis the other musket, and Tony opened fire.

As Travis looked at the spring through the sights, he saw a horse fall under a Mexican, dust kicking up around the other two horses. One of the Mexicans was returning fire from his horse; the other was struggling to free himself from his fallen mount. Travis heard a bullet ricochet off the rocks behind him.

Tony continued to fire at the fallen horse. He emptied his pistol.

Travis heard a shriek. He looked at the fallen horse. The man trapped under it was bleeding. Travis put his sights on the third man, who had now reared around and was in a full sprint back in the direction he had come, Chase's horse in tow. Travis put the gun sight on the butt of Chase's horse. His whole being, purpose, and training channeled into this instant. He pulled the trigger. Chase's horse stumbled and fell to the ground. The Mexican's horse stumbled; the tether rope broke free of his saddle, but the soldier continued to charge away.

Travis slowly lowered the rifle, his sense of everything else returning. He looked at Chase, getting to his feet over his convulsing horse. "Reload. We might have to finish those two off. Don't kill the colonel. We'll take him with us. He'll be a prize catch," Travis yelled, and grabbed the musket that Jim had just finished reloading.

Tony picked up his glasses and made a quick inspection. "Think they're both dead."

Travis turned to the spring. Neither of the Mexicans had moved. "Let's go down, but be cautious."

On Travis's words, Tony scampered from behind the rocks.

Travis watched as the Ranger slowly walked around the water's edge, pistol at the ready. Tony put two more balls into the Mexican under the fallen horse. Travis and Jim then came out from behind the rocks. Travis walked down to the spring to look at the colonel. His shot had hit the man mid-chest; all life had already departed.

"Boy, am I glad to see you," Chase said, walking up behind Travis.

"You don't know the half of it," Travis answered. "Santa Anna's going to massacre everyone at Goliad today. You were headed to a firing squad."

Chase only stared at Travis, seeming to have a hard time comprehending the words.

"You can thank Tony. He busted me out last night. We came looking for you. Can't believe we actually found you. It's our lucky day."

Chase turned to Tony, disbelief still written on his face.

"You're not home yet," Tony said. "We still have to cross that rope bridge and a hundred miles of hostile territory. The latter will be the easiest."

Travis reached down and grabbed the colonel's shako. "You can ride the colonel's horse. I get the real prize." He lifted the tail of his shirt and polished the insignia and unit markings on the cap's front. "This is a bad day for Texas. If that son of a bitch actually kills those men, we'll make him pay. He'll regret it."

Chapter 7

Banks of the San Jacinto River,
April 20, 1836

Day was descending to night, only a smidgen of violet in the eastern sky. It was a warm coastal night with a thick breeze. Travis turned to inspect the camp, housing some two hundred people: Texas regulars, volunteers, scouts, doctors, cooks, even refugees. The fires, twenty or more, gave the setting life—their orange spires waltzing wonderfully, sparkling embers eluding gravity, drifting like ghosts into dark nothingness. Out of habit, Travis looked up, locating the North Star and Orion, brilliantly hanging over the savanna.

A man approached, only an image in the uniform of the regulars: a dark navy jacket, white trousers, black boots. The soldier held a torch, its fluid flame constantly changing hue. He planted the long stick in the soft turf. "At ease, gentlemen. Gather around. I'm Captain Hoover—Houston's staff."

The dozen Rangers quietly formed a circle around the captain, amplifying the light. Travis knew them all well. Chase, Chester, and Tony stood across from him, their dirty, tattered clothes pulsing with the flame. The captain went down on one knee, and the Rangers followed as the officer unfurled a weathered map on the ground.

"What I'm about to tell you is completely confidential—you take it to your graves." The captain looked at the steely-eyed men. "General Houston has his army here"—the captain pointed at the map with a two-foot stick and spoke with an authoritative, professional tone—"at the confluence of Buffalo Bayou and the San Jacinto River. He's managed to maneuver Santa Anna to here. He's got him trapped. He can't escape. In the next day or two, General Houston plans to attack with all his forces. It's imperative to destroy Santa Anna's army here, not let it escape or be reinforced. To do this, we need to secure all routes to the battle, most notably this one." The captain again pointed with the stick to the map. "Urrea is here with the Yucatán, Cuautla, and Bajio Battalions. Those battalions have artillery. Some of you men served at Goliad and Refugio, so you know how capable these troops are. But their only route to rescue Santa Anna is this bridge over Oyster Creek. We need to take it and destroy it. I don't think it's in Urrea's hands now, but you can rest assured his scouts are out front with the intent of getting it. It's only a rough wooden bridge. Should be no problem to burn. Captain McAlister, you need to move there as fast as possible, with reckless abandon if need be."

"We're ready to move out now," Chase answered in a stern voice; he never had to raise his voice to be heard.

Captain Hoover looked at each man individually. A quiet settled over the group. "You are Texas's best, all her hopes and dreams. May God go with you." He extended a hand to Chase. "Once the bridge is destroyed, leave a couple of scouts, but the rest of your party should rendezvous at General Houston's headquarters. This is going to be a big fight. You will certainly be needed."

Travis took a deep breath. It would be an all-night ride to the bridge in question. He and his comrades were already worn thin, almost to their limits. It had been a demanding two months scouting and spying for the Texas militia. First, there was the demoralizing, deadly, and decisive defeat at Goliad, then the retreat in front of the Mexican army and its kill-crazy tactics.

The days had been long, with sparse rations, ammo and supplies always deficient, ubiquitous devastation and slaughter. The Ranger losses had been heavy. Travis looked at the lot. This ardent, resilient, individualistic group, just like himself, was more down and disheartened than he'd ever imagined they could be. The mood was somber, as it had been for weeks. He couldn't remember the last time he had heard the jaunty bantering once so frequent in the ranks. Travis, Chase, and Tony had already been spared death at Goliad, where almost every man, more than three hundred, had been massacred in cold blood. That alone may have been what pushed this group to where they were today. But maybe the end was near. Maybe this General Houston could save Texas. Travis wanted to go home to San Antonio and be with Mercedes, but he had no choice but to fight on. Defeat for him and his cohorts meant certain death, although they hoped it would be a quick one at the end of a rope or against a wall.

It was a burgundy dawn against the flat grassland and marshes. The dew was thick, the mosquitoes and gnats dense. Travis relaxed in the saddle, eyes haggard, shifting his sore bones and listening to the darkness as his mount casually grazed below. He heard some shuffling, but it was only an armadillo scurrying across the trail. The ten Rangers had paused to water their horses and wait for two scouts who had ridden ahead to reconnoiter the bridge. They had been gone for several hours, and Travis began to wonder if they would return at all. First light was the standard protocol for returning to a patrol.

Though he was dead tired, Travis felt a little tense but also excited, a miniscule rush. He and his party were about to undertake something important. While the job was often long, strenuous, and hazardous, these were the times that made it worthwhile. Deep down inside, he loved all this, the thrill, the camaraderie, the significance of his duties, making a difference. It was what kept him going.

"That must be them," Chase said softly, motioning up the trail.

Travis looked. There were two horses in the distance, one carrying a tall, wide man, probably Chester. Once the scouts got close enough to recognize the patrol, they picked up their pace and galloped ahead, steam rolling off their sweaty mounts.

"Bridge is about two leagues up this trail," Chester said, catching his breath. "It's unguarded. But Rayo's cavalry is in the area. We haven't seen them, but the ferry captain at Sims has. We doubled back that way."

"Rayo, huh?" Chase said, turning to look at Travis. "That old jefe sure likes to stay out front."

Travis's skin crawled a little. He hadn't seen his potential father-in-law since their meeting at the hacienda, but the Rangers had brushed the trail of his cavalry on several occasions. His worst nightmare was putting the *haciendado* in his sights. But at this moment, in this place, with Texas independence on the line, would he have to choose between the Rangers and himself, between Texas and Mercedes? Would she ever forgive him if he killed her father? His blood got cold.

Chase cleared his throat. "Lieutenant Ross, take four men and burn the bridge. The rest of us will move forward and flank the banks. Let's move out, a smart trot."

In thirty minutes, the group arrived at the bridge. The day was growing bright, the surroundings turning from a black void to light green. Chase left four men to guard the rear, and crossed the bridge with two more, fanning out to keep a keen eye out.

Travis dismounted on the bridge, slowly lowering his foot to the solid wood deck. It was so peaceful, the chirping of birds and bellowing of frogs drowned out the sound of his breath. He looked at the narrow bayou, only thirty paces in breadth, but surely necessitating a swim. "Get that whale oil and saturate the deck. Get underneath and wet the pylons. Don't want this thing to be easily rebuilt." Travis went down on one knee to study the support columns. But no sooner had he lowered his head than he heard one of the Rangers signaling the alert.

"What is it?" one of the Rangers asked.

"Don't know. Just keep working, but don't light it until everybody's back across," Travis answered.

A gunshot broke the silence; then two more rang out. Travis heard horses running and more gunfire—much more—from his rear. Two Rangers appeared from the far side of the bridge, racing toward the melee. Travis jumped on his horse, joining in pursuit. Populating the bayou banks were hundred-year-old cypresses spotted with moss; under these canopies, it was still night.

Travis could see the muzzle blasts coming from his right. He veered his mount toward the action, securing his Colt in his right hand. His small pony stalled and snorted. Travis looked down at the dark silhouette of a lifeless Mexican dragoon. He heard more movement: another man getting to his feet.

Travis lunged forward, spurring his mount violently, a three-step burst. His pony's front shoulders plowed into the soldier, tumbling him to the ground. A mutter of *"Me no Alamo"* came from the dark shadows.

With his pistol, Travis gestured the man forward, toward the firing, which now subsided. He urged the horseless cavalryman into a meadow on the banks of the bayou. The light got better, almost a morning glare. Standing against the water, all on black stallions and clad in their showy, colorful uniforms with gold belts and tall, brimmed shakos, four Mexicans brandished their long shiny lances. Rayo sat at their vanguard.

Under their tunics, the Mexicans stared at the three Rangers, on horseback, their pistols locked on the Mexican lancers. The timid eyes, Mexican and Texan, roved from face to face. Travis negligently rode forward, pistol still at the ready, his horse's steps the only sound. He motioned for the fifth soldier to join the others. "What you got, Tony?"

"We shot two of them," Tony replied without

removing his eyes from his sights of his weapon.

Travis looked at Rayo. "Señor Rayo, it appears that you ended up on the wrong side of this fight after all." Travis's voice was rarely serious, but this time it was downright grave. He lowered his pistol.

The old Mexican jefe did not reply, but rather gritted his teeth in anger, the veins on his face openly pulsing.

"What you want to do with them, Travis?" Tony asked.

"Let's kill 'em all," Chester said. "Just like they did at Goliad. Let God sort them out."

On Chester's words, the Mexicans tensed up, their horses beginning to fidget. Travis stared at Rayo, then his subordinates, before looking at the bridge, now starting to flame up. A smirk appeared on his face. "As beautiful as your daughter."

Rayo got more worked up, raising his sword higher, his body radiating rage.

Travis paused, tension in his chest, thinking Rayo might make a suicide charge. The scene was deathly silent, and stress hung in the air like a thick fog. Travis turned to Tony, whose face was rife with fear; he didn't want to pull the trigger, and he silently begged with his eyes. Travis twisted to look at Chester, itching, almost pleading to fire. Travis turned back to Tony. "Take their horses and weapons. Leave them their food and water. They can swim back across the bayou. Then swim the river back to Mexico."

Tony looked at Travis, wearing a grateful expression.

Travis wondered if the Ranger felt relieved for the prisoners or himself.

"What?" Chester interjected in a dumbfounded voice.

"You heard me. That's an order," Travis answered, riding off to inspect the burning bridge. On the banks of the bayou, he found Chase, on horseback, rolling a cigarette while joyfully eyeing the roaring fire.

Chester galloped up behind Travis.

"You boys get it all taken care of?" Chase said.

"Yeah, but Travis let the Mexicans go," Chester added, still appalled and staring at Travis, fury filling his eyes.

Chase put the cigarette to his mouth and looked at the bridge. He took a long drag, gratification exuding from his face. "Mexicans fight a lot harder if they think they'll be shot when they're captured. Besides, they catch your ass one day, you'll be glad we let them go."

As Travis listened to Chase, he heard some more horses lumbering in the trees. The group turned to look; then three gunshots broke the quiet of the dawn, kicking up turf around the horses. All three men pulled out their pistols and turned their mounts toward the trees. Travis saw some movement: three horses charging in their direction. Instinctively, he spurred his mount, charging toward the assaulters, Chase and Chester at his side. The Rangers fired three quick shots. The rest of the Ranger patrol joined in with a ten-shot volley from the side as they also charged forward.

Travis saw one of the men fall from his horse. He and his two partners jerked back on their reins to halt their mounts and fire again as two more shots came from the trees. The three Rangers' second volley dropped another man, only a dark silhouette. The third horse that had been attacking reared sideways, racing away into the trees. The Rangers emptied their pistols as he disappeared, blending into the darkness. As fast as it started, it ceased, the tranquil sounds of morning again descending on the swamp.

Travis dismounted to inspect the two lancers, both still alive and bleeding but not for long. Each had been shot in the chest, an almost certain death sentence so far from a doctor. He got a cool sweat as he recognized one of the men. It was Francisco. His mind got dizzy as he hurried down on one knee and turned the body up, ripping open the jacket and inspecting the wound. The bullet had pierced the high chest, through the lungs.

Francisco looked into Travis's eyes, unable to speak but nevertheless, Travis thought, aware of his surroundings.

"No," Travis moaned, putting a hand on the side of Francisco's cheek. He brushed his long hair back with his other hand.

"There's nothing you can do for him," Chase said, standing over Travis's shoulder.

Travis pulled out his canteen to give Francisco some water as the lancer's eyes closed and his breathing stopped, almost as if he were just falling asleep. Travis gently laid the head back on the ground. He felt empty, like his own soul was withering away, slipping out of his body. All his energy departed as he fell from his knees to his rear.

"We'll haul them up here to high ground and bury them proper before we go," Chase said, putting a hand on Travis's shoulder.

Two days later, the Ranger patrol slowly rode into General Houston's headquarters on the San Jacinto Plain. Travis had spent the days moping in the saddle, grief on his face, no longer fervent about his duties. He wanted to just ride off into the grassland aimlessly, wander around, and be alone. He felt as though he were only a body, just subsisting, taking in air, going through cumbersome motions. The Texas landscape all seemed to look the same: dull and depressing.

But as the Rangers rode onto the day-old battlefield, Travis's eyes, like those of all his comrades, filled with shock and disbelief. On the sunbaked fields lay bodies, Mexican soldiers by the hundreds. They were bloated, many stripped of clothing. The carnivores had feasted all night, and the buzzards, en masse, had descended from the sky for the easy meal. Over the sound of horses' hooves, millions of flies buzzed.

Travis smoked in silence, expressionless, and stared past the battlefield to a row of chuck wagons—the Texans' large camp, identified by the fires and hundreds of canvas tents, set in no discernible pattern. Above the camp, a few red, white, and blue flags of the new republic hung, limp without wind.

The group rode slowly past a guarded encampment of Mexicans, only a worn plot. The prisoners were bunched, hundreds of them, like pigs on the filthy ground. The smell of excrement became stronger than the morbid reek from the battlefield. Two doctors roamed the grounds, tending a score of wounded. A hundred more lay shoeless on their backs, having already taken their last breath.

Chase pointed to a large tent. Outside it and under a small oak, a man sat, smoking a pipe with his wounded leg propped up on an ammo box. "That's him. General Houston."

"Six hundred dead, six hundred more captured, only two causalities on our side? Incredible," Travis said.

Chase pointed again. This time at another man,

dressed in the clothes of a peon and bound in shackles between two sentries. "That must be Santa Anna."

A man approached on horseback, a Texas regular. He pulled back on his reins in front of the Rangers.

"Captain Chase McAlister and the Ninth Ranger Patrol, reporting as ordered," said Chase. "Do you know where Major Williamson is?"

The officer rubbed the stubble on his face before he spoke. "He's out chasing down the stragglers. We're 'bout done here. You boys get some coffee and food." The officer smiled and pointed to a distant tent, where a large group of soldiers congregated. "We got Santa Anna's stock of gold. General Houston's ordered that every man be paid up for his enlistment time."

"Pay?" Travis replied. "It's been so long since we got wages, I forgot we got paid for this job."

"Seven hundred Texans with three months' wages in their pocket," Chase observed. "The majority of battle casualties will be tonight, around the whiskey bottles and card games."

Chapter 8

It was the most glorious of days, the type that turn even the sad happy—not a cloud in the dazzling blue sky and a steady, cool breeze from the north. Travis slowly rode up to the Hacienda de Rayo del Norte. It had been two months since the battle of San Jacinto, and despite the fact that the Mexican army had departed Texas and that Santa Anna had agreed to its independence, the Rio Grande valley still idled in a state of war—many residents displaced, many still trying to decide on which side of the river to plant their roots.

Travis turned in the saddle to look back at the tall, magnificent black stallion in tow. The horse's mane had been trimmed and his coat brushed for this occasion. Travis smiled, pondering what response the horse's return would produce from the Mexican jefe. He also wondered how he would be received. Around him, the spring rains had turned the dry chaparral a dark shade of green and filled the hacienda's grounds with fresh wildflowers. But as Travis approached the main house, the lack of the livestock, hands, and activity that had been commonplace here for decades was conspicuous.

Travis trotted into the small garden in front of the house and dismounted. He tied his little paint to a hitching post and walked to the front door. A short, sun-seared mestiza woman, dressed in a rough calico dress and holding a pot, appeared in the doorway. She mumbled some quick Spanish and disappeared into the house. Travis, puzzled, turned to notice that the hacienda's yard had been unattended for some time, that displeasing weeds and untrimmed grass abounded.

Shortly, the servant reappeared. She scolded Travis with a look and barked some rapid Spanish in his direction. "Senorita Rayo will be down in a few minutes. She's making herself proper. You shouldn't show up here without notice. She's been waiting for you for over a week. About to drive me crazy." The woman shook her head, aggravated, and disappeared again.

Travis waited a full five minutes before Mercedes appeared, smartly dressed in a red and white charro dress. She paused a second in the doorway, then ran to Travis, gracefully folding her soft, sensuous arms around his neck. Travis returned the hug, feeling Mercedes go limp in his arms. She backed her head away from him and started to say something, but Travis put a finger over her moist, red lips, looking her over for a bit before speaking. "I brought your father his horse back."

"What took you so long? I spent all week making you a new jacket for your thirtieth birthday. You're turning into an old man." Mercedes snickered.

"I am sorry about your brother. You know I was there—"

"I know. It has been difficult for me. The most

101

difficult thing I've ever endured. But it's not your fault. You've probably suffered as much as I have." Mercedes brushed Travis's hair lightly, perhaps trying to comfort him.

Travis smiled. "You put some effort into your appearance. Men always like that." He paused. "Where's your father and everybody else?"

Mercedes exhaled an animated breath. "He's gone to his ranch in Coahuila. He's taken all the vaqueros and cattle there. Plans to stay there. Sell this ranch. He's not very happy about Santa Anna's capitulation."

"What are you going to do?"

"I don't know. I wanted you to marry me. We could go to Coahuila now that the war's over."

Travis paused, feeling his face turn an irritated red. "I'm probably not real welcome there. I've made enemies during the war. Especially that crooked *federale* down there, Paco. I so much as get in that river and he hears about it, there'll be a posse bearing down on me."

"I said I *wanted* to go there, not that I was going. I'm here, aren't I? My father has been lecturing me about staying here for you. He says in Mexico, women rarely get to marry the men they love. This is tearing me apart. You do love me, don't you?" Mercedes locked her eyes on Travis, studying his silent reaction, sincerity leaking from her face. "There's nothing so beautiful as the truth. Even if it's not what I want to hear."

Travis put his hand on Mercedes's cheek, caressing it lightly. "Yes, I do, but I don't even have a home now . . . I have to take care of a few things in town this afternoon. Why don't I come back tomorrow? We can go on a picnic down by the river."

"I can't see you today?" Mercedes's face filled with chagrin.

"I have to meet with Captain McAlister and the army tonight."

"All right, come first thing in the morning," Mer-cedes said, perking up.

Travis grabbed Mercedes's hands and backed away slowly, winking at her. "We've waited five months. One more day won't be hard. I'll be here for breakfast."

The next day was announcing its presence with the strong rays and long shadows of the early sun when Travis arrived back at the hacienda. As he had done the previous day, he parked his colt in front of the main house. But before he could drop the reins across the wooden hitching post, the elderly servant woman strode out of the mansion. Her face showed discontent. And Travis got an uneasy feeling.

"She's gone," the woman said.

"Gone? Where to?"

"Vaqueros from Mexico came and got her last night. Señor Rayo said she has to come home.

She not want to go. They had to tie her up and put her on a horse."

"What time?"

"About midnight."

Travis turned and looked south, toward the border. There was no doubt they were four or five hours across the river by now. "How many?"

"Six."

The merry mood and expectation in Travis's soul only minutes earlier sank to depression and denial. He saddled up, rearing his mount around and spurring his colt to a light trot in the direction of the Rio Grande, instantly thinking he would right this wrong, go after her, whatever it took. But as he scuttled along, getting closer to the river and thinking about a plan, his mind spun. He had trouble figuring out exactly what to do. If he rode hard, he would catch the horses in a day or two. But he would be deep into hostile Mexico all alone. Even if he didn't find the vaqueros, he could go straight to Rayo's ranch. But word of an Anglo traveling across the country would get out—not to mention the Comanches, who fell on solo travelers like bears on honey. It would be a menacing escapade, with little chance of succeeding. Did he want Mercedes that much, enough to take on such a daunting task? He would do anything feasible. But was this feasible? As he reached the river ford, he sank in the saddle, easing back on his reins, an almost painful sensation falling over him. His horse moved a foot forward, splashing the water. Travis looked ahead, took a deep, irritated breath, and veered his horse back to the north.

PART TWO

Chapter 9

Eagle Pass, State of Texas,
United States of America,
October 1846

Travis sat carelessly atop his fourteen-hand palomino mare, adjusting his bedroll and looking out at the herd of longhorns, five hundred strong—every animal in the M&R stock. The beasts forded up to the Rio Grande. Above and beyond the incessant moos, burrs, and settling dust sat the black hills, their slopes dotted with endemic ocotillo and pronghorn.

It had been a hard ten-day drive to Eagle Pass, across the stunning Chisos Mountains, but they had made good time. Travis turned his attention to the little frontier town, abuzz with activity, gusto, and tension. In the river, a hundred soldiers, U.S. Army soldiers, were constructing a pontoon bridge to the shouts of a few sergeants. Bunched up to the bank was a gargantuan wagon train, five hundred vehicles in all, stretching off to the horizon like an armada at sea. Travis turned to the army camp sitting against the river, a mass of hundreds of tents in a perfect grid. On a tall, skinned cottonwood, above the tents, hung a giant flag, the Stars and Stripes—the first Travis had ever seen over the Texas landscape. And floating through the camp was the whiff of savory spices drifting up from a long row of makeshift cooking pits. A dozen men in white aprons basted the line of grilling meat: beef quarters, whole javelina, deer, and antelope affixed to steel rods above the coals.

"It's about time we made some money out of this deal," Chase said, riding up beside Travis. "Army pays in cash. Hell, if you weren't much help at the ranch beforehand, you'll be non-existent after this payday."

"Our price was too low," Travis argued. "Especially for all the trouble and work we've put into these cows. There's not enough stock out here to feed this army. You should have let me do the negotiating on this. You're the labor, but I'm the brains behind this outfit."

"All the work you've put in! This is a pretty good deal for you. A pocket full of money for sitting around the porch, bitching and complaining all the time."

Travis nodded toward the town, only a few rundown adobe and wood hovels. "I bet somewhere over there we can get a drink, see some excitement for a change." He trotted off in the direction of town.

"We're not done here yet," Chase hollered.

"I am," Travis answered, continuing to ride away. "Come on. We've been on these damned horses for two weeks. Them cows ain't leaving that water. They haven't had a good drink in days."

Travis rode up to the drab, one-room cantina, a rough adobe building with swinging wood doors and a clay tile roof. He stepped up on the porch and waited for Chase, who was coming slowly behind him. The smoke-filled and dirty little bar, lit by candles, had six tables, all occupied. In the corner, a coarse old man banged on a piano over the sounds of boasting, bickering, and the clinking of glasses.

Travis and Chase approached the wood bar, stopping and leaning against it. A plump, unsightly country hag in her late forties leaned forward from behind the bar.

"We'll take two beers," Chase said.

"No beer or whiskey," the greasy-faced woman snapped. "Fifteen hundred men in town, mescal wine or nothing."

"Mescal wine it will be," Travis answered, scanning the tables, two of which currently hosted card games. The men in the bar were mostly soldiers, irregular-looking men, unshaven and in their grimy blue uniforms trimmed in yellow. "I ain't been in a card game with a white man in months. I may parlay those cows into a fortune before we leave this place."

Chase picked up a worn, week-old newspaper from the bar and scanned the headlines. "General Taylor's taken Monterrey. Maybe we should have signed on. Ben McCulloch and Jack Hayes are becoming national celebrities. That could be me and you."

Travis looked at the paper that Chase had turned to him. The headline read: *Rangers Storm Bishop's Palace.* Travis lifted his glass. "Here's to 'em *and* getting rid of those smelly cows."

"Hear, hear," Chase added, turning up his glass with an awful grimace. "Nasty shit. But I believe I'll have another."

"Me, too," Travis said as the bar suddenly got quiet and the piano paused. He looked at the doorway, occupied by a tall, impressive-looking officer, outfitted in a clean uniform and armed with a long, sheathed saber. The officer quickly inspected the room, then approached the bar, petulantly motioning for four men to vacate an adjacent table.

"You Captain McAlister?" the gray-bearded soldier asked, sitting down as the piano and conversation recommenced.

"I am," Chase answered.

"I'm Colonel Patrick, Third Dragoons." The officer curtly pointed to two chairs, instructing Chase and Travis to sit. He was obviously accustomed to having men jump to his every want and word. "You must be Travis Ross. So you two are the famous scouts and Indian hunters."

"*Infamous* might be a better word for it," Travis responded as he and Chase sat down. He took a long look at the officer, who was in his fifties with a humorless, serious face and long, shaggy eyebrows.

The colonel removed an envelope from inside his jacket and handed it to Chase. "For the beef. It's all there, cash. We're moving out in a day or so . . . to Chihuahua. We need scouts. And flankers to keep the Indians off of us."

"You don't have Lipans and Mexican scouts?" Chase asked, pausing and lighting a cigarette. "The Comanches and Apaches in Mexico make the Indians up here look tame. Mexico has a standing bounty of fifty dollars a scalp, keeps them roused up pretty good."

"Yeah, but I don't trust 'em. You can trust a Mexican about far as you can throw him." The colonel looked at Chase as if this were something the onetime Ranger should know. "You two have been assigned to General Wool—to lead us south, scout, and spy."

"Assigned?" Travis groused. "We've both been civilian for almost four years. With all due respect, Colonel, I'm not going anywhere but San Antonio. Got plans to squander as much of that money as possible—in debauchery—as fast as I can."

"I'm not asking; I'm telling," the colonel replied in an aggravated tone, reaching into his coat and pulling out another envelope. "All the other Rangers and scouts are already with Taylor, over a thousand. You boys are all that's left. Here's a letter from the governor. You two have been conscripted into the state militia, under General

Wool, to serve as spies and scouts." The colonel handed the packet to Chase.

"Can he do that?" Travis asked, peeking over at Chase with a sheepish glare.

"He can do whatever the hell he wants," the colonel continued, calmly but authoritatively. "Texas is a state now, operating under the United States Constitution. But it doesn't matter. General Wool has the authority, straight from the president, to requisition anything he wants down here, people or matériel."

Travis watched Chase read the letter. "What's it say?"

"It's from the governor to General Wool, suggesting us as Rangers in the area that might be of some help as spies. The governor places our services at the general's disposal." Chase put the handwritten note down. "I guess we're out of the cattle business anyway."

Travis looked at the colonel, who had pulled a third set of papers out of his jacket—enlistment papers. He was now filling in a few of the blanks. It was clear this matter was not up for debate or negotiation, at least not as far as the colonel was concerned.

Travis took a deep breath. He had actually been second-guessing his decision not to enlist for the past few months. In fact, in recent days, wandering the unfriendly, solitary plains, he had been second-guessing many of his decisions over the past decade. The worst kind of regret a man can have is regretting the things he didn't do instead of the things he did. Should he have gone to Mexico with the army? It had been a chance to get back across the border without being butchered and possibly see Mercedes. Maybe Providence had arrived, putting his decisions in someone else's hands; that could never be regretted.

"Enlistment is for six months," the colonel said, sliding the papers across the table. "You'll both get lieutenant's pay. I've given you five days to get your matters in order. We'll probably be across the river by then. Catch up and report to me."

Travis looked at Chase, who was scanning the contract. Chase picked up the pen, dipped it in a small ink bottle the colonel had placed on the table, and added his signature to the document. He handed the papers to Travis, who did likewise.

The colonel stood, waved the papers in the air to dry the ink, and extended a hand to both men. "I look forward to serving with you. You come well recommended. McAlister, you'll be in command of all scouts. Travis will be your second. You boys have a good frolic, but get ready to ride hard. We're going to punish these Mexicans. They've had it coming for some time. And you can rest assured General Wool has every intention of making them heel."

Chapter 10

With the pale blue Mexican sky overhead and the arid soil under their horses, Travis and Chase finally caught up to the army column four days later. The ride had been peaceful, with the simple pleasure of riding a horse through a scenic and unspoiled land. The open country, the thought of doing something useful and meaningful, a day's wages for a day's work, finally being a person of value, all excited Travis and made him step lively. But he also had misgivings. As he rode through a few cloud shadows, moving across the range and looking at the landscape, Travis wondered what was ahead, down the trail, in this exotic land. He had given up the gun. It was an unending internal battle; that which made him feel the happiest and gave him freedom also haunted him and conjured up his worst nightmares.

The land was flat, its once-prosperous fields now only a wasteland, swept by the howling wind and dotted with deserted, decrepit haciendas. Some of the ranches were only recently vacated, but others were almost archaeological sites, their tall lookout towers and majestic estates unoccupied for decades and falling into decay, almost like ancient Indian settlements.

The trail for Travis and Chase had been dictated by the need for water as always. They had crossed a few roaring rivers or passed periodic springs, usually bordered by a comfortable stand of trees. Game had been ample: whitetail, rabbits, quail, and dove. They had seen almost no one, only occasionally passing a few barefoot, wide-eyed, curious citizens politely waving from their doorsteps.

The two Rangers topped a small hill to get their first glimpses of the magnificent army, almost fifteen miles in length, now moving into the greener, more populated foothills. The column had been easy to find with its mile-wide dust cloud and hundred-yard wake of worn turf and battered landscape. At the rear of the procession were the wagons and support personnel— doctors, cooks, musicians, and quartermasters to name a few—trolling along slowly and guarded by a few pickets. In front of them marched the horse artillery, in three-men teams, each striding alongside three horses packed with a disassembled six-pound howitzer. In front of the cannons marched the main body, just behind the dragoons and cavalry. Out front of the main body were the scouts and skirmishers.

The army was a splendid, inspiring sight to Travis, with the men marching by fours, most with their royal blue jackets, crossing white chest belts, powder blue pants, and fatigue caps, all trimmed in vibrant stripes signifying their trade: blue for infantry, red for artillery, yellow for cavalry. The gold buttons on their belts and the black leather ammo pouches, attached to waist belts, all glimmered. The officers were identified by ostentatious embroidered cuffs, collars, and shoulder planks. Interspersed in the column marched the state volunteers—Indiana, Illinois, and Arkansas, among others—with their dazzling uniforms stitched of red, yellow, or green wool.

Travis stared at the column moving like a vibrant snake around the hills, its flags and guidons bobbing up and down against the distant mountains. How this mass of men and supplies made fifteen miles a day, Travis could only imagine. To him, it was a testament to the vigor and industry of his new country, one he felt proud of for the very first time.

"General Wool looks like he means business," Chase said, sitting his horse next to Travis and also admiring the formidable line of conscripts.

"This is nothing. Wool only has about three thousand men. Taylor has the main force in Monterrey, seven thousand men, I think, mostly regulars."

"Let's go see if we can find the good Colonel Patrick." Chase trotted his horse down the small hill.

After a thirty-minute trot, the two Rangers eventually located a group of officers, sitting on horseback under a twenty-foot brick tower at the apex of a thousand-foot hill the column now ascended. As they approached, Travis noticed a single star adorning one of the groups' flags, held high from the saddle by a cavalryman. Nearing the group, the

Rangers caught the attention of the officers, one of which was the solemn-faced Colonel Patrick.

"General Wool, these are our two scouts. Recommended by General Pickney," Colonel Patrick said as Travis and Chase brought their horses to a stop.

"I'm Captain McAlister, reporting for duty."

"Lieutenant Ross," Travis said, looking at the officers, all with hands and skin cleaner than anyone they had seen. General Wool was a gray-haired man in his sixties with a balding forehead. Travis could not help but notice the general's uniform, meticulously fit and freshly cleaned, but not adorned with any special awards or insignia save for the two star-covered plates on his shoulders, the double-breasted jacket with two columns of gold buttons, and the yellow sash around his waist.

The general gave a quick head bob and spoke in a gruff voice. "Where are all the Mexicans? Makes me feel like we're moving into a trap."

"Not likely, sir," Chase answered. "I'm sure all the local lawmen and *federales* have been summoned to the front. When that happens, all the *haciendados* and workers board themselves up in the towns because of the Indians." Chase pointed ahead.

Travis looked into the valley, a wonderful gorge bisecting the immense mountains far to the east and west. The terrain lay like a map, its rivers and roads easily read. Far ahead, maybe a dozen miles, sat a little white town buried in a green canopy, to the aft, a similar view of the country they had crossed.

Chase continued. "Santa Rosa's only about a half a day's ride ahead. I suspect you'll find the town overflowing. Not a worry, though. Most of the natives in this area are receptive—more than half of these haciendas are owned by Anglos. They hate Santa Anna."

"We've seen a few Indians, but none have dared to get very close," one of the general's juniors said.

"They're not likely to attack this train, but they'll jump all over any small patrols you have out," Chase countered. "I would recommend billeting in Santa Rosa tonight. There's plenty of water and food there."

"I see no need to slow down," Colonel Patrick said. "We're making good time."

"Just the other side of Santa Rosa is the Rio Sabinas," Chase said. "It will be a chore to ford. And the country gets much tougher—higher, less water and grass."

General Wool stared silently at the two Rangers for a few moments, sizing them and the situation up. He looked away before finally speaking. "Pass the word. We'll make camp in Santa Rosa. Colonel Patrick, send two of your men with these scouts to find good ground."

In Travis's experiences on the trail, whether fighting Indians and Mexicans, chasing bandits, or simply keeping the peace, he had always learned to settle into a daily routine. And the routine in General Wool's army that first week was the same every day: an early morning rise to scout the route for possible problems, watering holes, fords, and encampments, all the while keeping a sharp eye out for Indians or Mexican infantry. The days were warm and comfortable, in the seventies, but the nights hovered around freezing. About once a day, they entered a town, usually moving around it to come in from the south, giving the locals the feeling the village was already enveloped. The ground rose steadily. The days were long, riding up a hill, across a valley, over a stream, then back up a hill to repeat the infinite cycle. The only life outside the towns were a few shepherds tending their scant herds.

Travis and Chase were usually separated and each sent with two or three cavalrymen and a pair of topographic engineers. The engineers spent the days drawing maps and taking sun readings or compass readings with a brass transit. During the early evenings, they appraised the stars. In front of the column, the other engineers fanned out, building bridges or filling ravines. Teams of men with only hand tools worked all day, allowing the schooners to continue the endless advance.

The first week had been tense, hard movement as the determined column moved from the savanna up the steps to the Sierra Madre Oriental

Mountains. The pace had been slow, with always several wagons broken down, wheels or axles busted. Everywhere the army went, the locals warned of large forces with artillery massed nearby and ready to attack. Travis's experience on the border had prepared him for this ceaseless gossip, regardless of the location of the nearest army, whether across the next hill or a continent away.

On several occurrences, the pickets and patrols had engaged Mexican guerrillas, unruly outlaws usually outfitted in rough leather attire and brandishing primitive lances or sidearms. But the column had seen no sign of the Mexican army.

On the sixth morning in camp, Travis rose early, immediately noticing a cold, almost spooky breeze. The Lipan scouts seemed jumpy, the northern sky a cool shade of cobalt. He took a deep breath, sucking in the air as the campfires flickered in an eccentric dance; the grass fluttered, the tents clattered, the trees shimmered, almost bracing and awaiting the tempest. Travis knew the northers showed up fast and without warning, like a thief, raking the earth with savage winds and pelting, almost horizontal rain. He looked at the endless maze of tents and supplies, loosely lashed to the ground. He instantly moved in double time, heading for General Wool's headquarters, but before he arrived, two incredible bolts of lightning flashed across the sky, illuminating the camp and silhouetting the mountains with an instant white flash. The thunder shook the ground. As he opened the flap of the orderly's tent, a few peanut-sized raindrops fell on his jacket.

Noontime found the camp in total disarray, some of the tents scattered almost a mile away, twenty wagons on their sides, dozens of pack animals and horses missing. The storm had thrashed the earth for six hours, pelting man, beast, and the encampment with buckets of rain, cool gale-force winds, and apple-sized hail, terrorizing man and animal. The noncommissioned officers were busy trying to reassemble the encampment as the officers squabbled in meetings about the column's delay.

In search of the missing horses, Chase, Travis, and a squad of cavalry rode to the next village, only a collection of four haciendas, now criss-crossed by two muddy streets.

As the patrol approached the local church, a nice adobe building with a small bell tower, Travis saw a group of about twenty men, some tall and white, others short and brown, massed around the local priest. On the streets, a few of the larger ice balls remained under the shade of a few drooping and beaten sycamore trees.

Chase, leading the patrol, raised his arm in peace, halting them in front of the local church. *"Buenas tardes."*

One of the white men, middle-aged and in an American cowboy hat, walked up to Chase, removing his hat and wiping the humidity from his brow.

"We lost a bunch of horses this morning in the storm. Have any of you seen them?" Chase said in a conciliatory tone.

"Bunch of Indians raided the farms this morning," the man replied in educated English. He pointed to the pleasant houses. "They came while we were hiding from the storm. Got about five horses and two white women. We're trying to put a group together to go after them. They cut the throats of two of my vaqueros."

"Lieutenant Jones," Chase moaned, turning to the young-faced, spit-and-polish cavalryman Colonel Patrick had assigned to the Rangers as his attaché. "Bad news. Those Indians probably got our horses, too. Standard procedure. They come under the cover of one of those storms, scoop up the scattered animals. Just bad luck, that storm hitting while everybody was dozing." Chase turned to the *haciendado*. "What did these Indians look like?"

"About twenty of them," the man replied. "Looked like Indians. My vaqueros said one of them didn't have an ear."

Travis's stomach jumped, and he skipped a breath. The worst Indian of all had only one ear. "Any of these men see them?"

The man turned to the group and shouted, "José."

A little mestizo cowboy emerged from the group. "This Indian have a real small head and long black tattoo on his forearm?" Travis pointed to his own arm, describing the tattoo's location and size.

"*Sí.*" The little Mexican nodded his head.

Travis emptied his lungs of air and turned to Chase, now smoking a cigarette and staring out into the distant, quiet mountains. "Little Face."

Chase did not answer, continuing to take a few long drags.

"You know this outlaw?" the lieutenant interjected.

"Yes," Travis said, turning to the lieutenant. "As bad as they come, pure butcher. Half-breed: half Comanche, half Apache, the worst blood of both. Only thing he loves more than stealing horses is stealing horses and killing. Hates white men. We chased him for almost ten years on the border. Captain McAlister there shot his ear off."

"Only time I've ever missed in my life," Chase groaned, removing his pistol from its holster. The new Walker Colts were six-shooters, forty-four-caliber, fifteen inches long, and weighed almost five pounds. The imposing hand cannons did not require the removal of the cylinder to pack the percussion caps, powder, and balls. Travis watched Chase check his belt to make sure his second pistol was loaded and dry.

"We'll have to go after him, a serious pursuit," Travis continued. "If we don't show him we mean business, he'll prey on the column from here to Chihuahua. Lieutenant, I would send a man back to camp to report this. The rest of us should get on his trail now. He'll be easy to track on this muddy turf. It's only about a day's ride to Monclova. The general's planning to stop and regroup there anyway. We'll meet up with the army there."

The lieutenant nodded his head, and one of the cavalrymen took off at a trot.

"I thought you gave up fighting," Chase said to Travis.

"Not for this bastard. I'll gladly take up the fight."

Travis turned to the group of townspeople. "We'll track 'em. Try to kill 'em, send them all to hell. If there's any good news, the women should be all right for now. He intends to sell or trade them, probably for arms. We may be able to rescue them. Show us where Little Face killed these vaqueros."

The patrol walked a few hundred yards to be shown the two dead cowboys and the war party's trail, behind one of the main houses. Chase quickly studied the fresh tracks before remounting. He silently pointed to some rising foothills a few miles to the west and drove his spurs into his horse's ribs, riding off with a lumbering trot.

Travis goaded his horse with a soft "kee, kee," and led the remainder of the eight-man patrol out of the little village. He turned to the lieutenant, who was looking skeptically at Chase. "If there's a man in Mexico that can catch this group, it's him," Travis said. "Little Face killed his parents fifteen years ago. It's why he joined the Rangers, to hunt him down. We almost got him a couple of times, but after the Texas Revolution, the half-breed moved south of the border, where the Rangers couldn't get at him."

Travis and the patrol followed Chase for five or six miles, weaving through the tree-high hills carving up the Monclova Valley and under the shadow of the towering Oriental Mountains, encasing the basin like an impregnable wall. The terrain had turned tropical—piñon, juniper, and encinas starting to show up on the lush hills. The hostile party, with its twenty stolen horses, had left a straightforward trail, one that was effort-lessly followed from atop a horse. But as the patrol approached a long, bread-loaf-shaped hill, jutting a hundred feet above the valley, Chase slackened his pace.

"You see 'em?" Travis asked, bringing his horse to a slow stop.

Chase was leaning over the side of his horse, giving the ground and some horse tracks a thor-ough once-over. "No, but I'd say we're within a mile. Let's ride up this hill and take a peek. Keep the horses out of sight." Chase started up the hill without waiting for further discussion.

Travis and the patrol followed Chase up the palisade, slowly veering around several large boulders. Just below the summit, the squad hob-bled their horses, took to foot, and tiptoed to the hill's peak, where they flopped on their bellies. Travis pulled out his field glasses to scan the valley. In the distance, a half mile or more away, he could see a herd of horses. He focused the glasses on the single line of animals, noting the long, vertical spears, capped with white feathers.

"That's them," Chase said, removing his glasses from his eyes to study the land. "They're headed for that draw up into the big mountains over there. We can probably beat them there; those horses and hostages will slow them down. If we can box them into that draw, they'll have to make a decision between the loot and a light escape. The dumb ones will stay with the horses and women, but Little Face will probably cut out for the mountains, knowing he'll pick up more horses and women somewhere else. I guarantee you they'll split up. When they do, most of the patrol should go after the women and horses—kill all of the Indians if you can. Me and Travis will branch off and go after Little Face and whichever braves are clever enough to join him. We've got some business to settle with him."

Travis looked up at the sun; directly overhead, it cast no shadows. He wondered whether he had just been ordered on a one-way trip. He glanced at Chase's obstinate eyes, still scanning the valley. Travis knew his partner had waited many a year for this opportunity; he wasn't about to let it pass. But was he about to throw all prudence to the wind in his vengeful pursuit? The mention of this Indian was usually enough to stir Chase for several days. Would the famous Ranger keep pressing on until only he or Little Face rode away alive? And Chase could ride literally for days. He had an eye for horses, his mount always the best in the Ranger troop. He was legendary even among the Comanche for his stamina on the trail, his ability to ride hundreds of miles with little water or food. This could be a weeklong ordeal. Travis gathered himself. He would not be given time to gradually get back into his Ranger ways.

"They'll separate as soon as they see us," Chase said, starting back down the hill. "We have to push hard, make them abandon the captives and horses. But don't get lured into a trap by Little Face. Keep him at a distance. Little Face is sly, sneaky, the best; he can sneak up on an antelope. You'll never know he's there until you feel a quick sting in your throat."

Only seconds later, the group charged over the summit and down the hill into the open valley, a wilderness of waist-high grass. As Chase had surmised, the Indians, almost a mile ahead, immediately broke into two groups. Chase veered his horse toward five horses heading to the left, taking an angle to a breach in the mountains that narrowed the gap between the two parties.

Travis followed a few horse lengths back. "We'll get these," he hollered to the lieutenant over the jarring sound of horse hooves. He spurred his horse hard. The mare labored through the tall, thick grass. Travis bent low over her neck, trying to catch Chase, who was in a dead sprint for the outlaws.

Ten minutes with only the repetitive thud of hooves found the two Rangers at the mouth of the small valley. Trees were abundant in the chasm. As Chase raced between the lofty rock walls, he jerked back on his reins for a quick study.

Travis's heaving mount instinctively stopped adjacent to Chase.

"There," Chase said, breathing hard. He pointed to the back of the draw, where a group of horses slowly made their way up a precipitous hill through thick juniper.

Travis whipped his horse and drew his pistol, all in one motion, and continued the chase. As the Rangers reached the back of the small valley, they both emptied their pistols up the hill at the Indians, about to cross the summit and disappear from sight.

Travis heard some rustling and paused his pursuit to peer up the hill. "We got two horses."

Chase never broke stride, exhorting his colt up the steep slope. Travis changed pistols. A few seconds later, they passed the expiring horses, on their sides and hawing. But as the Rangers topped the apex, gunfire erupted, bullets zinging off the ground before them. Travis jumped from his saddle, landing flat-footed. He dived for the cover of trees. Leading Chase, he picked his way about halfway down the backside of the hill, bracing behind a rock outcropping where he could see the next valley, an open meadow fifty feet below, leading to a wide mountain stream, still raging from the morning's torrent.

"Hell," Chase said, arriving beside Travis. "We might have them pinned in. You can't cross that river on horse."

"Pinned in? There's five of them. We're the ones pinned in." Travis flinched as two more bullets rang through the trees. He raised his pistol and took a quick shot at some movement below. "The Indians down here are more advanced than Texas Indians. They've given up wasting all that time and effort making bows and arrows. Decided they'll just kill the white man with his own weapons. There's two down there. Just at the base of this hill. Probably the ones atop those two horses we shot. We've got a good line on them, but it's a pretty good shot." He then turned his back and slid to the ground, resting his head against the large stone as he spun his revolver on his index finger. Travis consciously noticed how easy the gun felt in his hands, how quickly and accurately he was drawing a bead. He hadn't shot at a man in years. But he remembered that gunplay came easily to him.

"Little Face?" Chase asked, strafing the area.

"I don't know. Can't see them very good, and I've only seen him once up close. That was ten years ago."

"Where you reckon the others are?" Chase was kneeling, exposing his upper half as he reloaded and looked for targets.

"Don't know. Probably hauled ass. Injuns are fickle comrades."

"There they go," Chase screamed, firing off a quick volley. "Little Face."

Travis jumped to his feet, looking below. Two men, with only scant leather around their groins and tall black hats on their heads, were skirting the rocks, making for the stream. Travis emptied his pistol, his barrage sending one of the outlaws to the ground.

"You got the wrong one," Chase cried, still standing boldly in the open.

"He's about to make the river."

Chase cupped his mouth with a hand and pointed his words to the fleeing Indian with all his voice. "Little Face! Don't get in such a hurry. It's me. Captain McAlister."

Chase's words stopped the heathen in his tracks. He twirled around, landing like a cat to scan the hill. He lifted his pistol, fired two shots, and yelled back as he scurried for cover along the stream. "I've been wanting to kill you for ten years," Little Face shouted. "Like I did your mother—squealing like a pig when I took that yellow hair."

"Here I am," Chase called, his teeth chattering with fury. "Going to get your other ear. I bet the

Comanche squaws love your scarred and ugly cheek."

Travis looked at Little Face as he dashed away, his long, stringy black hair bouncing with his strides.

"Keep him busy. I'm going after him," Chase asserted firmly.

Travis turned to his partner, whose lifeless expression announced he was game to die if he could plant this villain.

"Go get him," Travis said as Chase disappeared, reappearing shortly in the open meadow below. Travis's palms got damp and his heart raced as he watched Chase intrepidly, audaciously standing erect, walking slowly to the stream not more than a hundred paces away, almost daring his nemesis to come out and fight.

Chase raised his pistol and fired two shots into the little clump of tress on the bank. A shot came back from the bushes, and Chase ran forward, closing the distance, before diving into a small ditch. Travis heard more gunshots, not seeing either man. Then Little Face appeared on the bank and fired a shot before discarding his pistol and running for the creek. Chase emerged from the ditch, reaching for his knife. In a smooth, athletic motion, he reared back and threw the knife at the fleeing scoundrel, who ducked as he ran. The knife flew past Little Face, who dove into the river—out of sight.

Chapter 11

With the twenty horses and two women in tow, the Rangers and cavalry arrived on the outskirts of Monclova the next morning. After a four-hour chase, and under heavy gunfire, the Comanche band had finally abandoned the horses and women and fled for the mountains, unscathed. And the patrol had camped overnight at an abandoned hacienda.

As the returning group approached town, two sentries rode out to meet them. From these guards, Travis learned that General Taylor had signed a truce with Santa Anna and General Wool's army had been ordered to bivouac in Monclova, awaiting further orders. Travis and Chase separated from the cavalry and loped into town under a small brick arch.

"Sparring with Little Face get your blood stirring for a change?" Chase asked.

Travis studied Chase. His partner knew him as well as he knew himself, maybe better. Thinking back, he wondered if Chase had insisted on that cattle drive to Eagle Pass knowing the army would need scouts. He recollected that Chase had felt bad about talking him into the whole notion of running a ranch—and the dreariness it entailed. Maybe Chase wanted to put him back in an environment he was meant for. Whether he was happy about it or not, he wasn't sure, but he seemed appreciative that Chase was at least looking out for him.

"Yeah, a little bit. You sure were brazen back there. Looked like you had a death wish. I think you're the only white man in the country that Comanche's afraid of. He probably thinks you're one crazy son of a bitch . . . and I know you brought those cows up to Eagle Pass just to get me off that porch."

Chase smiled. "Not totally. We needed to pay some of the bills you've run up also."

Travis looked at the centuries-old, white-washed, provincial city of five thousand that sat nestled against the mountains, glistening in the sun, its flat-faced dwellings generally single-story adobe, segregated by vineyards, orchards, and gardens. Some of the houses had earth floors and no doors. The nicer ones had iron grilles on the windows. The roads were dirt, set in a grid around a large green hill that was topped, like in every other Mexican town, with a stone church. The town's air held a gold haze from airborne particles mixed up by the influx of hundreds of marching men and beasts; the streets were covered with fresh horse droppings.

Travis pulled back on his reins in the town's small plaza, overflowing with horses tied to anything that would hold a knot. Two yapping dogs and dozens of soldiers were watering in a fountain fed by a brick aqueduct and splashing water over a pyramid of black rocks. "Looks like we might be here a while. There could be worse places." Travis continued to look around. There were few native men in the streets; only the peons, held in eternal ignorance and bondage by their arrogant masters and by blind submission to the church. Travis sympathized with their predicament. What would just a smidgen of education and an honest government do for their lives? But the town's women, ranging from fair-skinned Spaniards to dark amber Indians, carried on their perfunctory chores among the hordes of flies and the begging adolescents who were pestering the mass of infantrymen. "I need a bath," Travis said. "Then, I'm going to find out where the fandango will be tonight."

"We need to find Colonel Patrick or General Wool. I want to put together a war party, go after Little Face," Chase answered.

"Always in a hurry to get shot at, aren't you? Let's relax a few days."

Chase turned to a soldier sitting on the fountain. "Where's General Wool's headquarters?"

"Big hacienda, down there," the young soldier replied, and pointed. "But he's at the town hall now."

"Where's that at?" Chase said.

"Other end of the next street."

Travis turned in the saddle and goaded his horse in the direction the man indicated. It was only fifty paces over to the next street. There, he saw the Casa de Monclova, a large stone structure, and its accompanying barracks. The town *alcalde* and the local officials, a dozen or so, stood outside of its grand front door, atop four feet of brick steps. In the street below, over the slow roll of the drums, an official surrender ceremony was under way. The best army regulars, two companies of infantry in their clean, meticulous uniforms, marched by the house in rows of four, muskets held vertical in their right hands. In a little square in front of the building, fifty more dragoons, on horseback and also clad in spotless uniforms, stood in a perfect line. Travis watched the pomp and pageantry. The officers and noncommissioned officers barked orders, heels clicked, and leather rubbed as General Wool and his staff dismounted and saluted. The group of Mexicans and Americans all stood at attention as the bugle blared the anthem. Atop the building, two soldiers unfurled an American flag and tied it to a tall pole.

"They like their formalities, don't they?" Chase said, sitting beside Travis and watching the scene.

The bugler stopped, and Travis watched the general ascend the steps to the peculiar little men. "Mayor must be turning the city over. Probably thinks it may save his hide."

"Wouldn't want to be in his position. Has to

suck up to the Americans. But if he's too congenial, the Mexicans will kill him after we leave."

As Travis's eyes lingered on the scene, something did not match. The general atmosphere of the army was rather relaxed; the town placid and enchanting. But he knew that this many trained men, this many resources, had not been sent this far for polite formalities. This army had been sent here to do the dirty work of its government. And that dirty work was coming sooner or later. He looked around at the innocent citizens. They had no idea what was ahead. It all just seemed too calm, refreshing, like the lull before a tempestuous storm. A shiver ran up Travis's spine. When would welcoming arms be replaced by deadly bullets?

It was a week later when Travis's morning was disturbed by Chase.

"Colonel Patrick wants to see us *now*," Chase said as he stormed into Travis's room.

"What for?" Travis answered casually from his bed, wiping his bloodshot eyes. He had been enjoying the peaceful morning, drinking coffee and staring out his window at the ranks drilling in an open field just outside. The movement of soldiers, clicking of heels, and barks of officers as the group constantly changed formations seemed to tug at his eyes for endless minutes.

"Don't know, but let's get a move on." Chase

looked at Travis, his hand on his chin. He then picked up a black paper mask on the floor. "What the hell is this?"

"It's a mask. Went to a fiesta last night—had to wear a costume. Young, enterprising lad on the street got a dollar from me for it. Party was good. I'm dangerous when I can move around anonymous."

"Maybe we're finally moving out. I hope so . . . before you go completely lame and fall in love with one of these courtesans."

"I deserve a fiesta after three years at the dusty ranch. But there's no fear of me falling in love. I'm not suave enough in Spanish, and I'll be out of money long before I am. Don't be in such a hurry. When's the last time you camped in a town full of women?" Travis slowly stood, slipping into his pants and shirt as he retrieved two empty wineskins hanging beside the bed. "Need to get out anyway. Get these refilled."

For the past week, the two had idled around town, enjoying the fruits of occupation. They had been boarded as officers, in the sturdy residence of an absent landlord, passing the time as the other soldiers did: days with a few scouting patrols and wandering the markets, nights at the cantinas or balls, dancing, conversing, and loving the town's daughters, who seemed amenable to the invaders' needs.

The little city's merchants, mostly citizens of the

northern republic, had welcomed the army like heroes, showering the soldiers with warm thanks and affection. They looked at the intruders more as saviors than as occupiers. The soldiers patronized their houses of sin; their restaurants; their shops of dry goods, food accessories, and items of need shipped from America. But the town's menfolk and gentry had largely disappeared, the few who remained eyeing the Americans with more mistrust and enmity each day.

An hour later, the two Rangers arrived at the large hacienda on the edge of town that General Wool had made his headquarters. The stately grounds were plush and vast and had been converted into a fortress. Freshly dug and well-manned parapets circled the estate. Around the main house, the other buildings—winery, barns, blacksmith shop, quarters, tannery, and storage buildings—had all been used to billet the general's staff. Peons were tending to the hacienda's lush gardens, shoeing horses, repairing wagons, and slaughtering stock under the watchful eyes of a few soldiers.

As the two Rangers arrived at the main quarters, they rode up to a small group of dragoons standing around the almost unidentifiable body of an American soldier. The poor soul had been stripped naked, tied up, and then lassoed to his horse and dragged across the rugged ground until there was little left except a bloody carcass. The horse had recently returned to town, and the soldiers were preparing the body for burial.

"Comanches?" Chase asked.

"Could be—or guerrillas. Who knows? It's different every day," one of the soldiers replied.

Travis turned away from the smell of decaying flesh, the teeming flies, and the somber faces, and headed for the colonel's office, a few strides away. He followed Chase between the two soldiers standing guard, pausing at the entrance. Travis looked inside as Chase gently knocked on the wooden door. The colonel sat alone, studying some maps and gnawing on a cigar.

Chase saluted. "Captain McAlister reporting."

"Good morning," the colonel replied, looking up and leaning back in his chair, the mood of his voice difficult to judge. He gestured toward two vacant chairs, then grabbed a towel and wiped the sweat from his face. The day was young, but the heat was already creeping through the thick adobe walls. "We plan to move out of here within the week. This city's terrible for morale—men sitting around all day bored, getting drunk, undisciplined. We've lost ten men in the last week—probably because they weren't paying attention, being careless. Nothing's worse for morale and combat readiness than this environment."

"You should've let me have a couple dozen of them to go after Little Face. I'll put them to work," Chase said in a disgruntled, insolent voice.

"Enough of that talk. He's no business of the army's." The colonel reprimanded Chase with a hard look, his veins pulsing in his neck. "Going to move the army south, to Parras. We'll wait for orders there. We'll be closer to General Taylor when the fighting recommences."

"Parras?" Chase said. "You'll have to go through Devil's Pass . . . with a wagon train. It's a dangerous gap. Two companies of infantry could hold your column up for a week."

"That's *competent* infantry. Not these bush-whackers and Indians we've been skirmishing with. The column moves ahead. We don't give up just because the terrain gets rough." The colonel pointed to the map.

"Captain McAlister, I want you to get a squad of cavalry and scout the route. You've got four days. Lieutenant Ross, get Lieutenant Jones to assign you a few men. You go to Saltillo and deliver these dispatches to General Taylor."

"That's over a hundred miles," Travis answered. "Over the mountains and through hostile territory. It'll probably take five days just to get there."

"We'll probably be gone when you get back. Meet us on the road to Parras." The colonel motioned the two away and picked up some official-looking papers. "Get on with it."

Travis's heart skipped a beat as he followed

Chase out of the office. The trip to Saltillo would take him through the little hamlet of Campos, where Mercedes lived. In the past ten years, he .more. Now he would possibly get a chance to see her, something he had hoped and longed for. But more disconcerting, her father was there, in uniform. So was Tony Flores. If the truce held, he might get to see them. If not, would he be asked to hunt them down? On the surface, it did not seem like anything to be fretting about, but something gave Travis the feeling he was about to descend into a fiery cauldron.

Chapter 12

Before daylight the next morning, Travis and four cavalrymen were in their saddles. With a week's sustenance secured to a packhorse and their forage bags full of barley and oats, they headed out of the still-sleeping Monclova. The morning passed quietly and without incident as the group crept up and up, around rocky fingers, through mighty passes, some with stunning views, into the sky and charming, beautiful mountains. The primitive mule trail weaved through open plains and thick forests, alive with squawking, tropical birds. As the elevation increased, the air lightened and the temperature cooled, first to a comfortable level, but soon the group was forced to don their overcoats.

Travis passed the time with a watchful, worried eye. He knew the broad, open slopes were visible for miles, and the restricted paths provided few options for movement or escape. Testament to this lay on the rough trail, where the group passed two sets of decaying bones, man and horse, murdered and left to be consumed by nature. Little Face also worried him. The Rangers had learned over the years that the outlaw rarely went far after a losing skirmish, preferring instead to lie in wait and assault on his own terms—exacting his own personal revenge.

In the half-breed's wildest dreams, Travis thought, Little Face could not have conceived a more auspicious ground to bait and capture his prey.

The day wore on, and the small, vulnerable horse train moved farther and farther from the safety and support of the main column. As they crossed ridge after ridge, enclosed by lofty mountains, peak after peak, Travis started to get the feeling they were being watched. Two times during the day, he thought he saw flickering silver on a far-off hill. Other than that, he had seen nothing out of the ordinary. But he had been ambushed four or five times in his career when all seemed much calmer than today. Finally, Travis halted the train atop a high salient, where the trail descended into a timbered draw.

"You see something?" the crusty cavalry sergeant in charge of the four troopers asked, riding up beside Travis.

Travis turned to the big, burly man, who had a dark red beard and a blithe Irish face. "No, but I don't like this. Something tells me we're riding into an ambush. I get the feeling we're being watched."

The sergeant turned to look at the hills, pondering internally, putting his hand on his beard.

Travis looked at the land. He didn't like it. What would he do? The burden of command weighed heavily on him. His and his men's fates might possibly depend on him. His decisions could mean their lives. "We're going to get off of this trail, skirt this ridgeline south until we find a better place to descend. Stay in open country as best we can. Might take us longer, but we'll probably get there. Tell the men to keep a good eye."

On the high slopes, day moved into twilight, a myriad of orange washing the blue from the sky. The temperature had plummeted forty degrees, a cool breeze now starting to cut through Travis's light wool jacket. They had been unable to procure passage off the ridge, which was narrowing and appeared to terminate up the trail, surely at an almost impassable rock face. Travis's worries had been justified. During the afternoon, the patrol had stopped on two high ridges to check their rear. On both occasions, they had clearly seen the hostiles, probably guerrillas, ten or twelve in all and maybe a half mile behind, stalking their trail, their muskets lying in their laps and ready for deployment.

Travis stopped to inspect a plunging, daunting gorge, appearing to provide access to the valley two thousand feet below. Passage looked chancy, but as he studied the terrain, it seemed to be the only option. With a big lump in his throat and his fears fully evident, he turned to the sergeant, his voice raspy and jittery. "We're going to have to take this valley. Those guerrillas are still following us. Looks like we're about to get trapped on this ridge. We'll freeze up here with no more clothes than we have. And we can't build a fire up here. It would lead them right to us, and we wouldn't have any night vision. That's probably what they're waiting on. It's our only chance."

The sergeant gazed down at the draw, shaking his head. "Hell, fighting the Indians or guerrillas could be a better option."

"Falling off this mountain is a mite better than what they'll do to you if they catch you," Travis answered, dismounting and leading his horse down the precipitous hill. The small rocks dislodged by his feet and tumbling down before him reminded him that any slip would be fatal.

As the group moved into the dense trees and enclosed cavern on the eastern side of the divide, total darkness soon took over. In no time, it got so black that Travis had to actually feel from tree to tree to descend, each step a perilous foot below the last. On a few occasions, when he found nothing to grab, he got on his hands and knees, feeling to make sure solid ground lay in his path. More than once, he bumped headfirst into the vertical rock. The small steps were not frightful, but they were time-consuming and taxing as the temperature continued to drop.

About three hours into the descent, his bones tired and cold, Travis heard a terrible ruckus—hooves clattered, a horse snorted and hawed, and a loud noise rumbled through the trees. He froze in his tracks, fear filling his heart. "What was that?" he whispered.

"Packhorse fell. He's gone," a hushed voice from the darkness responded. "How much further we got?"

"Don't know. Sure as hell can't go back the way we came," Travis replied. "This is a waste of time and energy. The next flat spot we find, we're going to stop and bed down. If the bandits want to climb in here and get us, they can have us. We'll starve in a few days without that packhorse anyway."

Icy and irritable, hungry and groggy, the group recommenced their journey at first light. Under the thick cover of the trees, they had shielded their camp with some limbs and built a small fire, probably the only thing that kept them alive through the frigid night. In the rays of the rising sun, the trip down the mountain was slow and foreboding, but never in doubt.

By noon, they reached an open valley, still up in the mountains, but safely below the treacherous high slopes. The warm, gentle rays of the sun were welcome, and to the group's good fortune, they stumbled onto a balmy spring.

As Travis and the men undressed to ease into the water and bathe their dirty skin, Travis noticed some Indian pictographs on the rocks around the spring's small pool, a testament that it had been a popular watering hole for centuries. After completely dunking his body, Travis hung his pistol around his neck and sat down on a rock just below the water. When he glanced at the water, he saw reflections from the hills. His heart skipped a beat. "Sergeant, we may have some company. Everybody get their weapons ready. Could be that group following us yesterday."

Travis put a hand above his eyes to take a look. There were five horses working their way down from the high mountains, moving at a slow pace and switching directions, reducing the slope by zigzagging down the hill. They were probably bandits or guerrillas, their glinting saddles were likely decorated with silver or other ornaments. Travis splashed his way out of the water, put on his boots, and walked to his horse, where he grabbed his field glasses.

"What you think?" the sergeant asked, also climbing out of the pool and standing beside Travis, both men completely unclothed above their boots.

"Don't know," Travis said, handing the glasses to the sergeant.

"That may not be them. We saw at least ten yesterday," the sergeant said, looking through the glasses. "They'll be here in five minutes."

"Maybe it's not them. Maybe the rest of the group branched off, or they're coming in behind us." Travis picked up his underwear and yelled to the men. "Everybody get ready, weapons loaded! Don't have time to get dressed. Just

cover the privates." Travis pulled up his underwear and looked at the sergeant, trying to make
light of the situation, but his somber voice
betrayed him. "I've never been in a shoot-out
naked."

The other men hustled to their horses and got
partially dressed. Then all took shelter behind
some rocks. In only a few minutes, the five horses
slowly moved up to the pool. Though the men
looked like savages, they rode with grace, ease,
and competence, Travis thought, expert horsemen. The guerrillas all wore leather pants; a
couple wore brown vests over their bare chests;
the others had black capes. All the men held
rifles, short escopette muskets, either in a free
hand or over their laps. Hanging from the horses
were the evil-looking, angled swords attached to
a thin piece of rope; they could be wielded or
thrown. And Travis noticed the brown, days-old,
dried blood on the shiny blades.

The guerrillas stopped a few feet from the
pond, and the ten men stared at each other for
few seconds, the only sound the trickling of the
spring. Travis turned to the cavalrymen, all
holding their pistols or muskets, eyes steady on
the bandits. The lead guerrilla, half a horse in
front of the other four, looked at the Americans'
horses. They were easily identified as an army
patrol: the blue uniforms lying on the rocks, the
unmistakable U.S. brands on the horses.

The same guerrilla leaned to the side of his horse and spat some tobacco juice on the ground. "You mind if we water?"

"We don't own the water," Travis said, locking his eyes on the man who had spoken. He knew him from somewhere, but he couldn't remember where—certainly from his days as a Ranger on the border. His face looked familiar, but the man had a scar, an indention, centered on his chin where a piece of flesh had been removed. Travis strained his brain, digging into his past, trying to recall if he had ever seen this man. Surely, he would remember such an unmistakable mark.

The guerrillas all dismounted gradually, their weapons at hand and their eyes cautiously locked on the Americans. Travis felt his blood pumping, his nerves unraveling. He took a slow, deep breath, trying to loosen up. He knew nothing motivated brutal, uncouth men like the sight of fear.

The guerrillas' horses all sank their mouths into the water as the bandits dipped their leather canteens, keeping their eyes on the cavalrymen. Travis looked into the eyes of the lead man; he could see the bandit still feeling out the Americans, deciding if their horses and weapons were worth a fray. He had probably expected to find just a small supply train, not five well-armed and ready men. If he wanted to fight, his face did not let on. Travis tightened the grip on his pistol, hanging beside his belt in his right hand.

"Tough and dangerous country for five men to be moving through alone," the chief guerrilla said, locking his eyes on Travis as he removed his canteen from the water. "If I were you boys, I'd move on."

As Travis stared at the bandit, he saw eyes that shined with hate and rage, the kind that made you give up your trust in the simple rectitude of man. "I might say the same to you," Travis replied with a calm face, voice austere and unflinching. He sensed that this man was searching his memory, as if he also were trying to figure out why the two knew each other. They both stared at each other with some unknown mutual discontent.

No further words passed, and the five guerrillas saddled up and rode out of sight. The cavalry scouts stood without a word for four or five minutes until the horses disappeared into the hills.

Travis's heart still beat fast as he finished dressing. "Let's get a move on. Get out of here, before they decide they want to water again."

"That one bandit sure was eyeing you down. You know him?" the sergeant asked.

Travis turned to the men, some still white as death. "Yeah, I know him. Don't know his name, but he used to run with this part-time bandit, part-time sheriff down here. Took me a little while to recognize him. I shot the sheriff's arm off. He's got it out for me. We should have shot the whole lot; would have done much to improve the Mexican pedigree." Travis picked up his glasses. He spent a few minutes combing the hills before climbing atop his horse.

Recharged from the bath, leery from the confrontation, and still hungry and without food, they rode on, hour by hour, descending to the east. Travis had an uneasy feeling in his gut the whole time. The scenery grew more arid, cacti and mesquite thrived, water became rarer, and not a person or track could be found on their virgin course. No game appeared in this bleak, inhospitable land. They camped a solitary second night along a dribbling stream.

The third day saw man and beast almost spent and near their limits. The climate had turned tropical, the sun beating down on their red necks, baking their brains, the atmosphere full of pesky, biting insects. But they continued to work their way down through the narrow passes of burned, lifeless earth, stopping several times an hour to lead the horses across a suspect ledge or down an abrupt incline. By late afternoon, they finally spotted a depressing desert village in a small valley. So tired and frayed were the men, they rode haphazardly into the town without the slightest concern for safety or military bearing. The village had only twenty hovels, palm huts with bamboo walls or arrangements of unfired brick.

"Maybe they have a hotel and some food," the cavalry sergeant said in an exhausted breath as the group came to a stop.

"Probably like the Grand in New Orleans," Travis said pessimistically. "Complete with a five-course meal delivered to your room by a Southern belle."

An old bowed-backed, leathery man approached on foot with eyes of contempt.

"Buenas tardes," Travis said, holding up a hand and a silver coin. "We need shelter and food. Have money, American money."

"We have hotel," the man said, raising his serape and pointing to a hut—a miserable sight it was.

Travis dismounted to find the owner, a grumpy old man, short and fat, lounging almost lifelessly in the shade of the hotel's porch. There were four dead chickens hanging from the porch and an antiquated musket leaning against the wall. "We need five rooms," Travis said. "Pasture for our horses."

With an air of discontent, like someone beaten down by a life too long and chronically filled with disenchantment, the old man extended a hand without getting up. "Twenty pesos. Any rooms you want."

"How far to Saltillo?" Travis asked.

The old man halfheartedly looked at the horses, turning only his head, as though trying to expend a minimal amount of energy. He pondered for a few minutes. "One-day ride. Down good trail. No bandits."

"Be there tomorrow, boys. Make yourselves at home for the night," said Travis. He dismounted, handing the man some money before leading his four subjects into the abject place. Travis's room was only five feet wide and the length of an average man, with a dirt floor and bamboo walls that barely kept out the sun. Its only adornments were a henequen hammock and a small portrait of the Virgin of Guadalupe, both hanging from the flimsy walls.

A young Indian girl soon arrived with a plate of sliced oranges. His body fatigued and his mind numb, Travis wolfed down the fruit and flopped down amidst the fleas and lice. As he closed his eyes, he heard the terrible rumble of thunder, making him appreciate the measly quarters as he escaped into his dreams.

Chapter 13

Stiff and sore, muscles aching, the patrol finally caught sight of the pretty mountain pueblo of Saltillo late the next day. With the evening sun at his back, Travis looked down on the town and the rugged San Juan Valley, running south from the city. From a high flat above, Travis could see that the valley, a magnificent, deep gorge, a natural anomaly, parting the mountains like a divine hand had opened them up for man and animal to amble through. It was the only passage between Mexico proper and the isolated cities of Saltillo and Monterrey. And Travis immediately saw why it was the focal point of the army's current defense. No entry could be made to either city without passing through the valley.

As the group moved lower, the white city of Saltillo came into view. Like the center of a wheel, the adjoining haciendas spread out from its walls, marked by huge plots of soil blocked off by green tree lines.

On the outskirts of town, Travis's eyes finally fell on the army camp, rows of white tents set under a large grove of walnuts. The grounds were set in a quarter-mile-square grid. The camp was alive, but with leisure instead of war, the men comfortably dressed, only light shirts and trousers, no weapons at hand. Travis thought he and his comrades had been almost magically transported from hinterland to town. The camp was a beehive of activity: men writing letters, telling tales, laughing, mending uniforms, throwing dice on a blanket, washing clothes. Travis looked over at the long line of horses being groomed and the bales of hay and piles of corn beside them. The cooks stood along huge tables, pounding coffee, cutting up chickens, or mincing onions and peppers. Indian or mestiza women and peons worked at policing the grounds. And dozens of vendors, Mexican and American, had set up at portable tables around the camp's perimeter and were trying to sell the troops everything from cigars to fruit.

Travis heard the roll of the drums, the call for dinner. He looked at his weary companions. They hadn't had a good meal in days. Their dirty and sun-parched faces scanned the surroundings with astonishment. "Sergeant, see if you can find the dinner table—for our horses, too. I'll see if I can find the general's tent."

With the early morning sun in their faces and fresh food in their stomachs, the ragged scouting party rode out of Saltillo the next morning bound for Monterrey. To the consternation of his soldiers, Travis had learned during the previous evening that General Taylor had left a quarter of his army in Saltillo and returned to Monterrey.

But Travis's group had slept deep and hard and were now refreshed.

In the indigo of dawn, confident the deplorable journey was almost at an end, the group trotted down Saltillo's paved main street, past its large, domed cathedral, encased by two bell towers, then around the large haciendas surrounding the city. In contrast to the camp, the town's streets were uncannily quiet, but had an air of bustle, anticipation, and impending calamity. Yellow candles and torches lit the buildings and side-walks as soldiers with humorless faces drilled and prepared defenses as part of sunup's chores.

The morning passed peacefully as the patrol moved along the broad, well-kept road to Monterrey. It bisected a large, scenic valley surrounded by tall mountains, the zeniths of which appeared to be individual hills, their sharp summits blotting the sky like a row of towering volcanoes. The road was flat, except at two locations where it moved through narrow passes and the mountains rushed up to the path. Trains of wagons, usually manned by overweight team-sters, holding artillery and other military supplies, crowded the road, moving between the cities. The busy traffic seemed to add excitement and urgency to the peaceful setting.

By late morning, the worn-out team of horses and men reached the outskirts of Monterrey. Though the trip had been fifty miles, it had plummeted from an elevation of five thousand feet to below two thousand, quickening the horses' pace. The Monterrey valley looked almost like a completely different country; in only a half day's ride, they had gone from temperate to tropical, from fields of cotton and wheat to stands of fruit and lush forest.

Travis looked up at two large hills, guarding the western approaches to the city: Independence Hill and Federation Ridge. Both were topped with strong, stone fortresses now flying the American flag. Pride filled his soul as he inspected the steep, rugged ramparts exposed to fire from the citadels above. Two months earlier, his beloved Texas Rangers had taken these hills at the vanguard of General Taylor's army.

By mid-afternoon, Travis found himself clean and fit, on a little narrow side street, looking up at a faded sign hanging from a whitewashed stone wall. He checked the wording on the sign against some scribbled jargon on a small piece of paper he had just pulled from his pocket. Confirming they matched, he returned the wrinkled piece of paper to the front pocket of his trousers and curiously opened the door. Inside, he found a small, empty cantina, a Lone Star banner hanging behind its bar.

He stepped back outside. It was the time of siesta, and none of city's fifteen thousand residents were about—only a few pigeons trolling for snacks. He looked down the cobblestone avenue to the imposing Monterrey cathedral, watching over the city like a giant castle. Little stone buildings crowded the street like a tunnel, their walls still riddled with shell blasts and scarred with smut from the three-day battle.

Travis walked back into the hotel, whacking his pistol butt against a small iron bell until a tiny old man appeared in a doorway behind the bar. "Any Texas Rangers here?" Travis walked behind the bar and secured a brown bottle. "And I'd like some tequila."

"Sí, sí," the man answered, wiping his hands on his white apron.

"Chester Woods?" Travis filled a shot glass and turned it up.

"Yes, yes . . . one minute, please."

Travis filled another glass, and sat at one of the bar's stools for a few minutes until Chester appeared, his shirt unbuttoned and an entrancing, black-haired señorita at his side.

"I'll be damned. What got you off the porch?" Chester grabbed the bottle and filled three glasses. He handed one to the young girl, her long, shiny hair a tangled mess and her soft arms around Chester's bare chest.

"General Wool requisitioned my ass," said Travis. "Chase's, too. Sent me over here to deliver some messages. Damn guerrillas shadowing me the entire way. After this war, the Mexicans need to get some Rangers. Dropped off my dispatches. Was told to be back in three days to carry more back. Cut the boys loose. Got a hotel, a bath, shave, and a shine. Decided to look around."

"Where's Chase?" Chester downed the drink and kissed the señorita.

"Out scouting the trail to Parras."

"Ya'll seen any action?"

"Nothing much. A few skirmishes. Ran into Little Face. Damn near got him. Chase is still pissed off. What about you?"

"Been quiet for a few months, but word has it Santa Anna is moving this way with a large army. Going to violate the truce, try to retake Monterrey. That's why Taylor occupied Saltillo—to cover our flank. He'll probably attack Santa Anna first. We've got scouts out in all directions. Not much going on now. The city's peaceful, but the countryside is getting more dangerous. Six dragoons found hung from a tree the other day . . . scouts always getting in scuffles. General Taylor's ready to do something. Troops are getting rowdy and tempestuous, especially the volunteers—good fighters, but an undisciplined and uncouth bunch. They'd like to slaughter and rape the whole population, officers as bad as the ranks. To tell you the truth, everybody here is pretty pissed off. That truce was a farce. After we took Monterrey, Taylor let all the Mexicans go with their arms. We'll all have to answer for that, probably sooner than later." Chester poured another glass of tequila and smiled at the señorita. He patted her on the rear. "This is the lovely but naughty Rosalina."

Travis nodded at the bashful beauty.

"After the battle, the Rangers were out on the hunt, looking for all the Texans that took up arms against us in the revolution. Burned a few houses and chased a few more down south, almost got that old mayor from San Antonio. But General Taylor put an end to all that. I'm still on the lookout for a few."

"What about Tony Flores? Have you seen him?"

"No, but I heard he participated in the battle. Your old buddy Rayo, too. There's an entire regiment of Mexican lancers right across the mountain. Camped there since the truce. Some of them come into town at night—out of uniform —or go back to their haciendas."

"He worries me," Travis lamented. "I know what a fighter he is, how he's not afraid to charge in with complete disregard for his safety. But fighting the U.S. Army's not like fighting a bunch of stupid outlaws or Comanches. And I get the feeling these American generals aren't going to have any mercy around here."

"They certainly have the means. This army's magnificent. The regulars and officers are impeccable. We never dreamed of anything like this in Texas. Took this city in three days, outnumbered two to one, population hostile, two hundred miles from our supply base. It was glorious. Wish you could have seen it. It can get contagious after a while."

It was late in the day when Travis rode up to the large Rayo house, his heart beating fast and his brain spinning with concern, anticipation, and delight. He looked up at the grandiose mansion, blocks of carved limestone set so tall and sturdy, decorated so extravagantly, they were meant to command awe for centuries. He got off his horse and trudged up the high stone steps to a wide, columned porch where three armed Mexican vaqueros guarded the house. The four men stared at each other, without words.

Travis looked at the door, but one of the men gave him a shake of his head and pointed to a garden beside the house. Travis walked in that direction, and stopped at the porch's edge, looking down at the beautiful courtyard where a woman knelt, tending one of a dozen impeccable flower beds adorning the yard. She continued to sprinkle the roses and daisies from a tin bucket as Travis stood quietly for a few minutes.

Apparently sensing someone watching, she turned to see Travis, then slowly came to her feet. The two stood speechless for what seemed like minutes before Travis descended from the porch. His movement caused Mercedes to walk toward him, slowly at first; then she picked up her pace.

"You have any idea what I've been through to get here?" Travis said with a smile, opening his arms to welcome a warm embrace. Travis got weak in the knees as he felt her feminine freshness, a stark contrast to the trail and the callous, hard men in the army. Her body had matured, gotten more accentuated over time.

Mercedes removed her head from Travis's shoulder and looked up at him, her eyes as big and zealous as ever. "Lieutenant Ross, you haven't aged much. You're as handsome as ever."

"Must be the blood because it's not the way I live." Travis pushed Mercedes an arm's length away, inspecting her head to toe. She had aged a tad around the edges, but in a good way, he thought, old enough now that her timeless splendor displayed itself—not just another looker in her teens. But she still had that inexplicable combination of dignity and a beguiling, promiscuous air. "Neither have you," he said. "I'm glad you're happy to see me. I was wondering if you even would."

Mercedes put a hand under her chin and looked up at Travis with a smile. "You haven't hitched up with another woman yet?"

"No, you would think I'd be a prize catch considering what little I require. Cook for me and sleep with me a couple of times a week and I'll be fine. I'll do the cleaning and dishes."

Mercedes grinned, her fair skin turning red.

"What's wrong?" Travis inquired politely.

"Nothing. My heart's just beating fast. Never thought I'd see you again."

"I have that effect on a lot of women," Travis said, pausing. "I guess your father is off fighting the barbarians from the north?"

"Yes, this is terrible," Mercedes said, her voice growing louder and more animated. "The Americans shouldn't be here. It's a crime. Mexico has done nothing. We do not deserve this. These evil American soldiers rape our women, kill our men, destroy our cities, treat us like serfs."

"There's nothing we can do about it. I tried to stay out of this, but the army forced me down here. I missed the battle. I'm with the army going to Parras. Everything is going to be all right." Travis paused to look at Mercedes. She was more alluring than he had ever remembered.

Mercedes put her arms back around Travis's neck. "You're still as levelheaded as always. Still have that quality of making your words believable. Gives people a temporary warm feeling that you're right."

Travis stood silently for a few seconds before speaking. "The biggest mistake I ever made was not coming down here to get you. It haunts me every day."

"No, it was my mistake," Mercedes countered with a disheartened face. "I could have come back. I wanted to. It's the one thing I wish I had done. I chose my family over you. I get sadder every day because of it." As her voice trailed off, she turned to two young ladies who were spy- ing on her and Travis with adolescent smiles.

Travis turned to look at the two younger versions of Mercedes, both as beautiful, one fifteen, the other sixteen.

"You remember my sisters, Doña and Maria," Mercedes said, waving the girls forward.

"Yes, but they've grown up." Travis stared at the two shy, innocent girls in pure white dresses that did little to hide their mature figures. He looked at the men on the porch and at the blood-thirsty countryside. They didn't fit in. None of the Rayo women did. *The girls are so fragile and helpless*, he thought.

The girls walked forward a few feet, waving, before running off, giggling, to play.

"They must mean a lot to you," Travis said. "Let's not worry about the past. I have two more days before I have to report back. Come to Saltillo with me tonight?"

Mercedes got a bewildered look on her face. "My father would have a fit if he knew I went to town with you." She put a finger to her lip for a second, her eyes roving with mischief. "Let me get a few things. I'll meet you out at the main road in fifteen minutes."

・・・

That evening, Travis led Mercedes to Saltillo's plaza and a large ballroom and bar owned by an American. He had been pointed toward it by several soldiers, who assured him he would have a good time. When the two entered the smoky establishment, the fandango was well under way. A ten-piece band, strumming all sorts of instruments, filled the room with festive music that bounced loudly off the stone walls. There was a large dance floor occupied with twenty or more soldiers, each dancing with a señorita clothed in a colorful, wide-skirted dress. Benches lined the walls, each also containing soldiers and girls.

Travis led Mercedes through the dance hall to a patio out back, where the two sat at a table shaded by a large banana tree. "These Mexican girls sure are a fickle bunch. They don't seem to have any problem taking up with the vile invaders."

Mercedes grinned. "Mexican women have a tough life. Their men treat them badly. They're looking for anyone to give them a better life. And they don't mind Americans. Don't look down on them. American women aren't saints either."

Travis ordered some wine and looked at Mercedes. She had been quiet for the past hour. "What's the matter? You don't seem very jolly."

"It's nothing. I am happy to see you. This place reminds me of the war and depresses me. I could

167

understand the war in Texas, but not here. Mexico has done nothing wrong."

Travis rubbed Mercedes's cherry cheeks. "It's just a big land grab. 'Manifest Destiny,' as the Americans call it. They want California and New Mexico. They've tried to buy it from Mexico, but Santa Anna won't sell. So they started a war to take it. I'll admit that most of the people in those areas would rather be Americans, and they'll be better off as Americans, but that doesn't make it right. Don't worry, though. The United States doesn't want Saltillo. They'll eventually leave."

Mercedes looked up. A young female waitress had arrived with a jug of wine and two glasses.

Travis took the jug and filled both glasses. "Does it still take a jug of this to get you to dance, to lighten up?"

"I don't know. Let's find out." Mercedes lifted one of the glasses. She looked at Travis over its rim and gulped its contents. She then replenished it. "I need to lighten up."

"Doesn't your father have another ranch in Durango?" Travis lifted his glass. He clinked it against Mercedes's and turned it up.

"Yes, he has a small ranch there."

"You and your sisters should go there. There will be no war there. You will be much safer."

"It's safe here."

"Don't be foolish. It's safe now, but who

knows what will happen? You should go, and come back when the Americans are gone. That will be no more than a few months."

"I'm tired of moving and running."

Travis filled the two glasses again, and the couple drank. After they did, he snared both of Mercedes's hands and lifted her from the small bench. He then grabbed her around the waist. With his free hand, he grabbed the wine jug. "Come on, woman. Let's go dance. I've been waiting on this for years."

The two spent the next few hours in the dance hall, bumping shoulders with the soldiers and señoritas. Late in the night, they stumbled outside into the cool, gray plaza.

Travis put his arms around Mercedes's waist and rubbed her lower back. He noticed her eyes moving curiously between him and the ground. He saw the confusion on her face, as if she were pondering the future, trying to decide between hope and skepticism. She seemed to project her worries onto him, and he brushed her hair over her ears.

"You managed to succeed in getting me drunk," she said. "If you're planning to take me back to the hotel and have your way with me, I'll consent." Mercedes arched her back, stood on her toes, and pulled Travis's head down to hers, bestowing a long kiss on his lips. She looked him in the eye.

"When my enlistment is up in a few months," Travis said, "I may come back here and woo you again."

"Just what I need, a brave Ranger to court and protect me and my sisters." Mercedes smirked.

"How many of these Mexican vaqueros am I going to have to fight off for you?"

"Don't worry. After I have my way with you later tonight, I'll put you in a fighting mood. But if I fall into your trap again, you're going to have to promise not to break my heart again."

Travis grabbed Mercedes's hand and starting walking off. "If I do take you in again, you're going have to be a more model mistress this time. Quit being so sassy."

"I thought that's why I was always the apple of your eye." Mercedes smiled, giving Travis a warm kiss on the cheek.

Chapter 14

"That's it," Chase said, sitting on his horse with both legs hanging over one side of his saddle.

Travis looked out at the daunting natural obstacle from the hilltop they were on. The road to Parras weaved through a jagged rift, like a keyhole, maybe three wagons wide, in a limestone precipice two hundred feet tall. Past the impasse, the Rio Nazas ran fast and deep, and on the other side of the river, a vertical slab of rock, several hundred feet high, had a steep diagonal ledge leading up from the river to the green Parras plain. A quick breeze channeled through the narrow pass, kicking up a few dust devils and making the pass look forsaken, ghostly, and ominous. In the distance, the quaint little town, glittering in the sun, cuddled up to tall, gray mountains.

"Engineers have been down there for a week throwing rock in the river, building a good ford. Wool plans to cross at first light in one day," Chase said. "Five hundred wagons, three thousand men. A dream for bandits and raiders, especially for any stragglers."

"We'll have our work cut out for us, especially if we don't make it during daylight." Travis looked at Chase, now wearing a tall, two-foot-wide straw sombrero. "You look like a damned bandit in that circus hat. You going native?"

"These hats work. Keeps the glare out of my eyes." Chase lifted the oversized ornament off his head and ran his hands through his hair. "How was your trip?"

"Miserable across the mountains. Like to froze and starved ducking the bandits. But I saw Chester *and* Mercedes. Monterrey and Saltillo are almost like New Orleans. Had a grand time."

"What's Chester up to? Bet he's loving this stuff. He hates Mexicans, and you know he's got a propensity to anger," Chase commented, suspicion in his voice.

"All the boys are doing fine. Loving the señoritas and fiestas. Looked to me like they've been having a party for the last two months. The citizenry and soldiers are in total admiration of the Rangers over there. But everybody's of the general opinion it's about to get bloody—even the populace seems ready to rise up and throw the wicked invaders out."

"You didn't run into Paco, did you? I hear he hangs out around Saltillo."

"No. Maybe somebody's put a bullet in his back by now. But damn near got into a gunfight with one of his pistoleros. That little greasy bandit that used to wear the beads in his goatee. Somebody must have cut it off because he had a little scar in the center of his chin."

"You mean Grunji."

"That's his name."

"That's Paco's main sidekick. Like brothers."

"When did you get back?"

"Last night. The road from Saltillo is long and dusty, two days, but nothing compared to the mountains."

"You haven't missed anything around here. Little Face is still around. The locals call him Uno Oído. He's hit us two times on the road from Monclova. I'm sure he's been waiting on us to get to the pass. I hope so. I've found a perfect ambush site for him."

Chase pulled himself back into the saddle properly. "Let's go. We've got a long day tomorrow. But you'll like Parras. It's the wine capital of Mexico. Weather and girls are just splendid. They don't even have mosquitoes around here."

It had already been a fourteen-hour day, prowling the barren hills around the pass, on the lookout for Comanches and guerrillas, when Travis took a furlough on a cliff above the foreboding gap to watch the train sneak along. The wagons, with their four strong mules, slowly strode over the bumpy path as the teamsters bounced on the wooden benches, slapping their reins and urging the animals with soft words. The picturesque scene of the army moving through such a hazardous, stunning obstacle riveted him. As Travis sat and watched the implausible feat, aghast, he thought how remarkable this was, a logistical miracle. Moving this many men, this many supplies, through such a perilous place in a single day surpassed anything he had ever witnessed.

But it was apparent that all of the army would not get to the safety of the far ridge until well after dark. Despite this, the general had decided they would continue until everybody and everything crossed. The later the day got and the more of the train that crossed the river, the more dangerous the gauntlet became. For it was difficult to come back through the tight pass, especially against the line of wagons moving up the ledge on the far slope. This left an ever smaller and smaller contingent of men and supplies isolated on one side of the natural barrier without hope of quick and reliable support.

Despite the Rangers' worries, the Mexican army had not arrived to defend the pass. There was not a more favorable location for defense in the entire country. *Perchance the Mexican army is beaten*, Travis thought hopefully. *Is this war already over?*

But at hand, there were still difficulties: fifty wagons left to enter the pass and five or six more broken down along the trail, with only a hundred isolated cavalrymen dispersed to protect them. And as he looked at the sun, already falling behind the mountains, the day waning and losing its light, Travis knew his work wasn't done. If the Comanches or guerrillas attacked, it would be in the next few hours.

Travis turned to look at a small, long hill to the

west, a geologic feature that the road weaved around. Actually it was two escarpments, separated by a small gorge, a perfect approach to the road from the mountains, with the late-day sun at any perpetrator's back. Chase had instructed the cavalry not to patrol the ridge. He was sure if the cunning Little Face raided the wagon train, it would be in the gorge. He had even requisitioned a stash of the regiment's finest horses and tied them up with grazing rope where the ridge met the road in hopes of tempting the bandit. If the Indian took the bait, Chase planned to swoop into the restricted gorge. He had happily remarked that the area looked ideal for a late-night coyote feast.

Finding all in order, Travis trotted back up the road a quarter mile to another hill covered with scrub brush. He slowly rode to its summit, where he found Chase, sitting comfortably in the bushes and scanning the ridge. "You see anything?" Travis asked.

"Not yet, but if he's coming, it should be any minute."

"Boy, I tell you what, you let Little Face get those prized ponies, General Wool's going to have your ass. Not to mention that underhanded Injun will swindle you again." Travis laughed. For the past couple of weeks, Chase had been engrossed in two running battles—one with Little Face, the other with General Wool, who had seen no priority in Chase's demands for men and equipment to pursue the Indian. But Chase had succeeded in one aspect. He had managed, with his constant, gruesome stories, to get most of the cavalrymen's attention focused on cap-tur-ing the outlaw. They were all aware of Chase's current trap, and if he managed to spring it, they were sure to abandon their duties and beat down the sage en route to the ambush; whoever got the prized Indian surely would be a hero in camp.

Chase didn't smile or find anything funny as he took a drink from his canteen. He picked his binoculars back up and steadied them on the wild country. "Look-a there."

Travis grabbed his glasses to look. In the dis-tance, against the twilight, he could see a little movement. There were objects shifting slowly with no definition at all. To an untrained eye, it could be cattle or maybe mule deer feeding. But to a competent eye, it was something else. Indians moved like game, slowly, alertly, blending in, something a white man could never master.

Chase looked at his pocket watch, then at the darkening sky, thinking, scheming, calculating. "Looks like there's only three or four of them. Go tell the boys. We'll storm that ridge in twenty minutes exactly. They should be well in there by then, trapped."

As usual under the circumstances, Travis felt a little nervous twitch. He looked at Chase. There was only confidence, eagerness, and no trace of concern.

"All right." Travis stooped low and crept out of the bushes quietly, leading his horse down the back of the hill to stay out of sight.

The twenty minutes passed slowly, tensely, in the wilting light. Travis looked at the thirty cavalrymen on their tall, remarkable horses, a few with pistols at the ready but most flaunting their long sabers, gleaming in the blue-black air; it was probably too dark to shoot at anything anyway. The work was certain to be close, dirty, and deadly. The horses fidgeted, their ears high and eyes still, as if they sensed peril from the men. The group formed a long half circle surrounding the end and both sides of the ambush area.

Chase looked at his watch and raised a hand. He looked ahead, dropping his arm. His horse charged forward, out in front of the line.

Travis joined the assault behind Chase. It took ten seconds to reach the ridge's apex. Only the sound of horse hooves on the bare land broke the silence of the night. He checked his mount as he reached the hill and looked into the brush-filled chasm, only a black belt, impenetrable to the eye. Shots rang out, and he could see a few muzzle blasts from the darkness. Travis looked around. Chase's plan had a flaw. The top of the hill provided a perfect backdrop, silhouetting the horses for the Indian eyes, already acclimated to the pitch black.

Chase fired two shots into the black void and cursed. He pulled his long knife from his belt and charged into the dark hole. The anxious cavalrymen followed, raising their lances high and whooping and yelling.

Travis also descended into the darkness. There were maybe sixty seconds of shrieks and hollers until his vision began to return. He recognized Little Face, unmistakable, his image now burned into Travis's brain. The bandit was discharging his pistol. Chase jumped from his horse onto the outlaw's back, slashing at the Indian with his knife. Both men fell to the ground and rolled in a tussle. Travis heard the moans and the grumbles. He jumped off his horse and dashed toward the scuffle. But before he arrived, a tall horse charged forward, a dragoon atop it swinging a lasso. The soldier threw the rope toward Chase and Little Face. Travis saw the American jerk back on the rope, then a grunt as his horse dashed backward a few yards, tightening the rope.

Travis and four dismounted lancers ran to the two bodies, still struggling but with less motion, the lasso tightly confining the two men. Chase expended all his energy trying to drive his fist into Little Face's mouth. Travis kicked a knife free from Little Face's hand. The soldiers raised their lances, ready to exterminate the bandit once and for all.

"No! No!" Chase yelled from the pile. "Let's take him alive. Torture him."

Chapter 15

When Travis and Chase walked into Parras's pleasant plaza the next morning, they saw a sight they had longed for, for many a year. It had to be the spectacle of the year in the remote mountain town. Centered in an army wagon sat a four-foot-square bamboo cage. Its only inhabitant was Little Face, bound in shackles, his eyes blackened, his face covered with fresh red chafes.

A platoon of soldiers stood around the cage, curiously eying the prisoner, the demon, who had terrified the column for several weeks. Little Face, with his one ear, long black hair, dark red skin, black and red tattoos, and chilly eyes, looked like a caged African beast on display at a circus, or maybe some gladiatorial show in ancient Rome. Though the soldiers were watching quietly, the town's natives, mostly Mexican women, with passion bursting from their inner depths as was so common with them, circled the cage, spitting on and cursing the heathen, the representative of the savages they detested to the bone. Occasionally, a woman would walk up to the cage and poke Little Face with a stick, yapping some loud Spanish.

Chase walked to the cage, his hands on his hips, a smirk on his face.

"What you think we ought to do with him,

Captain McAlister?" one of the cage's sentries, a young, bright-eyed private, said.

Chase grabbed a rope from a nearby horse. He slowly turned and faced the cage, jerking on the rope a few times, feeling its coarse twine as Little Face watched. "You're not going to get a rope or a bullet. That would be too good for you. I say we leave him right here. Let him baste in the tropical sun without food or water for a week or so. Let him die here. So the people he terrorized can see him suffer. Sounds inhumane, but it's nothing like the inferno he'll be in shortly."

Little Face lunged at Chase, crashing against the cage violently and jabbing his fists through the wooden bars, his shackles clanging. The crowd jumped back, oohs and aahs escaping. But Chase never flinched. He moved forward, his head only inches from the pin, and pointed down the street, a large grin on his face. "If you get out of that cage, I'll be right down there, in my quarters. Come see me. After that, you'll probably want to crawl back in here . . . if you can."

Travis let out a loud roar of laughter. The crowd, heartened, did likewise.

Chase turned and took off down the street, and Travis followed. From all appearances, Parras, with its ten thousand residents, was a jewel hidden on the Mexican frontier. Built around several plentiful springs and butted up to the tall mountains, today covered with a few clouds.

180

The streets were clean and lined with aged oak. The houses were shipshape, its haciendas and vineyards the grandest yet. Its fields were lush with everything imaginable: grapes, corn, olives, and melons. At an elevation of over five thousand feet, the climate was heavenly, but like every other hamlet south of the border, the dogs roamed the streets in droves, and the citizens seemed unaware that time even existed.

Travis looked up to a tall, stone citadel perched on the town's highest hill. It had been built to protect the town from Indians; it was no wonder Little Face was getting such a warm welcome. This day, an American flag flew over its ramparts, the soldiers currently tidying up its defenses and stacking bags of sand on its upper walls.

"Colonel Patrick gave us two days off," Chase said, stopping in front of the little hotel the army had rented to quarter the two Rangers. "Orders are to hold here and wait."

"Now that we've gotten Little Face, maybe you'll unwind a little. Enjoy yourself. I plan to," Travis answered, removing his hat and stepping inside.

First one week, then two, then a third antsy week, the army held at Parras, cooped up in the cantinas or impromptu massage parlors, drilling in the plaza, or hanging around town. For centuries, minutes had moved slowly here for even the busiest residents. And the troops were getting anxious, ready to do something—anything— march, fight, whatever would pass the time. The mood of many of the volunteers was almost mutinous. The only thing holding hundreds in their tents was the memory of the trip down, any journey north sure to be an ill-advised flight, the hills dense with guerrillas, bandits, and hostile Indians.

General Wool had terminated the circus in the plaza after a few days, ordering Little Face to be hauled out of town, shot, and then left to the buzzards. His body lay on the roadside, decomposing, an attraction for passersby. The town's women were plentiful and pretty, most not hostile, most of their men having long departed for a rifle and trench somewhere to the south. The town's merchants, as always, loved the paying customers, and after three weeks had started think this American occupation was not so egregious. But in the countryside, just out of town, the guerrillas and *haciendados* were becoming more rebellious, skirmishing with the patrols daily.

Travis stepped outside early one enchanting December evening to pass a few hours before a scheduled meeting with Colonel Patrick. He intended to stroll down to the cantina and get involved in a card game or maybe some storytelling. His reunion with Mercedes had taken away his desire for carousing. As he waited for Chase, he watched four mestiza women washing uniforms in the little stream meandering through town. Under an old stone arch bridge, they had laid the shirts and pants out on flat rocks to dry in the sun, all somehow strangely appreciative that they were being exploited. He also noticed two young Mexican lovers, probably not even fifteen, holding hands and frolicking on a shady bench, completely oblivious to the stress of their surroundings. In this isolated setting so far from the world, did they know something that Travis and this powerful army, with all it embodied, did not?

Travis smiled to himself as Chase tottered out of the hotel, giving the hostess, an old gristly woman, a festive hug and an energetic pinch on the behind.

"Maybe you should have joined the army years ago," Chase said to Travis. "This holding duty's perfect for you. Sitting around all day, milking your jug, playing cards all night."

"Don't have jugs here. They have skins." Travis began walking casually down the street. His destination was only a stone's throw from the hotel, and this evening it was overflowing. The cantina's small, energetic Mexican owner jumped between tables, filling glasses, lighting cigars, and passing out greetings as he cheerfully took in a few insults and derogatory comments.

To maximize his income, he had added an additional ten tables to the sidewalk out front, but they, too, were without vacancies. Across the street, a few soldiers relieved themselves in the bushes.

Parras was the closest thing to a city Wool's column had seen since it departed San Antonio four months earlier. And the men could not resist its charms, even under orders. Or the radiant, blushing, black eyes of the girls, irresistible to the hardened soldiers on the trail for so long. Travis paused to stare at the irregular men. There were essentially two armies in Parras: One was disciplined and professional, the regulars, officers, and West Pointers who had spent their careers fighting, living under the firm hand of the army. The other was rash and riotous, almost like disorderly children. The latter were the volunteers, independent men, with little military training or bearing. They were good soldiers when the time came, but during their free time, they were free to do whatever the hell they wanted—or at least they thought so. Each held the other in contempt, the volunteers continually complaining that the regulars looked down on them and gave them no respect. The regulars, especially the officers, derided the volunteers, forever singling them out for scorn or any less desirable jobs that happened along.

Travis entered the smoke-filled bar, Chase on

his tail, and scanned the seven tables for an open chair or a short stack of money. Muskets were against the wall, pistols on the tables, and a few spittoons sat on the floor. The room was loud and chaotic, with soldiers, a mariachi band, and five young waitresses, probably schoolgirls or domestic help only weeks before. The two Rangers leaned against the bar just inside the entrance as six trail-worn soldiers entered the room, still in their chaps, sabers dangling, apparently just in from a scout. Their arrival prompted a half dozen men, drunk and stumbling, to get up and embark for their scheduled duty.

An elderly-looking nag, probably only in her thirties but with aged eyes and skin, who was surely a prostitute, approached the two Rangers. "You lonely, soldier? You want woman?" She put her arms around Travis and looked up at his face. She brushed his hair with her fingers.

"No," Travis said, casually shooing the woman away.

The woman's face turned from pleasant to disdain. "What problem? Me good woman."

"I'm sure you are, but no, thanks," Travis said again, smiling at Chase.

The woman, in a black dress, put her hands on her hips, her face changing from scornful back to playful. "What problem? Me too much woman for you?"

Chase let out a smile, then a loud chuckle.

"Finally found a woman who can read you."

The woman turned to Chase. "You need woman? Maybe you buy me drink. Since he not man enough for me."

"You boys want a drink?" an Englishman behind the bar interrupted.

"Three tequilas," Chase said.

"We drink to your friend," the prostitute said, reaching over and picking the first of the three shots. She turned it up. "Maybe he find his manhood in the bottle. Come see me."

"I'll drink to that," Chase said, picking up his glass. "He's sure been looking for it in there for twenty years."

"Better drink up," the bartender said as the woman walked off to troll for potential business. "Hear you mates are leaving town tomorrow."

Travis turned to the patrons. "Tomorrow, huh? Must be what the meeting's about. I'd say it's time to go. Don't think Parras can take another week."

As Travis spoke, the bar got silent as a sudden hush descended, broken only by shouting. Travis turned to see two soldiers struggling to their feet, each yelling and pointing at the other. One of the two men, a middle-aged volunteer, graciously bowed, did an about-face, and stepped to the back wall. At the wall, he turned and gathered himself, spreading his legs and hanging his hands at his waist. With as much grace as he could muster, the drunkard pulled his blue wool jacket back to expose his pistol.

The seated crowd, all staring at the man, let out a collective breath and a few mumbles and curses.

Chase, a curious smile on his face, looked at Travis.

The other dragoon secured his footing, pulled back his coat, and exposed his own pistol, he, too, trying to convey a gentleman's manners. The bar got deathly quiet.

"I've never seen a duel before," Travis whispered, locking his eyes on the comical show.

The man against the wall clumsily drew his pistol, firing a shot before the weapon got above the floor. The other countered with two quick rounds, both splintering the back wall but with no danger of drawing blood. The two men then stared at each other for a few seconds, their unsteady pistols waving in the air.

A sharp yell from the back of the bar broke the hush. "I got ten dollars on Sergeant Taylor!"

"I'll take it," another voice replied. More gamblers entered the wagering, shouting and holding their money and bottles high.

"Let's get out of here before one of these drunks shoots us by accident," Travis whispered, stepping out the door as two more shots rang out.

Chapter 16

Two hours before sunrise the next day, Travis sat his horse outside Parras's citadel. He chomped on some hard cheese and drank some coffee. Only a sprinkle of light illuminated the town as the slow roll of the drums and the blare of a bugle indi-cated "boots and saddles." Travis turned to the fortress. Twenty or so sick and wounded were being moved inside. Some had yellow fever—"the black vomit," as the men called it. Others had dysentery, diarrhea, scurvy, or minor saber lacerations. In fact, diseases had been the biggest hazard thus far; almost twenty men had been buried along the trail. A company of infantry was being left to guard the lame. As the drumroll changed, "to horses, by fours march," Chase emerged from the citadel.

"You get any more details?" Travis asked.

Chase grabbed his saddle horn and swung a leg over his horse. "Santa Anna's moving towards Saltillo. We're going there in support. General wants us to cover the hundred and thirty miles in three days."

"Three days. That's almost fifty miles a day!"

"Only going to stop four hours a day to sleep . . . no camps. You're the only one that's been down the road."

"The road is good, but water is sparse—there's

only a couple of rivers. The Mexicans have destroyed all the water tanks along the way to keep the Americans from moving along the road. It was touch and go for water with five of us. It's doable, but I hope we don't have to fight as soon as we arrive. That will be a debacle." Travis looked up at the clear sky. "Going to get warm today. There's no meaningful shade the entire way."

"It might be rough. Hell, especially if you couldn't find shade. I've seen you shade behind a fence post."

With colors flying, all day the cavalry rode, the soldiers marched, and the mules lugged the wagons with their axles squeaking along the road at a steady pace. The country still stood big, the sky endless. It was toilsome work, the flies and dust harassing the men like a thick, black snow. The day was warm, the troopers' wool coats not fit for this duty. Watching the beleaguered soldiers, their faces parched and grim, loads heavy, Travis felt fortunate he was mounted. For the foot soldier, life was bleak, filled with the drudgery of marching or the tribulation of fighting. Twice during the day, the Rangers pulled tired troops who had fallen out of the line onto their horses, giving them an hour or so respite. A straggling soldier was easy prey for the savage Mexican guerrillas and scouts marauding the surrounding hills like predators on the hunt.

During the day, they crossed two rivers. Both looked impossible upon initial review. But the column was not to be held up. By sheer fortitude, ingenuity, and will, they forded the rivers. The engineers had lashed barrels to the sides of the wagons prior to their departure from Parras, ensuring they would float. Even with this, several were lost, swallowed up by the water, drowning the horses in a tangled mess of ropes and bridles, and forcing the heavier wagons to be unloaded and supplies carried across by horse. But the train moved on.

Ahead on the road, a tall, saddle-shaped mountain beckoned them on. As the column marched, hour by hour, the hill's apex seemed to draw no closer, as if it moved away at the pace of the column's slow strides. As Travis watched the parade from horseback, he had a constant uneasiness in his veins. The column looked as though it was moving through the valley of death—the high mountains encasing the road. What lay ahead of all these men? What would these men, himself included, look like in a few weeks?

But contrasting with Travis's worries was his delight to be going back to Saltillo. He would get to see Mercedes again. He had been thinking about her constantly since their recent reunion. He had thought it only a chance encounter, that maybe he would go see her again after the war.

Now he was headed in her direction again, probably for a long stint. This filled his soul with glee. But he first had to get there . . . alive.

An hour after dark, finally the bugler played taps, and the cavalcade halted to sleep in the road in battle order. The train had made forty miles this first day. With clammy skin and saddles for pillows, the two Rangers settled in for a short, scary night.

Early the next morning, only a couple of hours after midnight, Travis and Chase were rousted from their bedrolls. The night was still, only the remnants of a fallen moon washing a tad of blackness from the sky.

A young lieutenant, one of the general's aides, sat on his horse in the road looking down at Travis. "The advance scouts, twenty men, who were sent forward this morning got in a fray. Two men captured. General wants you two to go ahead with a patrol to look for them, report back by dark tomorrow."

Travis leaned up, bumping his head on the wagon he lay under. He winced and cursed. His eyes felt heavy, and he had to use his forehead muscles to open them as his dizzy mind begged to be left alone. He shook his head, then stood and stretched his arms and aching muscles as he comprehended the words. It had been a fitful, tenuous night, every minute noise causing alarm in his psyche. He looked up to the heavens, so dark and clear, the bright belt of stars bisecting the sky could be used for orientation.

As Chase also stood, Travis grabbed his saddle, throwing it over his shoulder, and walked twenty feet to his horse, standing just off the road. Water and corn had been given to the animals the night before to ensure freshness for the day's march. Travis patted the mare's worn back, looked at her dusty hide, then turned to the column. The officers and noncoms were already getting everyone up from the temporary rest to resume the march. Travis looked around at the darkness; he saw dozens of red embers—tips of cigarettes—bouncing through the night like fireflies. What could they possibly find before daylight?

In the late morning, after seven hours on the road, the twenty-man scouting party stood outside the small farming village of Patos. The country was still a *llano,* a high plateau, filled with mesquite and cactus and a few dispersed farms. Travis looked through his glasses at the town church and its tall tower. As was standard procedure, a single man had been selected to ride into town first. The lucky individual checked the town's status, then climbed to its tallest point to send a signal.

"Looks good," Travis said, seeing a white flag flutter above the church.

The patrol rode into the town, fanning out in three columns. Travis rode with Chase, the lieutenant, and three others down the town's main street, lined with unsavory-looking little dark men and destitute women, all undernourished. The men wore sandals; light, dirty clothes; and usually had a large knife or handmade *lazo* tucked in their belt. They stared at the impressive soldiers without reverence. Travis saw a collection of peons, hunched forward and carrying bundled straw on their backs, bound for some unknown location.

Chase finally led the patrol to the dusty plaza and ancient church.

Lieutenant Jones dismounted. "I'll go in here and see if they know where we can get some forage, if they've seen any soldiers."

As the lieutenant spoke, the soldiers were surrounded by a dozen begging Mexicans, some jawing in Spanish, others in an unknown indigenous dialect. The natives stared in amazement at the foreigners' strange green, blue, and hazel eyes. Travis looked at one impoverished woman, an ugly creature by all measures and skinnier than desert stock. Her hands were covered with calloused skin. Three young, filthy kids surrounded the woman. Travis reached into his pocket and pulled out a silver dollar. He put it in the woman's hand. Travis's charity caused ten more people to crowd the horses, yelping louder, pushing their open hands up in the soldiers' faces.

"What the hell you do that for?" Chase lamented over the background racket. "You haven't remedied any problems. Just given me a headache. Actually, you're exacerbating the problem, giving them something they can't depend on daily. Making them more dependent."

Travis looked at the woman, happy he might have helped her this day; she and her kids would eat this week. But he instantly regretted the contribution, for he might have to pull his pistol to back the beggars away. He lightly pressed his spurs against his horse, riding away, and turned to Chase. "Everybody didn't get your post in life, born into the Irish brotherhood. You didn't have any say in it; you're just lucky. You could have easily been conceived in a wretched land like this—or into blood further from God's graces. But they sure make a lot of noise. We'll go help the lieutenant interrogate the priest. Probably quieter in there."

After scouting the town for a half hour, the party ascertained from a few farmers, who'd been well paid for some barley, that about two hundred Mexican infantry and a small cadre of cavalry currently camped about five miles north in a small valley.

In less than an hour, the Americans found themselves on their chests, peering over a small hill and spying on the encampment. The Mexicans were a half mile away, their fifty tents in neat lines along a stream. A few fires released tendrils of smoke that rose vertically in the calm air, easily seen for miles.

"What you think?" Travis whispered to Chase, lying beside him.

"I don't know," Chase said, turning to look at Lieutenant Jones beside him. The lieutenant had become a regular on these patrols and seemed to be warming to the Rangers daily. "They might have the captives. We're only about ten miles from where they were purported last seen. These are the only Mexican regulars we've heard about. If guerrillas got the scouts, they would have probably shot them on the spot."

"We could just ride in there, guns blazing, lances high," Travis said. "Been my recollection that the Mexican army is best at turning tail, except for a few choice outfits."

"Can't do that," Chase added. "There's a truce on."

"I didn't think you took soldiers during a truce," Travis said.

"Well, we don't know that they did take them."

Travis turned to Chase, who was still studying the area through his glasses. "We need to catch a couple of their officers, then trade them."

"That's a good idea," Chase added. "You got any suggestions how to do it?"

Travis turned his glasses back to the camp and had an idea. "We need a couple of good-looking, obedient prostitutes. Send them in there for bait. Lure a couple of the officers out."

"That's the problem with whores," Chase said. "Never seem to have one around when you need 'em. Don't know where you'd find any around here anyway. And if you combed Texas, you wouldn't find an obedient one."

"If I was still in the mood . . . Put a couple with me on the trail. They'd be obedient in a day or so," Travis countered, and the group of five cavalrymen lying beside the two let out a hushed chuckle. "Unfortunately, we don't have time for that."

"Last whore I saw around you was throwing her shoe at you and digging around for a gun—ruined a good card game, if I recall," Chase added.

"It was just an idea. I don't fancy ducking those Mexican bullets any more than you." Travis removed his glasses from his eyes. "A couple of wagons of firewater would do the same. Hell, we'd have whole bunch by midnight."

"Firewater and prostitutes, huh," Chase chuckled. "Maybe you're in the wrong army. Sounds like you would have made a fine Mexican scout."

"Maybe so," Travis muttered, turning his glasses to a few buildings a half mile behind the camp. They looked like a ranch or plantation of some sort. "There's a hacienda over there. I bet those officers don't sleep here. Some of them will probably go over there to eat, or sleep under a roof. I bet about dark, we sneak over there, we can snag a couple worth trading."

"You're probably right," Chase said. "Let's double around over there, get the sun at our backs, and take a look. If it looks good, we'll go in right after dusk. Even if they don't have the scouts, we'll get some trading collateral to maybe find out who does."

It was an hour before dark, the sun just now dipping below the mountains and daylight beginning to diminish rapidly. Travis knelt on a hill, getting a final look at the three brick buildings and trying to stamp their layout into his mind. The men had scouted the farm earlier and had now returned to finalize their plans. As he had assumed, they had witnessed five or six officers come and go from the farm during the day.

The buildings were grouped tightly on only one acre and lay in open pasture, but a stand of trees hid the approach from their current location. Down in the trees below, day had already turned to night.

"Me and Travis will move around the side."

Chase turned to Lieutenant Jones and pointed to the farm. "Skirt these pomegranate trees, get in the open, and check everything out. Lieutenant Jones, ten minutes after we leave, take your men through this thicket. Be quite until you get about a hundred yards from the farm. Then charge in, pistols blaring; make a lot of noise. Any guards down there will think there's at least a company or two falling on them. They'll probably cut and run. Me and Travis will fall in with you then. We'll have looked the place over by then and can give you some direction. We just want a few prisoners. Don't go shooting the place up if you don't have to. Won't do us any good." Chase looked at the lieutenant, who gave him a nod.

"Well, let's get on with it," Travis said, and crawled back behind the hill. "Be too dark to see anything shortly."

As Travis followed Chase down the hill and around the trees, he sat lightly in the saddle. He secured his revolver in his right hand and felt his heart beat a little faster, his senses aroused, a nervous alertness filling his blood. The pasture that been golden during the day was now tinted a deep blue-red in the sun's afterglow. Ahead, approximately a quarter mile, he could see the buildings. Only open ground occupied the way. Travis narrowed his eyes at the ground and pulled back on his reins. He saw a disturbing sight: a black and white web on the ground. He whispered to Chase. "Your plan's got a defect. That's a prairie dog city in front of us. We can't ride through there. There's a hundred rattlers in there—too many holes. Might lose a horse."

Chase also gently pulled back on his reins and stared at the ground. He studied the area for few seconds. "We can't go around. We'd be seen for sure. Give our boys away. We're going to have to go through. The snakes are full by now anyway."

"I ain't going through there. If I get it, it's going to be from a Mexican, not a snake. Word gets back of that, my name would be ruined in Texas. Everybody would forget about all my heroic deeds. And you know how snakes terrify me."

"Come on, let's go. The boys are counting on us." Chase nudged his horse forward. "If we do get into some snakes, don't go making a bunch of noise."

Travis groaned. His body got agitated, and he almost had to reach down with his hands and push his unwilling heels into his mare's sides. He got shivers even at the thought of snakes, especially rattlesnakes. "You owe me for this."

Travis cautiously followed Chase, but only twenty yards into the maze of mounds and holes, Chase's mount hesitated. Travis's own horse froze, as horses are inclined to do when sensing something wrong, and tossed her head, snorting a few times. "I told you so," Travis whispered. "What we going to do now?"

Chase put a hand on his horse's neck and gingerly massaged it. He added a few soft words. The horse stepped forward. Travis heard the awful sounds of the rattling from the dark.

Chase's horse suddenly reared up, dumping him. The racket petrified Travis's impetuous mount, who jumped, bucked once, and lunged back in the direction they had come. Travis grabbed his pommel, not wanting to fall off into the frightful dark.

He heard a crack and a loud haw as his horse stumbled to her knees, then to the ground, her foot in a hole. Travis felt himself collide with the ground; then he felt the painful weight of the horse squeeze him. His mind rushed, fear blocking out the pain of the horse's fall as he grappled to free himself from the besieged, shuddering horse. Pinned to the ground, he heard gunshots in the distance, the cavalry charge.

He removed his pistol and shot his horse, whose swinging head had worked over his face. He put a second shot in the horse and looked at Chase, remounted and standing over him.

Chase extended a hand. "Come on. Jones may need some help."

Travis reached up and grabbed the hand. "Pull. Get me out of this snake bed." Travis tugged on

Chase's hand and worked his legs to no avail. "I'm stuck."

Chase turned the hand loose and removed his rope from his saddle. He slowly made a lasso to drop on Travis's horse's neck. He methodically worked the rope into a perfect circle, straightening the noose.

Travis could still hear a few rattlers shaking eerily a few yards away. "Take your time. I'm just lying down here with a horse on top of me in the middle of a snake pit. Not to mention, we're supposed be on a cavalry charge."

Chase continued to work the rope, in no hurry, his grin shining in the dark. He paused a few seconds before placing the rope near the dead horse's head for Travis to secure.

Travis, breathing hard, hustled the rope around the horse's head. "Go, get her off me."

Chase set his heels into his horse's sides, moving a few feet away before the lasso got tight. As the weight came off Travis, he wiggled free of the horse, stood, and sprinted for Chase. He leaped over the rear of Chase's horse, swinging an arm around his partner as he pulled his knife from his belt to cut the lasso. "Get out of here before we stumble on some more vipers."

In just a few minutes, Chase worked his way around the prairie dog field to the hacienda. The shooting had stopped, and five cavalry horses stood outside the largest of the buildings. Travis looked for guards, but saw nothing in the darkness. He jumped off the horse, pistol at the ready, and led Chase inside. As the two stormed up on the porch and into the three-room brick building, their footsteps reverberated up from the wood plank porch.

As Travis entered the room, he found Lieutenant Jones and his men pointing their pistols at three Mexican officers. Two of the Americans wheeled around and put Travis in their sights before recognizing him.

"What happened to you two?" Lieutenant Jones demanded, turning his eyes from the prisoners to Travis.

"Got a little sidetracked," Travis said. "Where's the rest of your men?"

"Forming a picket line between here and the Mexican camp."

Travis looked at the three Mexican officers in their haughty uniforms: white trousers, blue coats with a gold chest and long tails, and tall, ornamented shakos on their heads. The officers were young, in their twenties, and sat speechless, eyeballs roving over the Americans.

"They say they don't know anything about two American soldiers," the lieutenant said.

"I find that hard to believe," Chase declared in Spanish, stepping forward. He put his pistol to one of the officers' heads and cocked his hammer. "I bet if we shoot one of them, it might improve their memory." Chase put his hand on the trigger.

Everything got quiet. The young officers' faces got grave, a few beads of sweat forming on their foreheads.

"All right, we go check," one of the officers finally said.

Chase chuckled loudly.

Travis was familiar with Chase's aptitude for acting like a wild man. He did it so well, Travis often wondered if he was acting at all.

Chase continued, shaking his pistol at the officer he had in his sights. "We'll let this one go. The big mouth can stay here and pay if this one doesn't come back with the two Americans." He turned his pistol to the officer who'd done the talking.

Travis took a step forward and grabbed the white-faced officer who had just had the pistol removed from his temple. He jerked him up by his embroidered shoulder plates and shoved him out the door. "You've got two hours. And we want three horses."

Chapter 17

The prisoner exchange worked, the Mexican officer appearing a few hours later with the two captured dragoons. And two days later, late in the day, Travis stood on a hill, looking out at the column, which was covered with a brownish green cloud of dust. The men's faces were red and lethargic. All living creatures in the cavalcade stepped with a slow, lackluster pace as they moved into the campsite outside a hacienda called Agua Nueva, so named because it was built around ten freshwater springs. The column had managed to cross the 130 miles of hostile, waterless ground in less than four days, a march certain to go down as one of the most remarkable in the annals of the U.S. Army. General Wool had been ordered to camp here, in a mountainous valley, twenty miles south of Saltillo and wait for orders.

Travis inspected the large structures of the cattle ranch and cotton farm, as imposing as any he had ever laid eyes on, dwarfing the magnificent plantations he had seen in the American South. The buildings were enormous, made of stone, and surrounded by tall fences and lush gardens. Out in a field, beside the grand estate, a peon labored behind a plow pulled by two oxen as if it were just a normal day.

Colonel Patrick arrived at the little hilltop where the just-arrived patrol stood, inspecting the camp. He pulled back on his reins and looked the group over, rubbing his unshaven and dirty face.

"We got them," Chase said, pointing to the two dragoons at the end of the horse line. "But we almost lost one of our fearless Rangers."

Continuing to scratch his beard, Colonel Patrick looked the tired group over for a few seconds, then looked at Travis, inspecting the fresh abrasions on his face and his swollen nose. "What the hell happened to you? Looks like you got the shit beat out of you."

The line of cavalrymen let out a meek chuckle.

Travis's chest burned at the ridicule and at his current condition. "Long story *and* I don't want to talk about it. Not one of my finest moments, but I can attribute it to bad command decisions by your lead scout. Far as anybody knows, I stormed that Mexican camp and secured your two dragoons after rigorous hand-to-hand fighting."

"We're just getting settled in," the colonel continued. "Don't know how long we'll be here. You boys make camp as best as you see fit. Take the rest of the day off, but report to headquarters noon tomorrow. Captain McAlister, you might want to get your man over to the doctor, get him bandaged up."

"Will do," Chase answered with a smile, slowly leading Travis down the little hill to the camp. The soldiers had been arriving all day, and their appearance had returned life to the derelict hacienda. Skirting the grounds were rows of the familiar tents, carbines stacked, butts to the ground, barrels resting against each other as soldiers relaxed under the tall trees, recuperating from the march. Some slept, read Bibles, or cleaned weapons; others had removed their boots to doctor blisters. A large group was currently bathing in buckets of water hauled from the springs. The melancholy sound of a mandolin floated through the ranks.

Travis noticed a repugnant sight: a man, an American regular, lashed to a pole, chest first, his arms were spread, his shirt removed. Two small ropes, tied to the soldier's thumbs, were all that kept the man in his place. Beside the detainee, a tall, strong artilleryman made a few practice lashes with a long, black leather whip. The sound of its loud pop caused the barebacked man to shake and shiver. Travis also shuddered, wondering what seditious act had resulted in the flogging. He looked around; the fatigued soldiers were carrying on with their business, hardly noticing the preparations for punishment. As the big, healthy man reared back his arm, the tip of the whip dangled in the air like a satanic dagger. The whip's proprietor flicked his wrist a few times, displaying his command of the instrument, like a champion lancer brandishing his sword.

Travis turned his head and rode off as he heard the blow, the leather tearing into the skin. The man let out a horrendous shriek, and Travis cringed, almost as if feeling the blow himself.

For Christmas and the next six weeks, the army remained encamped around Agua Nueva. The area around the ranch consisted of high range, six thousand feet in altitude. The days were docile, but the nights were generally cold and windy. The main road, the only access from central Mexico and Santa Anna's army to the cities of Monterrey and Saltillo, bisected the range through a set of narrow gorges around the camp. And Wool's army had been placed in these passes to protect the occupied cities. The duties were light —scouting the high passes, mapping the area, always on the lookout for the Mexican army, rumored almost daily to be nearing, or skirmishing with the guerrillas and bandits. Travis spent many of his days in Saltillo or in the little of community of Campos with Mercedes, riding horses in the countryside or attending the theater or balls by night.

Late one cold February morning, he and Chase and five cavalrymen were scouting some farms and roads to the northwest of the camp when they came upon a small town. Chase brought his horse to a stop on the muddy road leading into the hamlet, which consisted of only a few farms, a store, a restaurant, a cantina, and some wattle houses, like any of dozens of other country villages under their dominion.

Travis tightened up the collar on his leather coat to shield himself from the frosty wind howling across this bleak land. He smoothed his mustache on his lip and turned to the cavalrymen. "We ain't seen much out here. What you say we stop and get something to eat? Get out of this cold. Captain McAlister will ride you to the bone if you let him."

Chase nodded his head. "It's impossible to ride you to the bone. You just won't do it, even at gunpoint." Chase laughed and led the group up to the restaurant, just a few tables under a thatch roof.

As Travis dismounted, he inspected the cantina down the street, where six horses were tied up outside. A group of six or seven men were exiting the establishment, mingling around the porch in a loud, drunken state. Travis thought he recognized one of the voices. He stared at the men, searching his memory. They were a hundred yards away. His chest got tight as he saw a face he would never forget. It was Paco, his missing arm removing any qualms. Without uttering a word, almost innately and uncontrollably, Travis slowly raised his pistol over Chase's shoulder and fired two quick shots.

The action spooked the cavalrymen, who all wheeled around, pistols drawn, as the group of bandits scrambled around, some to their horses, others for cover, like a bunch of stirred-up wasps. Two shots were returned, sending Travis and the patrol for cover behind the nearby brick wall of the town's store.

"What the hell you doing?" Chase yelled, ducking behind Travis.

"Paco," Travis yelled, peeking around the corner to see Paco getting on his horse. Travis stepped out from behind the wall bravely, exposing himself, and fired another shot that found Paco's horse. It fell to the muddy street. Travis turned to look at the Americans, hiding behind the wall. "Come on, let's go get him. I just shot his horse."

Chase reached out and grabbed Travis by the belt, pulling him behind the wall. "Get back over here."

"That's Grunji with him. Let's kill them both now." Travis knelt and took another peek around the corner. He saw the bandits saddled up and charging forward in the street. Paco rode double behind another man. Travis dipped back behind the building. "Here they come," he bellowed as he heard the horses nearing, their hoof thuds growing louder. He looked at Chase, and both men cocked their pistols, as did the soldiers, pressing their backs against the wall.

Then the horses stampeded by and both groups sent a barrage of lead at each other. One of the rascals' horses fell. Travis heard a grunt from one of the cavalrymen as he looked at the street. The bandit atop the fallen horse had gotten to his feet and was raising his pistol. A bullet from Travis buckled him over, and the bandit fell to the street. Travis turned to the fleeing bandits, charging out of town. He emptied his pistol to no avail. He quickly reloaded, expecting to give chase. But instead of riding hard, the bandits stopped and turned around, safely out of pistol range.

Paco leaned sideways on the horse so Travis saw him. "I heard you were down here, Ross. I won't rest until you're planted. Hope that makes you sleep well. I'll be looking for you."

Travis stepped out into the street. He gazed down at the bandit on the ground, in the fetal position. He looked like any other Mexican bandit—long, black, greasy hair, leather attire, a tall sombrero. Travis pointed his pistol at the still-heaving bandit, blood generously flowing from his chest and mouth, dying a hard death. Travis looked at a broken bone protruding from the wound. He thought about grinding the bone with his boot. He looked back at Paco. "Is this another one of your brothers?" He then put a bullet in the stricken bandit's head, the blood splattering onto his pants.

Paco screamed and emptied his pistol, only kicking up mud in the street. Then the group of horses charged out of town.

Travis turned to the cavalrymen, all tending to the wounded man. To Travis's relief, the soldier had only a minor leg wound, and Chase was already cleaning it. Travis looked at the soldier, who gritted his teeth but took the pain admirably.

"He'll be all right, but we need to get him to the doctor in the next few hours," Chase said.

Travis moaned, "I guess that bastard's going to get away again." He walked over to his horse and removed a white cotton cloth from his saddlebag. Tearing it into two pieces, he handed it to Chase to bandage the wound.

"Sounds like you'll have a chance to get him. You won't even have to search for him. Looks like he's learned to shoot with that other arm," Chase said.

Lieutenant Jones stood and looked at the Rangers. "You two sure have a lot of enemies down here. I'd hate to ride with you in Texas. I suspect you duck more than just women throwing shoes."

"Get him loaded up. We'll make a beeline for camp. Maybe we won't run into them," Chase said.

Chapter 18

The next morning, Travis and Chase were summoned to see Colonel Patrick. They had managed to make it back to the camp the previous day without further incident, and to Travis's relief, the prognosis from the camp doctor was good for the injured soldier, a dozen stitches and a week of light duty. As they entered the large stone building housing General Wool's headquarters, the day looked normal, only a few officers and orderlies fraternizing on the grounds. In the colonel's office, they found him occupied with some dispatches. The two Rangers waited patently for him to finish reading. On the walls hung mosaics of hand-drawn maps of the entire region, a one-hundred-mile radius around Monterrey. Travis didn't need to study them, for by now he had traveled through the entire area, leading many of the engineers who had drawn the maps.

Colonel Patrick finally put the papers down and stood. He walked to the maps on the wall. "We're starting to get reliable reports that Santa Anna's moving this way. Could be here in a day or two. Natives in Saltillo are all disappearing, a sure sign something's coming. When he does attack, we're going to fall back and defend these passes. General Taylor will be here tomorrow with his forces; we'll number five thousand then. And he has twenty-pound artillery. Reports suggest Santa Anna has twenty to thirty thousand men. Taylor has all his scouts out. All the Rangers and most of my cavalry are out looking for them also. They're reconnoitering these roads south." The colonel pointed to random spots on the map, then tapped his finger on a crossroads. "I've got a spy. Name's Cervantes. Owns a little store here. Supplies stuff to the Mexican army. He'll sell anything for money, including his soul. He's given me some good information in the past. You two flush out to the west. Don't have any cavalry for you; go alone. Find him. See what else you find while you're out." The colonel reached under his desk and pulled out a small leather sack. He tossed it on the table, and the gold coins inside clinked loudly.

Chase picked up the loot.

"Bring him back with you. He's fickle. Won't say much until he's here. And he's crafty. Don't give him all the money up front. Pay him a little and show him the rest. His eyes will get big. Hell, you two were Rangers. You know how to bribe these bastards. You made a living out of it. Go about fifty miles and report back to me."

By early afternoon, Travis stood on a tall ridge, finally observing what he and Chase had been in search of for months: Santa Anna's army. Looking infinite, it spanned all of the three valleys in sight. From this viewpoint, almost two miles away, it was only a hazy image, large blocks of earth, colored brightly, shifting and stirring up dust. But the sight was still awe-inspiring. This was the bulk of the Mexican army. Travis trained his glasses on the lead elements, marching by sixes up the road that wound through the imposing hills. On the hill-tops, huge fires blazed, iridescent orange shining against the horizon—the signal for war. The wind howled over the hills, but the day shone clear, without a cloud blotting the sky. Travis felt as if he were in the belly of the beast, looking outward.

"I'd say they're fifteen miles south of the camp," Chase said, looking through his glasses. "Probably won't make it there today, but they will tomorrow. Looks like infantry and artillery. The dragoons and cavalry are probably ahead. I wouldn't be surprised if they're not already skirmishing with our scouts. Let's go see if we can find this spy."

It was almost dusk—the mountains turning a dark gray, the air cooling, the breeze increasing—when the two Rangers finally found the small crossroads Colonel Patrick had pointed to on the map. Travis looked to the east. The horizon was covered with cloud fingers, placidly turning from pink to plum as they fell away. Underneath the spectacular Mexican sky, he knew the ground was busy. Travis leaned back in the saddle, looking at the two buildings straddling the road. One was a general store; the other looked to be a residence. Both buildings were red brick with stucco facades peeling away to show some of the masonry. Travis saw not a soul, but in the half-light, a lantern shone through the store's only window.

"What you think?" Travis inquired. "You reckon the good Cervantes is around here?"

"This might be a big goose hunt," Chase answered, looking around wearily. "We're going to have to ride back through these mountains after dark—with the entire Mexican army on the move. I'd say it's at least a three-hour ride. We may have to find him just to help us get back. Let's go in this store and see what we find."

Travis dismounted and walked into the musty store, the door veiled only with a serape. He parted the cloth and led Chase inside. The floor was dirt, the room dimly lit. There was a large stone counter against one of the walls of the empty room. Travis removed his hat, then banged his pistol butt on the stone bar a few times. "Anybody here?"

"Sí, sí," a voice sounded from behind the building.

Travis turned to see a man filtering through a second curtain covering the back door. He was a short, chubby, aging mestizo with a devious-looking face.

"We want some tequila. And Cervantes—in a hurry," Chase said.

"Yes, I have drink," the man said, and hustled behind the counter. He removed a bottle and two glasses.

Chase filled a glass. Setting the bottle down, he turned up the tequila. "You Cervantes?"

"Yes."

"Good. That part was easy. Colonel Patrick sent us here. He wants to see you tonight," Chase continued.

Cervantes stopped refilling the glass and stared at Chase before moving his eyes to Travis. "I know nothing. Mexican soldiers don't like me talking to you. They find out, and they come here and steal my forage. Beat me up."

"I don't give a damn about all that," Chase said. He removed the sack of gold from his pocket and tossed a five-dollar coin on the counter. He then shook the bag a few times, listening to the money jingle. "You've got two choices: You can have this sack if you come tell the colonel what he wants to hear. Or we can take you . . . shoot your ass if you're too much trouble." Chase threw the bag on the counter.

Travis watched the old, gray-haired Mexican's eyes get big. Cervantes looked at the bag, then at the two Americans again, then picked up the bag to inspect its contents. Travis stared at the Mexican, thinking he would watch Cervantes struggle with the decision, his own conscience feeling a little ashamed that their task for the day was coaxing a man into betraying his country—the sort of feeling that comes over most humans when they trick somebody into doing something they don't want to do. Instead of seeing indecision or confusion on the storekeeper's face, Travis saw joy.

"My memory is getting much better," Cervantes said with a smile.

Despite the fact that this man had information that might save the lives of hundreds, if not thousands, of Americans, including perhaps Travis's own skin, Travis immediately looked upon him with disdain. Cervantes had hardly hesitated, and had not bartered at all. He had no heart, no conviction. He had sold out, not only without resistance, but with pleasure.

"I can see you're a good Mexican, easily bought," Chase said, patting Cervantes on the shoulder. "Get your horse and let's go."

After a six-hour ride that included outrunning a nasty, unfriendly group of horsemen early in the night, the Rangers and the spy topped a hill on the perimeter of Agua Nueva. For several miles, in the post-dusk dark, they had seen the red glow over the hills. Travis had feared the worst, but from some outlying pickets they'd discovered that the army had already moved out into their battle positions around the narrow passes. Reports of Santa Anna's advance had arrived earlier in the day. The army had left two companies of cavalry volunteers to guard the rear, load up all supplies, and burn anything left behind, including the ranch. Travis stared in amazement at the impressive complex, probably constructed over hundreds of years, its support buildings, storage houses, large church and steeple all in flames. The scene was ghastly, evoking episodes in the Texas Revolution when the Mexican army had left almost nothing standing.

Around the burning ranch, soldiers moved at a fast pace, almost panicky, as a few officers tried to calm the jittery troops and organize an orderly retreat. In the darkness and the cool evening air, the Rangers continued on at a fearful trot, more worried they might be shot by jumpy pickets than marauding Mexican cavalry. On several occasions, they saw movement ahead on the trail and yelled out, informing the pickets they were friendly.

Chase led the group through the tight passes. So dark was the night that the natural obstacles could not be perceived, their eyes able to see only the dusty road beneath the horses. The narrow road brimmed with soldiers marching, supply wagons, and twenty-pound artillery bumping along or being coerced up side trails by laboring mules and teams of grunting men. Past the mountain gaps, the land opened up and visibility returned to shouting distance. From a few pickets, the patrol learned that headquarters had been set up a mile to the rear, in a large hacienda called Buena Vista.

Thirty minutes later, the Rangers rode up the tree-lined drive to the ranch. All the windows in the hacienda's five buildings glared with yellow candlelight. Travis noticed all the horses tied up out front, at least fifty, and figured a war council was surely meeting. He looked at the orderlies, adjutants, and junior officers milling around the main house's porch. Their faces were solemn and serious, as was the mood of everyone else. Around the house, the atmosphere was electric. Soldiers moved at a deliberate pace, stacking cotton bales or unloading ammo boxes. The aura sent a nervous chill down Travis's spine. He had seen it before. When men of this much importance got this somber, the business of death, usually on a vast scale, was close at hand.

One of the orderlies instructed Travis and Chase to lead Cervantes to a room in one of the houses. The room had six or seven other Mexicans already lounging around. Apparently, Cervantes wasn't the only native willing to turn on his countrymen for a month's wages.

After an hour's wait, Travis and Chase were escorted inside to meet with Colonel Patrick. As almost always the case, he was standing over a table covered with maps. Four lanterns, the only light in the room, sat on the table's corners, their shadows shifting and illuminating the cool room. Travis looked at the maps, the country familiar, but not the fresh marks indicating the location of friendly units.

Colonel Patrick removed a pipe from his mouth. "We should be in position by daylight.

The Mexicans only have two routes to Saltillo: down the main road or over these ridges to the east. As you can see, we're defending both. Artillery is being placed on all the high ridges. Reserves scattered on these two ridges where they can easily access the battle. You two will join Taylor's Rangers, about sixty, here on this high hill where General Wool will command." The colonel paused and put the pipe back in his mouth as he pointed to the maps. "You will serve as dispatch riders or support if it's needed. You'll camp there tonight and be under their command for the battle. I would suggest getting on over there. And try to get some rest. Tomorrow will no doubt be a long day."

The colonel's look and tone gave Travis an unsteady feeling. His stomach got queasy. He thought of the vast army he had seen on the horizon that morning, somewhere out there in the night, descending on them at this very moment. Though the air in the office and outside on the ranch stood still and quiet, he sensed the energy all around him. What would tomorrow bring? Certainly there would be death on a grand scale. If the Mexicans did surround the outnumbered Americans, there would likely be little quarter given. The Mexicans, like the Americans, had old scores to settle, to make amends for the disgrace of the Texas War of Independence. Travis thought back to Goliad, the bloody battle on the prairie, and also San Jacinto. Tomorrow was sure to surpass anything he had seen before. Unlike those other times, his heart did not race with excitement or anticipation, but trembled with fear—not just for himself, but also for his friends and comrades. What would tomorrow bring?

Chapter 19

It had been a near-sleepless, cold night on the commanding hill. No fires had been permitted, and the wind, blowing down from the mountains, scooted swiftly over the exposed ground, cutting to the bone. But with the dawn, the morning calmed as the slow minutes ticked by. Travis looked out at the battlefield below as the sun started to transform it from black to blue to magenta, and finally the green and brown of the hills.

The pass below was still dark, shadowed from the rising sun. But it looked formidable. It was barely two wagons wide with steep, vertical sides hundreds of feet high. To the west lay a swath of impassable gullies, but east of the pass were high, wide ridges, their slopes abrupt but not impassable. The American artillery was scattered along three hilltops, the brass howitzers gleaming in the sun. And the five thousand Americans stood in their combat lines or sheltered behind outcroppings in the pass and on the ridges. Along the line, the only movement was the incessant white breath from the horses and men, dumping into the cold air and rising before dissipating. It gave a hint of the strength massed in the hills.

Travis turned to the rear. Behind the pass were the wagons of ammo and the field hospital. The surgeons had lined up the wood bunks, covered with white sheets, outside the tents. Beside the tables sat the boxes of bone saws, iron probing rods, razor-sharp blades, and jugs of whiskey and disinfectant. In the distance, the docile hacienda of Buena Vista was surrounded by hundreds of wagons.

The anxious morning brightened with no sign of the enemy, only the large dust cloud approaching from the south. On the hilltop, behind the Rangers, a battery of artillery silently sighted its barrels, stacked balls, and arranged powder canisters. The lifeless slopes were quiet until mid-morning, when a shout went up at the arrival of the commander—not General Wool, but General Taylor—riding high in the saddle, his colorful uniform and guidon visible for a quarter mile. He was surrounded by a party of a dozen mounted guards. His arrival roused the troops, who welcomed him with loud cheers and wholehearted screams from the lines.

The time passed slowly until early afternoon, when Travis finally saw the Mexican army marching up the road, a half mile distant. Through his glasses, it was a spectacular but sinister sight. The Mexican drums rolled, and the cavalry fanned out in front of the artillery and lancers, marching in a steady, proper, and choreographed column along the roundabout road. The sight of the two armies pumped Travis's adrenaline and tightened his chest. It somehow made his fears seep from his soul, replacing them with bravado. That reaction could be induced only by a setting like this, with all of America represented on the hills. Though he was all alone in his thoughts and his actions, he felt as if thousands of eyes were watching his every move. Travis turned to the sixty Rangers in their distinctive buckskin jackets with frayed sleeves. Chester was there, and a dozen more Travis had served with. The steadfast group added to his confidence.

A single Mexican cannon fired, its ball whistling over the line, harmlessly exploding in the rear. The shot caused the American lines to applaud, wielding their muskets and lances. The minutes passed, the ground in front becoming more and more crowded with the enemy. Travis wondered where Santa Anna was. Where were Rayo and his old friend Tony Flores? Surely they were out there. Somewhere on the field was a battalion of Irish deserters, taking up arms for the Mexicans. If they were engaged, there was sure to be a fight to the death. They were on the list of those to be punished. Off to the left, Travis could see the Mexican lancers and infantry, afoot, climbing the hills to the bluffs.

Then, in the road, he saw a single rider approach from the south. He rode fast under a flag of truce. The thousands of Americans got silent; not even a whisper was uttered as hundreds of field glasses locked on the man. The rider approached the American lines and was escorted by two pickets up the hill, right by Travis and the Rangers. Reaching the summit, the foreign soldier reached in his pocket and removed a piece of paper that he handed to a sergeant.

Travis watched as the paper was delivered to General Taylor, clearly in sight but just out of hearing range. The two hundred men on the hill seemed to hold their collective breath as the general read. It was so quiet, a few birds could be heard cutting through the air overhead.

General Taylor raised his hands in disgust and responded. The men again shouted approval as word came down that the response was something on the order of: "I don't care if we're surrounded by twenty thousand men. Tell Santa Anna to go to hell." Travis looked off at the plateau. The Mexicans were still ascending the hills, and he saw the dust trail of two American cavalry units riding in that direction to shore up the friendly lines.

General Taylor instructed one of his adjutants to scribble out a response, and the Mexican emissary was sent on his way. The general then barked a few orders, and three officers jumped on their horses and dashed away to the rising beat of the drums.

Not thirty minutes later, a few shots commenced on the high plateau, just distant pops and puffs of smoke. All afternoon, the Rangers on the hill, the artillery, and the officers watched the small skirmishes on the hills, only little bands fighting at close range, just a fraction of the armies waiting to engage. Runners came and went with reports. The Rangers stood by their horses, ready to ride at the shortest notice. The artillery rarely fired, the warring parties too intermingled for either side to lock in a sure target. As day elapsed into night, the lines remained static, as the bulk of the Mexican army moved closer, growing wider and deeper on the horizon.

The night was again frigid, but also rainy, a wintry downpour that pierced the skin, as Travis and the Rangers stayed on the hill, breaking for sleep under canvas tarps and waiting for the new day, which would surely be a climax to all the waiting.

When the next day did arrive, the Rangers were roused by the sound of Mexican drums. Travis looked toward the valley; the Mexicans were still in formation, holding a prebattle Mass. The priests, in their long, white capes, rode along the column, blessing the men and showering the army with holy praise. Some of the Americans removed their hats, reverently taking part in the ceremony from afar.

Soon, the clerics disappeared. In front of the array of soldiers, the officers were visible in their bright, almost partylike uniforms, laced with insignia, belts, and ropes. Boldly and alone, a few rode forward, two within range of the American lines, to have a look before returning to their ranks, unmolested.

The morning hush ended with the sound of Mexican artillery. First a few volleys, then long barrages screeched overhead and landed in the friendly ranks. The Mexicans moved forward en masse, first on the high plateau, then down the road. For almost an hour, the Americans hunkered down behind the cover of rocks, hills, whatever they could find, not firing a shot as the Mexicans drew closer.

Then it began. After a few shots of American artillery, almost the entire line engaged at once. Shortly, the battle transpired under a cloud of black smoke hanging over the scene like a dense fog. Both sides advanced, then wavered, the falling shells ripping through the ranks.

Travis heard a loud voice.

"Here they come."

He looked down the road, not a hundred yards away, where the trail turned out of sight. The Mexican lancers, dressed in white, their polished barrels shining, assaulted the pass. Travis looked below. The dragoons were mounted, their drawn sabers pointing skyward from their waists, shining like a row of deadly toothpicks. In front of the dragoons, the infantry knelt, carbines clasped firmly at the ready. All the men's faces looked eager and strong. Where else could the masses so easily become heroes? The officers moved about on horseback, high in their saddles. This was sacred work for them.

Travis heard the air scream, first in the distance, then getting closer. The hill exploded; the ground shook so hard that he almost fell. A wind gushed forward, then retreated. The dirt fell like rain, stinging his skin and covering him with mud. Over the screams and the dissipating energy of the falling ten-pound balls, Travis's horse jumped and grunted, but he stood erect, the reins tightly in his hands. He looked at the other Rangers, doggedly standing, and the artillery battery, keeping to their dirty work, answering volley with volley.

Then the order came to descend the hill. Travis never heard it, but followed the men, on foot, taking cover behind some rocks thirty feet above the road. There they pointed their pistols and carbines toward the pass.

As the Mexicans moved forward, the American artillery homed in with deadly accuracy, charring the earth and maiming the bodies. The bold enemy continued to advance, moving around their fallen comrades.

All the Americans began to fire their light weapons. Travis fired six shots into the line of men, aiming only at the collective throng. He heard the balls slapping into flesh and the screams resonating through the pass as he reloaded his Colt. The fleeting minutes passed with only a few

Americans falling. Travis emptied pistol after pistol into the pass as the battle raged. Finally, the road was only a pile of bodies, hundreds of bodies.

As the Mexicans retreated, the order came down the hill to cease fire. Travis wiped his burning eyes and silently looked at Chase, his face now caked with black smut. He looked at the slaughter, almost spellbound, feeling a little ashamed. What was, only minutes ago, a proud regiment, now lay as a mangled mass of death. The Mexican soldiers, mostly Indians or mestizo peons, lay clad in their beautiful white and gold uniforms, the bottoms of their feet covered with sandals. Though their uniforms looked daunting, they weren't the select specimens of the American ranks, who were much larger, better trained, more motivated, and more disciplined. Travis looked at the Rangers as he struggled back up the hill. He knew that this little victory had not been secured by superior weapons or the officers, albeit spirited and courageous they were, but by the quality of these men.

Atop the hill, Travis guzzled a canteen to quench his thirst and took a seat among the quiet Rangers, resting on the ground. He looked at his watch. His mind was whirling. The past couple of hours had passed like minutes. Out on the plateau above the pass, the epic battle still raged—maybe still in question, or tilting to one side or the other. He saw only heaps of men and little puffs of smoke and heard the distant sound of cannons.

A captain rode up to the tired Rangers, his uniform dirty, his face sweaty and red. He jerked back on his reins and yelled, "All reserves, follow me to the ridges. The Mexicans are breaking through."

The Rangers ran to their horses, tied up atop the hill. They followed the officer down and around several deep draws, ducking around sage, then up, down, around, and through more gullies, a labyrinth of red dirt, for ten more minutes that garbled any sense of direction. Finally the group emerged on the high range. A few hundred yards distant, the battle thundered and pandemonium reigned. Companies of Americans retreated, while others charged into battle. Muskets roared; cannons screamed; officers yelled. Along the ridge, the small Mexican lancers, by the hundreds, were appearing from the ravines like ants emerging from their nest.

Travis looked at the bloody terrain, alive with activity like waves on an ocean. Horses charged; dirt danced from the cannonading; sabers glittered; the white of the gloves flickered like flags in the wind. He saw an American soldier, missing an arm, grimacing in pain and fleeing to the rear. A dragoon raced forward, reached down, and jerked the man onto the butt of his horse. Far afield, on the next ridge over, more Mexicans were attempting a further flank to the east. American reinforcements stirred up dust racing to meet them.

The captain raised his saber and pointed ahead. "Those gullies there—that's where most of them are coming from. Let's fall on them. Chew them up and cut them off."

Travis looked ahead toward the long, thin ravines splitting the battlefield. He turned to the willing Rangers, their horses' tails standing high, ready to scamper.

Chase rode forward, lifting his pistol. "Chester, half of you get the first one. We'll take the farther one." He then lunged forward in the saddle and took off at a full gallop.

As the Rangers unleashed mighty yells, Travis spurred his mount, leaning over her neck. Half the horses veered off to the right, disappearing as the ground fell away. As Travis approached the second draw, he brought his horse to a sudden stop, kicking up some loose rocks on the rim. Down below, the Mexican infantry, as many as fifty men, were running through the barren crevice to a gentle slope at its back. The twenty Rangers commenced shooting. Travis lifted his pistol, briefly having difficulty locking on a target; there were so many. He fired twice, only having to wait for the pistol's recoil to dampen between shots. Beside him, the Rangers were all emptying their Colts. Over the roar of the firing, the running Mexicans screamed and fell to the ground like ducks shot on a pond.

"Give the greasers some cold steel," one of the Rangers yelled.

Travis turned to look at the men. Instead of reloading, they drew their sabers. Travis holstered his pistol and pulled his lance from his hip, then followed the group, charging down the precarious slope. The air turned to dust. Travis saw a Ranger fall. The mass of rushing horses plowed over the dozen remaining Mexicans, pounding them to the ground with a wall of stock and sharp steel. Travis's horse trampled over several men as he wielded his sword. His agile beast reeled around, ready to charge again, appearing to enjoy the rough play. The animal had not the slightest inkling this was deadly fun. A Mexican lancer turned and raised his musket at Travis. Travis rushed forward, impaling the white outline with his saber, feeling only a minor resistance as the pressure of the hot flesh collapsed on the steel. Travis retracted the blade with a jerk, and the young, dark-skinned Indian fell away.

The screaming slowly stopped, the sound of horse hooves the only noise in the draw. Travis looked at his lance; dark crimson blood dripped from the blade. He felt his horse breathe, her lungs contracting and expanding between his knees. He looked at the Rangers; two had fallen. The rest sat on horseback, panting and looking at the ground, which was covered with corpses.

Travis drew in a sharp breath. He currently felt no fear or sympathy. He was only a pawn. It was them or him. But days later, after he settled down, he knew this sight would reverberate through his brain, a nightmare that would go on and on, wetting his palms. He wiped his lance on the uniform of a dead Mexican and sheathed it neatly. Travis reloaded his pistol as he looked at the two fallen Rangers, both already dead. He swung his eyes to the Mexican bodies, some still squirming. He sighed again, not wanting to carry out the inevitable duty of finishing the soldiers off. In a sad way, it did them a favor that they most probably wanted. He knew that, but still had no wish to take part in the horrific work. He looked around, trying to discover some other worthy task. In doing so, he saw some movement, probably more Mexicans making their way up the draw, but stealthily veering off into a small side draw.

"Psst," Travis whispered, nodding in that direction, his mind still whirling. He motioned to Chase with a silent hand, then gestured to the other Rangers, instructing with hand signals that they should ride back up to the plateau. He pulled out his watch, tapping it with a nail and put two fingers up, implying that he and Chase wanted to get in position before they commenced their assault. Travis led Chase down the ravine to the smaller gully, branching off from the one they were in. Travis crept forward, peering into the cove. Twenty Mexican lancers were crammed together, bunched up in the draw, only a hollow with walls too steep to climb. Travis raised his pistol, pointing it at the Mexicans, only fifteen steps ahead. "Halt!" he yelled.

Just as he spoke, the twenty other Rangers appeared overhead, looking down on the Mexicans, ready to fill the hollow with lifeless flesh.

Travis exposed himself, straining his eyes through his fuzzy vision. Above, he could hear the hammers cock. He saw a fearful sight. "Tony Flores, for God's sake! Put those guns down right now."

As Travis spoke, his old friend turned to look at him.

"It's not worth it," Travis yelled. "Your war's over."

Tony looked right at him, then at the Rangers above, the fronts of their horses covered with blood. He surely knew some of them. Tony's face flickered with confusion and astonishment. Thirty seconds passed without a word.

"Travis," Tony finally replied. "I always fought for what was right—most often with you. Now I have to fight you for it. I would gladly give my life for what I believe, but not the lives of my men." Tony's rifle fell to the ground as if he had lost the facility of his hands. His soldiers, most unable to understand the conversation, soon followed suit, and the little hole in the Mexican earth got quiet for a few seconds before it was broken by the sound of stampeding horses.

Travis shook, and the Mexicans cowered, a few

reaching for and picking up their rifles. Travis looked up. The other half of the Rangers had arrived, Chester in the lead. Their horses were bloody, their guns and sabers drawn. They paused but a second before falling into the chasm, so precipitous most of the men jumped from their mounts.

"No!" Travis yelled with all his energy as he watched the men raise their lances—too bloodthirsty even to think of their pistols.

Travis felt himself go numb, his surroundings turned into a dull glare, no detail at all, as he watched the massacre. In only a few seconds, it was over. His stomach nauseated, feeling as if he were about to vomit, Travis stepped forward, raising his pistol. He pointed it at Chester, a few feet away and still slicing flesh. Travis walked slowly, his pistol extended the full length of his arm. He stopped and locked his eyes on Chester, his body shaking with fury. No one spoke, and Travis felt the eyes. The Rangers all got quiet. The seconds passed slowly.

Chester looked at Travis over his bloody sword. "Do it. You don't have the balls," he said with panting breath.

Travis leaned forward, cocking the hammer. He jammed the barrel into Chester's upper body, still not uttering a sound.

"Don't do it, Travis," Chase calmly said, walking up behind Travis.

Travis put his finger on the trigger, then whipped

the pistol back, whacking Chester across the forehead with the barrel. Chester staggered back. Travis dropped the gun and delivered another blow, a fist full of knuckles to Chester's cheek with all his fuming strength. He swung so hard, he felt the hard bone on his balled fingers, then added a left to the ribs. The punches sent Chester to the ground, and Travis dived at him, arms swinging, groans escaping from both combatants. As Travis landed two more blows to the groin, he felt two men grab him and wrap their arms around his waist. He slung his fists in all directions as he felt the strong arms tighten their grip.

"Cut it out," Chase said with a growl, securing his arms around Travis.

"Let him go," Chester said, getting to his feet. He wiped some blood from his mouth. "I was about to teach him a lesson. He's tight with these greasers anyway."

Chase slung Travis behind him and grabbed a handful of Chester's shirt. "One of those was Tony Flores. And they had all already surrendered." He shoved Chester back.

"He should have known what he had coming when he took up sides," Chester retorted. "You better watch yourself, Travis. You're not immune from your actions."

"Ya'll get out of here. All of you. I'm going to talk to Major Richardson about this later," Chase said.

Chapter 20

The little gully was quiet except for the swishing of Travis's horse's tail. The sounds of the battle raged above only in the background, like mockingbirds chirping in trees overhead. Travis had a pounding headache, and his midsection ached as if he had been kicked in the gut. He looked at the pile of bodies, the white uniforms now tainted with dark, almost black blood, their fabric torn and frayed from the sabers.

He stepped over two dead soldiers and pulled a few bodies back, looking for Tony, hoping he might still be alive, at least barely so he could say something. But Tony was only a lifeless, limp carcass with bones. Travis knelt, realizing painfully the time between the two was over forever. There was nothing he could do about it. He felt hopeless, helpless. Travis sat silently for a few seconds before he grabbed two handfuls of Tony's cotton shirt, jerking on it, having to pull three times to unfetter the corpse from the pile.

"Tony was a man," Chase said, stepping forward to help Travis. He lifted Tony's feet as Travis lifted his torso. The two were alone in the draw, holding Tony parallel to the ground. "He knew what he was getting into and the consequences of it. Thousands of men will die today. He was one of the minority, here by choice."

"I know," Travis said, lifting Tony up and dropping his upper body over the back of his horse. Travis's hands seemed to have no sensation, no feeling. His body felt numb. The sky—everything—didn't seem real. It all felt unimportant, like a figment only in his brain, just thoughts created by his mind. "But it doesn't make it any easier. Every time I take up the gun, I regret it."

Chase looked at Travis. "You take it too personal. It's not your fault. But this is the only thing you're good at—and you're damned good at it. This is the only thing that excites you, gets your juices flowing. You were miserable on that porch. Every man has to find his own meaning, purpose in this world, whether it's sweeping a bar, running cattle, or Rangering. You don't like your meaning."

Travis removed some rope from his horse to secure the body to his saddle. "I am in a bind. The only thing I'm good at, I hate. I guess I'm bound for eternal misery."

"We'll bury him proper tonight." Chase patted Tony's leg and let out a small smile as he helped Travis with the rope. "You might get bailed out one day. Maybe you'll take up with a woman that will settle you down. You'll enjoy lying around the house, doing nothing. I know where there's one at."

"If we get out of this mess. We're surrounded by twenty thousand Mexicans." Travis saddled up and started to ride up out of the sheltered ravine. "I really don't care about this anymore."

As Travis topped the banks of the gully, the environment changed from quiet to pandemonium, as if stepping off a peaceful street into a rollicking saloon: cries, bullets, cannon blasts, movement everywhere. They trotted to the top of a little hill where the Rangers had congregated.

"Orders are to stay here until we're needed," one of the Rangers said, signaling with a raised hand to Travis and Chase as they arrived.

For the next three hours, Travis watched the battle. The entire line became engaged, and ebbed and flowed as each side made progress. The scene seemed to continually repeat itself, the Mexicans, pouring men incessantly into the field, breaking the line, only to be repelled a few minutes later by charging, reckless American reinforcements or a timely artillery barrage. The Mexican causalities mounted, piling up on the high plain. From Travis's view, the Mexicans looked fearless, even more so than the Americans. But the Americans' ability to communicate, rapidly send reserves to a critical point, move and shift artillery efficiently, and deliver the shells accurately overcame all the nerve and numerical superiority of Santa Anna's army. *What a travesty,* Travis thought. *What a senseless waste.*

As Travis watched the carnage from afar, the spectacle looked like a tragic opera. The scene reminded him of Goliad. These same people were killing each other again. Though their appearances were a trifle different, they were essentially the same, the same wants, needs, aspirations. Travis thought the battle resembled one of those watercolors, maybe of Yorktown, or Waterloo, absent the hawks, condors, and vultures circling overhead, waiting for the smoke, noise, and men to depart—or the Mexican soldiers stealing the Americans' boots, clothes, or weapons as they fled. That wouldn't be glorifying the victors or doing justice to the foe's heroism.

By late afternoon, the battle had become critical. The Americans were bloodied and exhausted, their lines almost caving; the Mexicans poured more and more men onto the field, their ranks and lines growing in strength. Just when it looked like the Americans might finally be overrun, defeated in disgrace, General Taylor appeared on the plateau, his guidons and standards riding high. Just the sight of him, riding the lines exposed, sent jubilation through the American ranks, rekindling the men's spirit and will. It was just enough to make a difference. The Americans fought off the final Mexican push of the day. The scene made Travis wonder what would have happened if at that vital moment, a Mexican general, maybe Santa Anna, would have had the courage and wherewithal to do the same.

In the waning hours of daylight, the Rangers were ordered to the rear to repel a flanking move endangering the supply wagons and headquarters.

As had happened all day, the poisonous American artillery came to the rescue, tearing flesh and ground, demoralizing the enemy, and stacking the dead. The Rangers had only to mop up after the salvo.

By nightfall, the lines had stabilized almost where the battle had been joined; the slaughter had decided nothing. As the sun fell, the ground turned blue, while the artillery still sang in rapid volleys, its canisters streaking across the sky, an orange stream, strangely almost normal, going unnoticed by the men.

As Travis rode through the rear camp, looking for a place to bury Tony, he noticed the wagons and ambulances trudging back to town. In them were the bodies, concealed in blankets, or the wounded soldiers, covered with fresh bandages, usually sitting upright and smoking an opium pipe or clutching a bottle. Travis heard a few dismal, drawn-out screams from inside the wagons. The scene was gloomy, one of those that would stick in the mind.

A couple of hours after dusk, Travis finally found a small grove of oaks, where he stopped and spent an hour digging a grave. The events of the day still tormented him. He was having trouble believing what had transpired. It was like a bad dream, a nightmare, but he was not waking from it. The screams from the gully had been real.

His body was exhausted, his legs cramped from dehydration, his mind numb as he labored with the shovel, all alone. He removed Tony from the horse and gently placed him in the small pit, having to fold his body up to fit it in the undersized hole. After refilling the earth, he saddled up and looked around. He had left no cross or monument, fearing bandits or soldiers would rob the grave, but he promised himself he would return on a later day. He quickly visualized a humble tombstone:

TONY FLORES
TEXAS RANGER & MEXICAN LANCER
DIED VALIANTLY HERE THIS DAY
FEBRUARY 23, 1847

Valiantly didn't seem to gibe with what had actually happened, but it mattered little, Travis thought as Chase arrived.

"He have any family?" Chase made a cross on his chest with his hand. He raised a gourd and took a long drink of water, then put a piece of hard beef in his mouth, offering some to Travis.

Travis shook his head. Despite the fact that he had not eaten all day, he had no appetite. "No, he was a bastard son. Mother's dead. I think he has an old grandmother in Chihuahua. Maybe I'll write her a letter," Travis said in a soft voice. "What's the word?"

Chase looked into the shadows. "We're going back to that hill. Picket duty. Wait till morning. They may attack again. Last of the reserves are coming down from Saltillo. We should be back up to prebattle strength by morning."

"And the casualties?"

"Guessing about seven hundred dead, twice more wounded, missing, or deserted for us. Three times as many for them. Plus we've captured about three hundred."

The night was again cold, with the Rangers dispersed in two- or three-men groups between the two armies, at all viable avenues of attack. Travis had been allowed to sleep the first four hours before being sent with another Ranger to the lines. The ground was dark; no moon shone down. It was almost too black to see more than twenty yards, but the turf was alive with suffering. Grunts and groans from the no-man'sland between the two armies, in English and Spanish, drifted out like a fog. Men, some almost delirious, hollered for help or for water to extinguish the fire in their throats. Occasionally, a few dull shots rang out from the darkness, probably a soldier from one of the armies turning a carbine or pistol on himself— better to be shot than scavenged by the coyotes and wolves that surely roamed the ground. In spite of the pleas from the darkness, it was doubtful any of the pickets, Mexican or American, were bold enough to brave the ground and save a comrade.

Travis was tired, so sleepy he could hardly keep his eyes open. He fought a perpetual war between consciousness and pithy naps in the saddle, only waking when suddenly startled by the chilling hoot of an owl or some other shuffling in the dark to wonder how long he had been away. He half felt like just succumbing, falling asleep, leaving his future to fate.

Despite his depleted body and mind, the minutes passed, one at a time. Travis had trouble deciding if he wanted the night to hurry by or try to stall daylight's arrival, not wanting the morning and subsequent killing to resume. He and his partner spent all night not saying a word, too worried it might give away their position to a Mexican picket. Instead of standing watch over this cold cauldron of death, Travis wanted to be with Mercedes. In the cold, dark night, he found his thoughts and focus constantly shifting from the blackness to thoughts of her. Where was she? Was she safe? He wanted to finish this dirty work, so he could go back to her. Her arms were the farthest things in the world from this misery.

As the night retreated, the eastern mountains started to come into view. First, they were only faint images, but with the passing minutes, the scarlet outlines became more and more defined. The morning stood still and clear; the sounds of birds began with the rising sun. But as the sun rose, the battlefield looked the same, even more disastrous than the day before, and totally at odds with the new dew of the day.

Certain there were no enemies nearby, Travis led his partner back up to the hill where the Rangers had rallied the day before. On the hill, the grass had been worn bare or burned to nothing from the embers expelled from the cannons, beside which lay heaps of empty boxes of powder and shell. The big guns, the day before a polished brass, were now dingy, dull, and covered with blast residue and burned powder. Down below, there was no Mexican army in sight, only a few soldiers on the far ridges. To his rear, he saw the American supply wagons, slowly making their way forward to an army thirsty for bullets, powder, bandages—everything.

"We think they've pulled out," Chase said, approaching. He handed Travis a little tin cup of coffee, steaming in the cold air.

Travis took a big gulp. He swished the coffee around in his mouth before swallowing it. The aroma stimulated his senses. The caffeine seemed to instantly revive his mind, and the sultry liquid trickling down his throat warmed his bitter, frosty stomach. He shivered and looked down at the day-old battlefield. Most of the American bodies had been stripped and now lay half naked on the ground. *Who were the barbarians?* he thought.

"Don't know where, but Patrick is putting together a patrol. Wants us to join it. Move south and see what they're up to . . . if they're turning tail or just regrouping. Get some food. We pull out in an hour. We might be gone a couple of days."

Chapter 21

Later that morning, the patrol wound its way down the main road south. The rudimentary dirt passage was riddled with charred craters, swollen bodies, abandoned weapons, and dead horses, some still hitched to wagons or artillery.

The day had warmed; Travis felt the sun on his back as he turned to look at Lieutenant Jones and the three other cavalrymen behind him, riding in combat order, spaced two horses apart. Travis looked ahead to Chase, leading the group.

The patrol had stopped in the road at a pile of dead Mexican infantry, a platoon, probably sixty, literally stacked so thick that they blocked the way. They had surely been bunched in a tight combat formation when the ruthless American artillery had locked in. The flies buzzed over the fetid flesh.

Travis looked twenty or thirty paces to each side, where a few men lay, having tried, unsuccessfully, to flee the certain death from above.

Travis shook his head, loathing the scene. The American officers could be cruel, stubborn, and uncaring in ordering their men to senseless deaths, but he could never remember an American or Texas soldier left on the battlefield to rot. The Mexican officers cared little for their men. Fallen or still fighting, these peons were only fodder to achieve a means—at any cost.

By midday, they had traveled ten miles, and paused on a hilltop to observe the Mexican army, camped at a now-burning farm in a broad valley. Another cavalry patrol, having captured a few Mexican officers, had told them that Santa Anna had paused here, hoping to lure the Americans out of the fortified hills. But with morning gone, he had now decided to move farther south and disengage. The patrol made camp on the little ridge, all afternoon watching the Mexican army march from view. Travis was still in disbelief. How could an army outnumbered five to one, in a foreign land, among a hostile population, win such a battle? He thought of Cervantes and Santa Anna's incompetence. They were only small, insignificant pieces. There were many others. Only the culmination of all of them would produce this.

The next day, they continued south in front of a three-hundred-man, thirty-wagon detachment that had been sent forward to set up an advanced camp. The ride was slow, the ground stripped and desolate with no livestock or forage along the way. Most of the houses had been ransacked, as if a swarm of locusts had purged the ground. Small groups of stray but harmless Mexican soldiers stumbled along the road, usually running for cover at the sight of the Americans.

By noon, the column entered what had surely been the peaceful, picturesque city of Farias a few days earlier. The little village of five hundred had forty nice houses, a warm plaza, an elegant old church, and a single street paved in brick. But in the wake of the retreating Mexican army, it was in total disarray. Hundreds of wounded, bleeding Mexican soldiers lay about the town, in the plaza, outside the church, under homespun blankets, or on wooden tables; some lay only on the ground. Twenty of the town's women tended to the men as best they could, providing water, bandaging the wounds, or applying only a couple of gentle words or a soft touch. The sour smell of mortality filled the town, overtaking the sweet fragrances of the plaza's many trees. The populace looked not much better, hungry and deprived, their faces wearing the strain of the tragedy.

Travis looked over into a well, a deep hole encased by bricks in the middle of the plaza. It was dry, the seemingly endless supply of water already bucketed out. He looked around as the American detachment moved into town. An enterprising young dragoon officer took charge, ordering the two doctors to tend to the needy and the quartermaster to pass out food and supplies. What first brought a rare appreciative glance from the town folk, soon almost turned into a riot as the residents crowded the wagons, screaming and swinging at each other. The old priest, a dignified-looking man, ran out of the church and, eventually, helped the soldiers restore some sense of order.

Travis nudged his horse and slowly rode over

to the town hall, a square stucco building in the shade, where Chase, Lieutenant Jones, and a few other officers were standing outside, discussing the situation.

Chase looked up at Travis. "Sounds like Santa Anna's moved all the way down to El Salado. The column will stay here for now. Whole valley's pretty desolate . . . looks like the gates of hell. We need to get out, find some farms. The town, including us and animals, will starve in a few days here. Find some grain, stock."

Travis removed his hat and ran his hands through his hair. He looked up at the serene sky, spotted with pristine cotton-ball clouds, a complete contrast to the funerallike ambiance of his surroundings. He turned and gazed at a scrawny, young mestiza girl, not fifteen, with dark skin and bare feet. She was breast-feeding a baby in the plaza. Her eyes were not wistful, only indifferent, accustomed to hardship. He wondered what would become of her, not just in the near future, but as the years passed. Her husband, if she had one, was probably dead. This was a pitiless, unforgiving land, even in peacetime. "We'll take a look," said Travis. "Didn't see much on the trail that looked very promising. Hell, we might have to fight just for food and water around here."

By early afternoon, Travis and Chase had been riding several hours, hopelessly searching the deserted haciendas and little villages for stores of grain, livestock, green grass—anything that could be foraged. They approached a lovely, large ranch, sitting on a little hill and surrounded by well-kept gardens. The grounds showed promise. The contiguous fields were flush with tall grass and a few cows grazing on the hills. As they trotted up the rise that led to the main house, Travis saw six horses tied up outside, the first they had seen all morning.

"Looks like somebody's here. We finally found some life," Chase said.

"I think you're right," Travis answered as the two slowly rode into the house's yard, shielded by tall trees. Travis studied the horses cynically. They were American stock, U.S. brands on their front quarters and big saddles, uncommon south of the border, on their backs. "What do you think?"

Chase took a cautious glance around. "Could be some volunteers looking for shelter and food—or deserters. Or Mexican bandits who stole the horses." Chase slowly dismounted.

Travis looked at the front door. It was partially open, a few inches of air between it and the jamb. Travis noticed the handle was shattered, probably from being kicked in. He pulled his pistol and whispered, "Let's go see."

Chase hunched low and tiptoed to the door, putting his shoulder against the wall to eavesdrop. Travis joined him. Inside, he could hear some talking and a few shouts. Chase put a hand to the door. He looked at Travis with a finger over his mouth, then gently pushed the door open.

Travis looked into the room, which was much darker than the day. It took a couple of seconds for his eyes to acclimate. His first sight was a volunteer cavalryman in his dirty red uniform, his pants around his boots. He had a young Mexican girl bent over a table, her dress up around her back, her mouth bound with a rag, her bloody wrists lashed above her head and tied to the table. Three more soldiers stood in the room, one casually pointing his pistol at an old, gray-haired man in his sixties with a fresh black eye, sitting in a wooden chair. So preoccupied were the men, none even noticed the two Rangers walk in.

"What the fuck is going on in here?" Chase yelled, hysteria in his voice.

Travis saw all the men and the girl look at Chase. He himself looked at Chase, whose eyes filled with fire, his loud voice uncommon. The veins in his neck pulsed.

The man behind the girl turned to Chase with a sick smile, continuing his business. "Choice stock, get in line, or there's another one in the back."

Chase stepped directly to the man, raising his pistol. He lashed the man with its butt across the forehead before he ever knew what was coming, all his powerful, inflamed energy put into the blow. The soldier fell to the ground with a wince. Chase pulled his knife, then reached over and cut the girl free.

Travis looked at the other soldiers, their mouths hanging open, their eyes now filled with fear where he had seen amusement just seconds earlier. He pointed his pistol at the three, more gesturing than aiming, his own disgust now manifesting itself. "The fun's over. Get out of here now. You don't want to tangle with us, especially when Captain McAlister is wound up. I can promise you, it will be short and painful." Travis looked at the man on the floor. "You, too, before I plant my boot in your bare, ugly ass."

Travis turned to look at Chase, his jaw firmly clenched. He walked over and helped the girl to her feet, straightening her dress and brushing her hair. The young girl had beautiful, alabaster skin, long ebony hair, and dark brown eyes that were probably once enchanting. Now they were lifeless, fearful, and plain, as if all her essence had been stolen. The girl looked at the floor, too embarrassed to make eye contact. Travis shuddered, tightness in his chest. The four other men made their way outside, and the room got still, a weird quiet. As Travis's mind stopped rushing, he heard the voices from the back laughing and jostling.

Chase turned to the hall, striding in that direction with all haste. Travis followed. The scene looked similar, two more men and a lovely woman in her twenties on a bed. Chase entered the room, this time sparing the occupants the conversation. Travis stood awestruck, watching the events unfold. Chase grabbed the man on the bed, pulled him to his feet, and forcefully jerked his head down to Chase's rising knee. He then rammed the man's face into the hard adobe wall, grinding the big, hairy brute's nose against the stone a few times before shoving him out the door.

Chase's fury and wrath filled the room, sucking in Travis's attention and further bringing his own anger to the surface. Travis saw some movement behind him, only a glimmer in the half-light. He turned around to see the other man raising his pistol. Before it had even gotten above the belt, Travis pumped two bullets into the man's chest, not really even cognizant of what he had done, the reaction automatic. As the deafening echo of the shots faded, the man buckled over without a word, his red wool jacket filling with blood. He hit the ground, burping some crimson saliva onto his big black beard.

Travis turned to Chase, whose own pistol had been drawn, but not in time to administer justice. The two looked at each other, then at the woman, whose mouth had not been gagged. Travis cut her hands free from the bedpost, and she shriveled up into a ball, covering herself with a blanket.

Travis left Chase and walked back out of the room. The other cavalryman stood in the hall, blood dripping from his now-pale face. The tall, lean man looked at Travis, his hands dangling over his two holstered pistols. Travis stopped, looking at the man's eyes. The hall was quiet, only a light wind singing through an open window. "Go for it. If you get me, and I don't like your chances, you'll have to deal with my partner. He'd love that." Travis nodded to the room behind him.

The man stared at Travis, his face vexing, his rotten teeth showing. Travis saw he wanted to draw, but the soldier had to know even the slightest twitch would send him to his Maker. Still, the man pondered a few seconds before relaxing his hands and turning around. Travis hurried forward and kicked the man in the rear with a two-step skip. The action sent the soldier to his knees. "Come on, pull it. I'd like to clean up the Kentucky blood," Travis yelled as the man scrambled down the hall on his knees before regaining his feet and fleeing the house.

Travis turned to Chase, now in the hall and wearing a cheerless leer. In the house's front room, the old man held the young girl in a hug, the only sound the shuffling feet of the fleeing volunteer as he walked out the front door. Travis moved to a window to look outside. The first four men had ridden down the hill. Travis nodded to the back room. "What about him?"

"We'll drag him outside. That poor girl back there doesn't need to look at him." Chase walked in that direction. "Don't worry about this. The entire army knows what outlaws the damned cavalry volunteers are."

Travis turned to the old man. He still had the young girl's head buried in his chest. Travis tried to say something, even started to move his mouth in a quick, indistinguishable murmur, but he paused, realizing nothing he could say would comfort the two. Only his departure might aid in their grieving.

Chapter 22

Travis sat in a rocking chair on the porch of a lesser building, near the Buena Vista ranch. Around him, the grounds were flourishing: hundreds of white tents, dozens of wagons with their tan tops and U.S. markings, hundreds of troops grooming horses, mending tack, constructing new buildings, or unloading supplies. It was two weeks after the battle. The Mexican army had retreated south more than a hundred miles. The American army had given up the field, now ensconced in the fortified cities of Monterrey, Saltillo, and here in the pass guarding those cities. Though there had been no formal fighting for the two-week span, the countryside was more lawless than ever, the guerrillas and bandits roaming the hills and administering their own form of vigilante justice with terror and robbery. The areas outside of the encampments had become so hazardous, any movement between the camps and cities required a large force; the decomposing bodies of solo dispatchers or foolish troops trying to go between the towns dotted the sides of the county roads.

The cavalry and scouts spent their days patrolling the countryside, scouting, constantly combating the ever more intrepid vandals, and trying to guard and protect the restless, inhospitable inhabitants, their homes and farms perpetual victims of these foraying, ruthless bands. In the past week alone, two wagon trains had been attacked, with more than thirty Americans dead. The generals had told the troops, in no uncertain terms, to give no quarter to the guerrillas; any misdeeds would go unnoticed.

But today, the headquarters area had a strange tenseness, for a general court-martial was to be convened after lunch. Travis looked at the grounds. Scattered about were the tools of punishment: a pile of foot shackles and accompanying twenty-pound balls attached with a chain, a steel brand with a D on its end, and three wooden coffins, empty, their tops open—the future resting spot for three American soldiers, a dishonorable death in a faraway land. Above the coffins, the wall was peppered with shot marks from the firing squads. Travis looked at two drums lying beside the coffins. When would executioners and condemned, all in their ceremonial dress, arrive? What reprehensible crime had occurred? Deser-tion, repeated insubordination? Travis wondered.

He looked at the door of the little dusty building behind him. Chase had appeared from inside, an easy look on his face.

"You're next," Chase said. "I'll wait on you."

Travis stood and quietly walked inside to an office where Colonel Patrick sat at his desk.

The colonel shuffled some papers and looked up at Travis. He casually spoke. "Have a seat, Lieutenant Ross."

Travis slowly took a seat, locking his eyes on the colonel.

The colonel picked up his cigar, studying the hot end for a few seconds before he began. "Captain McAlister gave me his version of what he saw in the gully that day. Sounds like it was just a big mistake."

"Big mistake?"

"Do you know how many Texans and Americans the Mexicans murdered in cold blood during the Texas War? Weren't you there? The only reason they haven't done it down here now is because they haven't had the chance."

"I was right there. The Mexican lancers had clearly already surrendered."

The colonel moaned, putting his elbows on the table. He puffed his cigar and set his gaze on Travis. "Shit just happens in war sometimes. I don't like it, but that's the way it is. They were on an open battlefield. The bastards have no honor. They sent out a white flag during the battle trying to dupe us. This happens from time to time. And as it always does, it's going to be swept under the rug, where it belongs. Can't change it. Won't do anybody any good to worry about it now." The colonel paused a few seconds. "As for this Kentucky Volunteer you shot . . . Everybody knows what a bunch of miscreants they are, but they're good fighters."

"They were raping two girls. And the son of a bitch threw down on me. Like you said, shit just happens sometimes."

"I know. I'm not worried about it. Nothing's going to come of it. It will go under the rug, too. But if I were you, I'd be looking out for myself. Those bastards will be out for you. Wouldn't get out in front of them if we have another fight. Hell, we've already found a half dozen officers with American grape in their behinds. Wasn't any coincidence that they were all hated by their men, or somebody had a score to settle with them."

Travis raised his voice a tad. "So nothing's going to be done to Chester and the others for that massacre?"

The colonel snuffed out his cigar in a tray and turned his eyes to some papers on his desk. "That's all, Lieutenant."

Travis stood and walked back outside. Dispirited, he lazily dragged his feet on the wood planks. Outside, Chase stood on the porch. "You hear anything different than I did? Like nothing happened as far as they are concerned," Travis asked him.

"I got the standard rhetoric also." Chase stepped off the porch, leading Travis to their horses. "Best thing we can do is put it all behind us, especially you. You're not making any friends around here. And you've alienated most of the Rangers. Chester's got it out for you. Just lay low a couple of weeks, everything will be fine. It may take a little longer for Chester to settle down. General Scott landed at Vera Cruz last week. I hear we're going to Isabel in a week or so. Then to Vera Cruz by ship."

"Vera Cruz? We don't have but seven weeks left on our enlistments. And General Taylor's been honoring all of them."

"I know. I guess they plan to make us earn our wages the last month. Hell, I may sign on for another six months. I'd like to see Mexico City."

"Not me. I'll be done." Travis put a boot in his stirrup and climbed up on his horse. He looked at the sun. "There's a supply column leaving for Saltillo in an hour. We better make it if we want to go to the big ball tomorrow night."

Looking out across Saltillo's vast plaza, several hundred yards wide in both directions and covered with stone, Travis felt a little gratified. He looked at the ancient church, stunning, and towering over the plaza. From its steeple hung five bodies, a rope around each man's neck, their feet dangling four feet above the ground. The guerrillas had been shot that day and put on display here, the exhibit intended to appease the restless natives, warn the bandits, and boost the morale of the soldiers. General Wool had ordered that all guerrillas and bandits be allowed this formality. These weren't the first at this locale, and probably would not be the last.

In the plaza, the citizens moved about, barely noticing the corpses. They tended to their business and carried on with daily chores—life trying to return to normal. Travis noticed two American soldiers on crutches, each missing a leg, the severed limb still covered with a large white bandage. On the other side of the plaza, Travis saw an old, dark-skinned Mexican, also without a leg, certainly having lost it in some faraway battle years before. The Mexican hopped along with a crutch and a small tin can, begging for change. Travis turned away, hardly able to the look at the sad scene. The two brave soldiers had little to look forward to.

It was late in the day. The air had a cool nip, but the gray stones all around still radiated heat from the sun's work. Travis reached over and grabbed Mercedes's hand. She sat on a horse between Travis and Chase, also staring at the hanging men. Travis flicked his reins and rode over to the church. He looked at the fresh blood puddle on the ground, then up at the guerrillas, hoping one was Paco or Grunji. All five looked the same: dark, stringy black hair and leather clothes. To his dismay, he did not recognize any of the faces. He turned to Mercedes. "You ready to go to the party?"

"Nothing like a few hanging dead men to make the mood jolly," Mercedes said condescendingly. "You're not going to keep me around all those drunken, obnoxious soldiers all night, are you?"

"You women sure are a lot of trouble. Not sure you're worth it," Travis said.

"Yes, we are." Mercedes smiled.

Travis paused a few seconds, admiring Mercedes's long red dress. "I guess you're right. We wouldn't keep coming back for the punishment if you weren't. And no, we won't stay long. But all the officers will be there. It will be very formal; even the governor and mayor will be there. No drunkenness. That will be later tonight." Travis turned and looked at a row of large, handsome, exquisite Spanish domiciles along a side street. He laughed. "But poor Saltillo will surely suffer before daybreak."

Mercedes reached over and brushed a speck of dirt from Travis's clean, freshly starched white shirt. Then she looked at the two Rangers in their new trousers and shod in polished boots. "You two cowboys sure look nice this evening. You should do it more often."

"I almost forgot how opinionated and forward of speech your woman was," Chase added with a smile.

"You sure don't have to solicit an assessment. It just comes out, no matter who's around," Travis said as Mercedes urged her horse off down the side street that weaved around a large hill dividing the town.

"What about your father? Has he showed up yet?" Travis asked, trotting his horse up beside Mercedes.

"No, he's still in the hills. He'll fight on till the end. I think he's got a death wish. These wars are going to take all the men in my family before they are over."

"I'm going to see if I can find him. See if I can talk some sense into him. The war around here is over. As soon as Santa Anna capitulates, the Americans will leave and everything will be back to normal. No sense in doing anything stupid in the interim. General Taylor is pardoning every Mexican that will go back home and mind his business." Travis pulled back on his reins as the three entered a second plaza, a smaller version of the one they had just left. He looked at the grand governor's mansion, where the ball was already in full swing. And what a sight it was. Outside, in a perfect row, stood the tall staffs flying all the regimental flags. Beside the mansion's two immense doors stood a pair of sentries in their formal dress uniforms. Around the building, the other hotels and cantinas were all open, at least a thousand attendants moving among the plaza, the party, and the other establishments. It was like roaming a fair as the sounds of the orchestra inside could be heard. In the crowd were soldiers in clean uniforms, American civilians dressed in their finest suits, and Mexican gentry—merchants and land-owners—all also dressed in their most excellent attire. Many of the soldiers walked happily with the docile señoritas, hand in hand.

A tall, large bearded soldier walked toward Travis, stopping ten paces away. "Buggies and horses over there." The sergeant pointed down a little street to a park.

Travis handed a young barefoot Mexican boy a dollar and got off his horse.

"Better drink up tonight. We're leaving for a three-day scout tomorrow," Chase said, helping Mercedes off her horse.

A few hours later, Travis, Chase, and Mercedes strolled down a dark street to Saltillo's small seedy district. The little patio bars were all bulging with soldiers and natives, drinking the night away. The sounds of the loud talk and bottles clinking drifted through the city. Each bar had its own clientele, some crammed with the state volunteers, others officers or Mexican merchants, some even with the scoundrels from the bush, probably bandits or guerrillas by day. Armed army soldiers, not fortunate enough to be off duty, ensured tranquility on this formal night, sharing the street corners with bands playing in front of tin collection cans.

The group eventually walked into a large park lit by scores of cresset torches, where hundreds of people, mostly natives, danced or congregated around a ten-piece band. The throng of jovial humanity sang along to the choruses of the festive music, clapping and swaying in the cool night. Four or five proprietors had set up small bars around the park and busily made a week's wages selling drinks to the mob.

Travis grabbed Mercedes's hand and wedged his way through the mass of flesh to one of the hastily built bars. In the crowd, the air was thick and humid. He leaned against the bar and ordered a bottle of mescal as Mercedes put her arms around his neck. Travis handed Chase the lavender bottle. "You don't have any friends that Chase can court? Might relax him some. He takes all this too serious."

As Travis bent over to kiss Mercedes, he looked over her shoulder to see a bulging, hideous image at the end of the bar: Paco, the bandit's threadlike beard, wicked scowl, ostentatious gold necklaces, and black leather outfit unforgettable. Travis let go of Mercedes and grabbed the bottle back from Chase. He took a few gulps directly from it. Normally, the sight of the bandit might have made the hair on his neck stand up, but the alcohol filling Travis's blood only emboldened him. He looked at Chase and nodded at Paco.

Chase turned to look. "The hooligans are out."

Travis let go of Mercedes completely and locked his eyes on the guerrilla with an inert stare. He took another sip from the bottle. Paco finally felt the penetrating eyes and turned to face Travis, his truncated arm against the bar, his nefarious eyes piercing. Travis fought an urge to pull his pistol and send the bandit to hell, but there were too many people around to risk gunplay; any fight sure leave the ground covered with the innocents.

Travis moved a few steps down the bar, stopping only a few feet from the bandit. He wiped his sweaty brow.

Paco laughed loudly.

"Who's that?" Mercedes whispered in Travis's ear.

Paco turned to look at Mercedes, an immoral, wily grin on his face. His eyes roved like a snake's, cold, unblinking, ready to strike without a moment's notice.

"The scum of Coahuila," Travis admonished with a liquor-induced slur, loud enough for Paco to hear him. "Next time you see him, his ugly one-armed ass will be dangling from the church."

Paco did not look at Travis, but continued to stare at Mercedes, narrowing his eyes. Travis could feel her quiver as she put her arm around his own wide frame.

"I hope you go home and have a good time

with your mistress," Paco finally said. "After I kill you, I may try her myself."

A rush of anger filled Travis. He lifted his arms and lunged at Paco, but got only a half step before he felt a strong pull on his collar. Chase jerked him back.

"Let him go," Paco said, turning his eyes back to Travis. "I'll go ahead and put a knife in him. Then I can enjoy his mistress tonight."

Mercedes grabbed Travis's hand, squeezing it tightly. "Let's go somewhere else."

Travis turned his back to Paco, shielding Mercedes from his eyes and leading her away from the bar.

Chapter 23

It was high noon the next day when Travis led the twenty-man patrol into a little village sitting on a salt flat about an hour ride southwest of Saltillo. The ten-structure town sat at the intersection of two major roads, under a tall windmill, its only enterprise vice. The village had two rough cantinas and a large hotel that doubled as a brothel and a site for fandangos after dark. The nameless settlement was a frequent haven for soldiers on pass and guerrillas squandering their fleeced money on mescal and women. And in the past month alone, on its dusty streets or in its dark, damp saloons, a half dozen shoot-outs had taken place among bandits, soldiers, and local vaqueros.

The patrol had spent a quiet morning riding the farms and haciendas between here and town. A few were occupied, but most were deserted, their administrators dead or having already fled to the safe confines of town. The only activity of the patrol that morning had been dispersing ten volunteers pillaging a small farm, rounding up a few chickens, and dismantling the wood porch of a small shack for firewood.

Travis looked at the tan adobe buildings, all square, plain, and with one story. The day was clear and dusty, the brisk spring winds starting to appear. In the town, all was quiet, the only sound the creaking doors of three wooden outhouses on the village's perimeter, banging back and forth with the persistent gusts.

"Doesn't look too rollicking right now," Lieutenant Jones said, sitting his horse between Travis and Chase.

"It gets going a couple of hours before dusk. Place will look like Galveston in a few hours," Chase said, and moved out in front of the column down the windswept red road between the buildings, only a washed-out hallow. "Back when we were Rangering, if a bandit wanted to get Lieutenant Ross off his tail, all he had to do was ride through a little town like this. That alone would put five hours between him and intrepid bandit hunter."

"I can't disagree," Travis answered with a chuckle, following Chase up to the hotel. "Sometimes, a man that serves is needed in two places at once. He just has to decide where his valuable services will be needed and appreciated the most." Travis looked up and read the weathered sign painted above the wooden door out front: CASA DEL DORADO. As he did, he heard the terrified scream of a woman. He looked at Chase, whose face had transformed from humor to concern. Travis dismounted, leading Chase and the lieutenant into the moldy cantina. The room was dark, and he narrowed his eyes. The dusty, wood-plank floor squeaked beneath his feet. The screams came from the back of the bar, where a young girl, twenty or so, lay on a table. She wore a long white dress, now covered with blood. Over her stood a man with a bottle of clear alcohol and some bandages, cleaning a wound.

Hearing the footsteps, the man turned to look at Travis before resuming his work; each stroke with the soaked cloth caused the girl to writhe and holler. She kicked her feet as the man tried to hold her still, his free hand pushing down on her chest. Another man entered the bar from the hotel. He was a mestizo, short and wiry, in his forties. Travis knew him. Poncio Fragos owned the establishment. He was a shaky figure with a deceitful, scheming face. Travis had long thought he was half bandit, half hotel owner, and always looked upon him suspiciously.

"What the hell happened to her?" Chase said, walking behind the bar and pouring himself a shot of whiskey. He quickly downed it.

"*Bandidos* came this morning," Poncio said in English. "All drunk, in rage, after all my customers gone. They mad at some of my girls—two that have taken up with norteamericanos . . . cut their ears off. Got all the rest of my girls stirred up. Five left this morning. Say they not come back . . . this not good for business."

Travis looked at Poncio, incredulous that the man was so unconcerned for the harlot, now screaming and suffering on the table, her head maimed for life—his only concerns related to his pocketbook. As Travis got worked up, he was reminded, as he was daily, of a woman's station in this land. He walked over to the girl and looked down at her. Her eyes were closed tightly, all her facial muscles working. Travis put his hand on her forehead; it burned hot. He grabbed the man tending her wounds firmly by the arm. "Who are you?"

"He's the store owner," Poncio interjected from behind him.

Travis again looked at the girl. The man had shaved the sides of her head, and tried to clean the wounds before covering them with a torn cotton towel. "Where's the other one?"

"She's in the back," Poncio answered.

"Take them down to our camp. Let the white doctor look at them." Travis pulled out a little piece of paper and scribbled on it. He handed it to the storekeeper.

"They'll be all right," Poncio insisted. "Hair grows back, nobody will ever know the difference. They don't need ears in their profession."

"I said take them down there now," Travis told him, his voice loud and rankled. He walked over and grabbed a handful of Poncio's shirt, lifting the man's ninety-pound frame off the ground a few inches. "And don't give me any back talk."

Travis sat Poncio back down in a chair and

turned to the girl. "You, storekeeper, get a move on now. And take both of them." On Travis's words, the man took a large rag and wrapped the girl's head, her face included. He then helped her to her feet and led her out of the saloon. Travis turned back to Poncio. "Who did this and how long ago?"

"I know nothing. I was asleep . . . with my mistress. I had late night last night. American soldiers drink all night. My girlfriend very frisky afterwards." Poncio chortled.

Chase and the lieutenant walked up beside Travis, crowding Poncio. Travis took a big swig from the bottle and stepped forward, his chest bumping against the devious little innkeeper's nose. Travis stared down at Poncio, who was now looking for somewhere to retreat. He shuffled back a few inches in the chair until his back touched the bar. Poncio's shoulders drooped, and he got an uneasy, edgy look on his face, his eyes shifting nervously.

"I want some answers," Chase said. "General Wool would love for us to shut this place down. I doubt anybody would mind if the little greaser that runs it comes up missing. Sure wouldn't bother me at all. I'd probably volunteer to make him disappear." Chase took another swig of whiskey and pulled out his ten-inch steel knife, its blade shining in the half-light of the room. He put the long, jagged edge of the cold blade to

Poncio's neck. "We close this place down, it will solve half my problems anyway."

"All right, all right," Poncio said, leaning back from the blade and talking fast. "It was about ten bandits—never seen them before."

Chase laughed, a long snigger, as he leaned forward and grabbed a handful of Poncio's hair. He held the knife up in front of Poncio's face and twisted it in random motions. "This is the deal. You're going to tell us where their hideout is. We're going to go there and look for them. If you've given us a line of shit, I'm going to come back here and kill you. If you run off, I'm going to hunt you down. I'm not supposed to be back in town for a couple of days anyway. I've got twenty bored dragoons outside. It will help us pass the time."

Travis watched as Chase put the blade back to Poncio's neck, point first. He turned to Lieutenant Jones, watching intensely and content to let the Rangers finish whatever business needed finishing. The regulars despised the guerrillas more than most, since they were more likely to be the guerrillas' victims. Chase gradually pushed on the knife until the skin retracted a tad. Travis watched Poncio's eyes fill with panic; his face beaded with sweat. Chase pushed a little harder; Poncio leaned his head back until his skull hit the bar. Chase continued to push, his face now directly over Poncio's, looking down at him, nose to nose, until the knife drew a speck of blood.

"I'm dying to do this," Chase called out with an expressionless face. "Clean up the greaser blood."

"I'll tell you! All right!" Poncio screamed, fear in his voice.

"We're listening," Chase answered, not removing the knife, but moving it side to side across Poncio's neck, still applying pressure.

"There's a deserted hacienda, two valleys west. Follow the second river south from the Parras road. I hear they go there sometimes. That's all I know. I swear."

Chase removed the knife and put it back in his scabbard. He looked at Poncio. "To tell you the truth. I hope you lied to me. I'll come back here and be the boss of this place for a few days. Always wanted to run a whorehouse."

All twenty soldiers sat on horseback in knee-high gold grass atop a foothill. Travis looked down at the hacienda, a quarter mile into the valley. They had scouted it late the previous day. It looked like all the haciendas: part house, part fortress. This one was broad and single-storied. It was surrounded by six buildings and a tree-shaded yard. The main house was made of thick stone, all the windows barred with iron, the building's square, flat face rendering all approaches subject to gunfire from within. It probably had thick, robust doors. The building had been constructed as much to comfort its owner as to protect the entire farm and workers from the Indians. Not much of an obstacle for an army with artillery, but a menacing task for twenty mounted dragoons.

Down in front of the house, the twelve horses they had seen the day before were still tied up. Though Travis could not see them now, the day before, two men had stood guard on the roof. Travis looked to the east at the mountains, the sun only now peering over their apexes, brightening the day with first light. Maybe the guards had fallen asleep after getting drunk during the night. Travis hoped it was so. He turned to the soldiers, all army regulars—stalwart, tested troops, their eyes sturdy and their bodies strong—in a line along the ridge. The horses stood, side by side, stirrups a foot apart, bridles toward the hacienda. Most of the men already held pistols in their shooting hands as they casually conversed.

Lieutenant Jones slowly rode ten paces to the front of the line. He turned and faced the men, his actions ending all talk. "No quarter for the greasers. Kill them all except woman and children. If the hags fight, kill them, too. I can promise you they'll give us no quarter. We'll hang them in that little lice-infested village for all the army to gawk at on liberty. Hang them low for the coyotes to feed on." The lieutenant raised his pistol. "This ones for our two Rangers, their dedicated service to the republic. They're leaving us for Vera Cruz in a few days to do more of God's work." The lieutenant lowered his pistol and turned his horse toward the valley. He spurred his mount. "With all speed."

Travis took off at a full gallop, urging his horse with a whip of his reins. Falling down the hill, the cavalry line gained ferocious speed by the time it hit the valley floor. The hacienda raced forward, bouncing in Travis's vision. As the assailants entered the yard, two shots rang out and a dragoon fell from his horse. Travis looked at the roof, where two men stood, firing their pistols. A ten-shot barrage from the yard sent both to their deaths, one falling forward off the roof. Travis dismounted and charged the front door. He fired a shot at its iron handle and drove his shoulder into its center. The bullet only sparked as it bounced off the thick steel. The door did not even budge at Travis's assault. In disgust, Travis turned to see dirt splattering in the yard and arms poking out of the hacienda's windows. The bandits were firing pistols from inside without even aiming.

"The roof," Chase, still on horseback, yelled. He wheeled his horse around, a lasso swinging in his right arm as he scanned the awning for somewhere to anchor the rope.

Travis dived to the ground, feeling the cool dirt

on his face as he heard another voice from the back. "The dumb bastards left the ladder up. We'll pull the roof up. Half ya'll stay out here. If they flee, gun them down."

His ears ringing, his body flinching uncontrollably, Travis looked to see a dozen cavalrymen scattering around the house, a safe distance from the sporadic shots. One of the horses fell to the yard; its rider jumped off and scurried for the cover of a tree. Travis got down into a squat and jogged to the back, where four men were already climbing the ladder. By the time he arrived on the roof, the soldiers had already dislodged twenty of the clay tiles and peppered the room below with pistol fire.

"Cover me," one of the soldiers declared, reaching into the hole and grabbing a rafter.

"Open the door first," Travis yelled as the man swung into the hole and disappeared over a rapid volley fired by the soldiers into the room below.

Travis hustled forward and to his knees. He peered into the hole and saw two bloody bodies on the floor. He looked toward the trees. Six more dragoons were running for the front door. Travis grabbed the rafter and swung below. His first sight upon entering the room was the door opening and the men charging inside. Fleet of foot, he moved through the building's convoluted maze of halls and rooms. As he did, he heard the roaring gunfire and the shrieks resounding through the house, bouncing off the solid stone walls—the sounds of death continuing for what seemed like minutes. Travis finally found a small room at the back of the house where three unarmed bandits, accompanied by two young black-haired women, only girls, were trying to unhinge a massive door. Travis cocked his hammer. The bandits turned to look. Travis flipped his head back in disbelief, unadulterated pleasure pouring over his soul as he recognized the tiny scar on the chin of one of the villains. It was Grunji, standing in the center of the group.

Travis smiled as one of the bandits stepped forward, trying to utter a word. Travis squeezed the trigger and quickly shot him in the forehead. The bandit fell, his blood splattering on the others. The two girls screeched and balled up on the floor, kicking their bare feet and waving their hands. Travis quickly shot the other bandit without remorse, then stood, silently watching Grunji, bare of chest and panting, standing over the two dead men and quivering girls. He pointed his pistol at the bandit, enjoying the moment too much to pull the trigger.

"Where's your buddy at?" Grunji smiled. He was the devil in person.

Travis heard footsteps behind him. His heart danced, a nervous shimmer, cold sweat forming on his forehead. He didn't want to turn and look, not daring to remove his eyes or barrel from the bandit.

"How many you get?" Chase said.

Travis exhaled a long breath at the familiar voice. He relaxed his trigger finger. "Why don't you sound off before you barge in behind me like that? If I didn't have such a prize in my sights, I might have swung around and shot you. You know how that cramps me, you son of a bitch."

Chase stepped forward beside Travis, a grin on his face. "We got them all, ten, not including these two. Two more women. Why haven't you shot him yet?"

"Going to take him with us. For bait. Maybe Paco will try and come get him."

Chase again smiled. "I like that. Pretty ingenious. You always said you were the brains behind this outfit. This is the first proof I've seen in twenty years. Can I have some fun with him first?" Chase stepped forward, raising the barrel of his heavy pistol and raking it across Grunji's face with all his might. The bandit heaved over, and Chase kicked him in the face, his hard boot sending the ruffian's head back upright.

"That's enough," Travis implored. "We'll have some more fun with him later."

Chapter 24

Travis rolled the light paper around the tobacco, meticulously twisting the ends tightly. He held the cigarette up and licked the paper, then sealed it before putting it in his mouth. He struck a match on his boot and leaned back in the rocking chair on the porch of the Casa del Dorado to look into the street. An old woman was dumping some dirty dishwater off a porch as she watched the parade of soldiers enter town. In the middle of the ten horses walked Grunji, his hands bound behind his back, two separate ropes around his ankles, above his bare feet. The two ropes were each lashed to the saddles of two different horses, ready to jerk him down and tear him apart with any misstep. Grunji walked at the pace of the horses, the ropes sliding down the road in front of him. Beside the horses, two of the girls who had been with Grunji's group walked along slowly, each smoking a cigarette.

The day was still only a few hours old, but the dew had already gone. The damp streets hardened, and the wind and dust picked up. Across the street, five more soldiers were stringing up four of the bandits to the windmill. Two black buzzards pecked and paced the ground below their sagging boots.

"Don't let their blood drip in the tank," Lieutenant Jones yelled at the men, sending the buzzards hopping into flight. "Don't want to contaminate our horses or any of the population with that bad milk."

"This must be a dream come true for you," Chase said, standing behind Travis. "Sitting on the porch, the jefe of the whorehouse, watching the criminals marched down the street."

Travis looked at Chase without a smile, then stared back at the road and the dead dragoon, lashed over the back of one of the horses, on his way to a proper grave.

"Why did you insist on leaving them two gals?" Chase said. "Should've brought them back to town. You won't be in the prostitute business long like that."

"Left them there on purpose with a couple of those bandit horses. We brought the pretty ones with us. One of them is probably Paco or Grunji's girl. The other two will ride off and tell Paco. Maybe he'll show back up here wanting them or Grunji back." Travis looked at his watch, calculating the time. "Been three hours. Hell, anybody can ride to Saltillo and back five or six times between now and dark. He may be here any moment."

Lieutenant Jones arrived at the porch, but did not speak.

"Sit him right here beside me, sir," Travis said. "We'll lash him to one of these posts where the whole town can see him."

One of the soldiers untied the rope from his saddle and tossed it to Chase.

Lieutenant Jones pulled out his watch and looked at it. "We've got to get back to camp tomorrow morning. I'm not going to order you two to come. You've got your own orders, but you're supposed to be back by first light. Orders to be cut for movement to Isabel. We'll cut out of here a couple of hours after lunch. Stay as long as we can."

Travis did not respond or even look at the lieutenant. He raised the cigarette and took a long drag, then looked at Chase, now tying the rope to a post. "Do what you got to do. Soon as I finish my business, I'll be in."

"I know you've got some personal business. It's no business of ours," the lieutenant said, and walked inside.

Travis turned to Grunji. "Might as well sit down, you dumb bastard. Unless you want to stand in the sun all day."

On Travis's words, one of the soldiers shoved the bandit forcefully to the porch. Grunji locked his cold eyes on Travis and slowly sat in a wooden chair. Travis felt none of the reactions in his body induced by fear. He picked up a jug of mescal from the porch, half filling a tin cup. He turned to Grunji. "You want some mescal?" Travis lifted the glass, flipped his wrist, and splashed the liquor in Grunji's face.

The soldiers laughed.

Grunji stared at Travis through his bruised face, never flinching, licking the mescal off his lips.

"If he doesn't show up, we're going to have to shoot Grunji and get back to camp," Chase said, leaning back in his chair. "Guess we'll just march him out of town and shoot him on the road."

Travis set his elbows on the table and looked around the cantina. A few of Jones's men played cards; others cleaned or loaded their pistols, carefully packing the powder and balls. A few more men sat on the porch, keeping an eye on the hostage. It was mid-afternoon, and the cool wind refreshingly blew through the bar's open doors.

"Probably not a good time to get rambunctious," Chase continued. "After that incident with the volunteers. Half the Rangers are pissed off at you. Sure wouldn't want to tempt the bosses with desertion."

"I'm in pursuit of a guerrilla," Travis answered.

"But if you miss that trip to Isabel, that's what they'll call it. I'll probably ride back with the boys. Me and Lieutenant Jones will cover for your ass. We've probably got a few days before we leave. But you'll have to be back by then, with or without Paco."

As Chase spoke, one of the soldiers entered

the saloon. He looked at Chase and Travis with an unsmiling face. "We got company."

Travis jumped to his feet, sliding his pistol up from his holster a few inches, then lowering it to check its freedom. He led Chase out on the porch and looked toward the town's periphery. Just out of shouting distance on the road stood nine horses. Travis's stomach jumped. He let out a slow breath. On three of the horses sat Paco and two more bandits. There were three horses without riders. But on the other horses sat three women, their white and blue dresses and golden hair standing out against the tan and brown mountains in the backdrop. "Everybody hold your fire," Travis said emphatically, his voice crackling. He stepped off the porch and mounted his horse.

"What the hell you doing?" Chase asked, his own voice with a rare touch of rasp.

"I think that's Mercedes and her sisters," Travis turned to look. "If the son of a bitch kills me, start shooting. Try to save the girls best you can." Travis raised his pistol and trotted off in the direction of Paco. As he got closer, he saw the three ropes, each hanging around one of the girls' necks, the other ends tied to the saddles of the three bandits' horses. Travis stopped twenty yards short of the bandits, holding his reins in one hand, his pistol in the other. Paco sat on the lead horse, a musket in his left hand, the barrel pointing upward, the butt on his thigh. He had the reins of Mercedes's horse wrapped around the stub of his missing arm, just below the elbow. Travis took a long, slow breath. An icy chill, as he had never before experienced, went through his body; for a moment everything was a blur.

"Easy," Paco said. "Sure would hate to stir our horses."

Travis did not reply, his mouth hanging open. He continued to look at the ladies, their hands bound behind their backs, their mouths gagged. A piece of tumbleweed blew by, and the dresses fluttered in the wind. Two bandits sat on horseback behind the sisters, their pistols lazily pointing at the backs of the dresses. Travis looked at Mercedes's two sisters; both had their heads down, staring at the saddle horn between their legs. But Mercedes had her eyes locked on Paco, no apprehension on her strong face.

"What do you want?" Travis said, his throat thick, almost too thick to even pass air. He rode forward, his horse moving only one foot at a time.

"I want Grunji. And the girls back. I might give you these. I've already tasted all of them. Good stock but not my type . . . not feisty enough. But it was the first time I've ever stroked a yellow pussy." Paco smiled, exposing his stained, brown teeth. He turned to Mercedes and caressed her cheek with the back of his hand. He lowered her gag and leaned over, kissing her lush, soft lips.

Travis looked at Mercedes. Her expression did not change. She didn't move, didn't react or resist; she just sat lifelessly, her eyes locked on Paco.

Travis spoke to Paco, although he still looked at Mercedes. "Your girls aren't captives. They can go anytime they want. Only low-life, fucking scum would horde women. What's the deal?"

"Let Grunji go." Paco leaned over his horse and spat. "I'll be at that hacienda. You can come over and get the girls. But don't be too long. I may get bored—make them earn their board while I wait, or cut their little ears or hands off. They would be even more beautiful then." Paco reached over and massaged the neck and ears of Mercedes's youngest sister. "I'd leave the cavalry here if you ever want to see them breathing again."

Travis squinted his eyes, anger washing over his body, filling his soul. He started to get dizzy. He reached to his saddle, grabbing his canteen. He poured some cool water in his mouth. "You can have Grunji. But if you harm any of these three, you will regret it. Don't worry about me; I'll catch up with you. If not today, soon. Very soon." Travis wheeled his horse around and rode back to the saloon, where all twenty of the soldiers had their muskets or pistols drawn on the three bandits. Across the street, fifteen of the town's stewards also stood outside, watching the scene. Silence prevailed in the town, the squeaking, turning windmill the only noise.

"Let him go," Travis said, nodding to Grunji. "He's got Mercedes and her two sisters, ropes around their necks, tied to his horses. He wants me to come over and get them at that hacienda we ambushed."

"You going?" Chase said.

Travis did not respond, but stepped onto the porch. He pulled out his knife and cut the ropes around Grunji's ankles and wrists. "You better get out of here before I change my mind."

Grunji slowly stood. He looked at Travis, pulled back his fist, and delivered a handful of knuckles to Travis's cheek. Travis lifted no hand in response. He barely flinched, barely felt the blow, his skin still numb. Chase grabbed the bandit and threw him off the porch. The town got quiet as Grunji boldly walked down the street, the sound of his footsteps drifting in the air.

Chase finally broke the hush. "You going over to that hacienda?"

"No, it's a trap. He's not going to kill them, though. He's knows I'm coming after them. That's what he wants." Travis poured some more water over his hoarse vocal cords.

"I'm going back to camp," Chase said. "Check in. I'll catch up with you on the trail tomorrow or day after. Leave a good trail from that hacienda."

"No need for a trail. I'm going to find Rayo. It won't be long before he hears about this. Find Rayo, you'll find me."

Chapter 25

It was two days later, late in the morning, and Travis lay in the tall green grass on a little knoll looking at the Mexican camp, only fifteen tents along a river. He moved a piece of grass to the side as the sun dipped behind a cloud. He looked up at the sky with suspicion. *Rain?* he thought. Then he froze as a pebble tumbled below and behind him. Travis scrambled around, his thoughts racing. He grabbed his pistol, ready to shoot, and stared at the little meadow behind him. He raised his left hand and cupped his ear.

"Psst. It's me," Chase said.

"Come on up," Travis answered in a hushed voice, and turned back around.

Chase stumbled up the hill and fell down in the grass beside Travis.

"You're getting old . . . or lazy," Travis cautioned. "I heard you."

"That Rayo's camp?"

"Yes. I think. Lazy bunch. Not hardly a soul moving and it's ten thirty. What'd you find in camp? Am I in a shitpot full of trouble?"

Chase plucked a piece of long grass from the hill and put its end in his mouth. "You and ten more Rangers are leaving for Isabel tomorrow. You're officially absent without leave since muster call this morning. I talked Colonel Patrick into letting me stay behind a few days after the main party departs, so I've got a few days. Me and Jones explained everything to him. Didn't seen too worried about it, but if you don't show up tomorrow, you'll be considered deserted. Chester and a couple of those Kentucky boys volunteered to bring you in if you don't show. He's got it out for you, for sure. Colonel Patrick denied their request. Think that's why he let me stay. But if they get their hands on you, he'll have to act. And you can bet they'll be looking for you."

"I won't be back until I get Paco. I guess I'll be a deserter tomorrow morning. I've been every-thing else."

Chase scooted up beside Travis and returned his eyes to the camp. "What's your plan?"

"Just going to ride in there with a white flag. Only been waiting around for more of them to get up, so I don't spook 'em. Looks like Rayo's only got about thirty men."

"Let's get a move on. I've got to be back at camp day after tomorrow. You may not have any trouble tempting the flogger, but not me. I'll be there."

Travis stood, picked up his field glasses, and started back down the hill. "We'll ride in from here, so they can see us easy."

In just five minutes, Travis and Chase were on horseback, approaching the little camp. Travis held his musket high, a white shirt tied to the tip of its barrel. As the two drew near the camp, they stopped a hundred paces from it. Their approach had caught the camp's attention, and two men had saddled up and were riding out to meet them, lances drawn.

The two Mexicans stopped a few horse lengths in front of Travis and Chase. Travis looked them over. They wore the colorful uniforms of Mexican cavalry. Travis held his free hand up, palm toward the two Mexicans. "We want to see the generalissimo, Rayo."

The two soldiers gazed at Travis with a strange look, neither contempt nor curiosity on their faces. Travis felt a little perplexed as he spoke. "Tell him Travis Ross, Texas Ranger, is here to see him."

One of the soldiers nodded to the other, who rode off back to camp. Travis looked at Chase and slowly removed his pistol, its handle toward the Mexican. He dropped it on the ground, then did the same with his lance. Chase also surrendered his weapons. The Mexican soldier slowly turned his horse around and motioned with a hand for the two Texans to follow him.

In the camp, Travis and Chase were removed from their horses and ordered to sit on a flat stone outside a tent, the largest in the camp. No other words were spoken. In the camp, the soldiers were stirring, and a few pots of coffee or iron pans hung over the fires. In less than a minute, a man emerged from the tent. It was Rayo, in full uniform, saber sheathed. Travis had not seen the man in almost a decade. He noticed the Mexican jefe's hair had grayed, his stomach now with a modest pooch.

"The war's over up here," Travis said in a casual voice, not getting up from his seat. "Hasn't anybody told you? You've all been pardoned."

"War's not over until all the invaders are off our soil," Rayo snapped and stomped his foot.

"That's not why I'm here," Travis continued.

"I know why you're here. You're wasting your time. I'm going to kill that rogue this afternoon. Just waiting for my scouts to get back, confirm his location."

"We've got vested interest also. You could use us. We're going to tag along whether you like it or not." Travis finally stood.

"You're the reason my daughters are in this mess. I heard you've been seeing her. It's disgraceful for a Mexican woman to fraternize with the invading filth."

"The women down here sure seem to enjoy it." Travis smiled, his voice thick with sarcasm. "Maybe it's your problem. And if you hadn't've cowardly hauled your daughter off to Mexico, we wouldn't be in this bind. And I have honorable intentions with your daughter. I always have. Don't care what you think about it." Travis's voice rose.

"I'll see you in hell first. I still owe you . . . for my son." Rayo pivoted and backhanded Travis.

The desperate blow rocked Travis. His face burned, but it was the ferocity of the swipe that troubled him. Its force announced the old man's pent-up anger. Travis watched Rayo turn to the side, away from him, and stand without speaking for few moments. Travis noticed the old man's mind measuring, his soul bleeding, his hands wringing, intentions baffled. Travis raised his voice again. "I don't need you anyway. I'm going to kill that bastard with or without you."

"I'm thinking about shooting both of you right now," Rayo snapped.

Travis drooped his shoulders as he heard the words, as they sank in. He looked at Rayo and his resolute face. He knew him well enough to know he was serious. Travis looked at the camp. The men were just now getting up, but thirty on two was no match for even the steadiest Ranger. Travis felt the seriousness of the situation, but not the nervy sensations he usually felt on such occasions, his burning desire to kill Paco much greater than any want to live. "He doesn't care about the girls. It's me he wants. Bring me along, and you'll get him. If not, he'll just run off until I show up. He wants to kill me as bad as you want to cut his throat. I killed his brother and shot his arm off."

Rayo thought a little more. He looked to the hills, his face growing redder. He finally turned to Travis. "All right," he said in a tired voice. "Their camp is about a three- or four-hour ride.

We'll leave in about an hour. But I call the shots. Any funny business, and you two will meet your Maker by way of a Mexican sword."

Mile by mile, Travis rode, picking through the tall hills and rock passes, the country growing higher and more arduous. Around him, the sun shone on the mountains, assuming every shade of color. As he rode, Travis was at a loss for direction and distance. Though they were moving west, Saltillo in the valley below, visible from the promontories, seemed to stay in the same place. The seven horses rode in a line, with Travis and Chase at the rear. The two Rangers had now been following Rayo and his four men for almost three hours.

Travis rode with vigilance, eyes continually scanning every crevice, shadow-draped draw, high ridge in front and back, without the conversation he was known for on the trail. As the monotonous time passed, Travis thought of that episode, ten years earlier, when he'd had Paco in his sights and had let him get away when he'd had a chance to kill him. It was a painful thought that bludgeoned him in the heart. Why had he fired that shot to taunt Paco? A moment's indiscretion had led to this, his worst nightmare, many years later and a world away. Travis looked up. The sky was clear, but to the west, where they were headed, a few thunderheads floated over the lost land, their dark underbellies gloomy, ghostly above their trail, a portent of things to come—not only a change in the weather, but the momentous task at hand. He felt that all his life had led him here, down this trail.

"Might get a rain. Probably a bad one," Chase said, breaking the silence and looking up at the hills. "I get the feeling we're not only in pursuit, we're being followed."

"I got the same feeling," Travis answered. "Any idea who it is?"

"No telling. Could be some of Paco's gang, or just vaqueros moving through the mountains, wanting to stay back from us."

Then Travis saw the buzzards ahead on the trail. His heart ceased to beat for a second. Out in front, Rayo and his men picked up the pace, but Travis slowly moved forward, fear of what lay ahead almost holding him in place. He did not want to cross the next ridge and find out what had drawn the birds.

The first thing he saw were two dead mules, fallen within the past day. They had been shot in the head from point-blank range. The blood had dried hard, but the flies and buzzards had only now started to indulge. Travis looked beside the trail, near a rock projection. There were two bodies. To his relief, neither was Mercedes or one of her sisters. They were a pair of middle-aged Mexicans, half-breeds more white than mestizo, in cattle-working clothes.

Chase got off his horse to inspect the tracks. The nearby turf was trampled with dozens of boot prints, but outside the immediate area, there were more tracks, horse tracks, on the trail. The signs showed at least eight horses coming and going. Chase studied the arcane maze of marks for a few minutes before speaking. "Hard to say. Doesn't look like they were ambushed. Looks like they rode up here toward the bigger party. Got shot without much of a struggle. Then the bigger party, eight or ten, moved on down the trail. Looks like they took two horses with them . . . without riders." Chase picked up a handful of the rock-strewn earth. He let it sift through his fingers and pointed to the smutty remains of a small fire. "I'd say last night or early this morning, before daylight."

"You mean like somebody saw a suspicious party with women bound, rode up to investigate, and got shot."

"Something like that," Chase answered.

Travis turned to look at the somber-faced Rayo, smoking a small Mexican cigar. He and his men still sat horseback, looking at the two dead men. "You know these two men?" Travis asked.

"No. Never seen them."

Travis looked at the men, lying facedown. Both had been shot in the back. "I'd like to stop and bury them. But we don't have time. This bunch is on a killing spree."

"Their camp is just an hour away. We'll know soon enough," Rayo said, turning his horse down the mountain trail. He motioned for his men to move ahead.

Travis put a cigarette to his mouth, tasting the tobacco through the thin paper even before he lit it. He looked down at his saddle and lifted his shoulder, trying to shield the match from the wind as he struck it. He could smell the days-old stench of sweat on his shirt and his oily skin. He looked up ahead; the powerful storm was ready to engulf them. The sun was nowhere in sight, hidden behind the black, fluctuating clouds. A cold burst of wind shot almost straight down from the heavens, putting out the match before he could light the cigarette. "I need a bath anyway," Travis mumbled to himself as he felt the first drop of rain, followed by a dozen more. Disappointed, he removed the smoke from his mouth and discarded it on the trail. Two bolts of lightning streaked across the sky, and his horse snorted in terror.

"There's a cave up this hill," Rayo said, riding back to Travis. He looked up at the sky. "The camp's just over this next hill. Me and one of my men will go scout it. This is a good time. They'll all be taking cover."

"I'm coming with you," Travis demanded, reining in his skittish horse, the rain now pelting his body. He pulled his hat firmly down on his head.

"No. One of my men will lead you to the cave. We'll wait there until after dark," Rayo objected.

Travis looked at Rayo, his face stern and sincere. Travis next gazed at his men, standing beside him. All looked at Travis, their obedience to Rayo unquestioning. "I want to go now. Attack Paco in this bad weather before he moves on."

"No," Rayo snapped. "He's not going anywhere in this storm. We go at night, with cover, when they're drunk or asleep. Moon goes down at midnight. Not going to take any chances. I'm in charge. I told you that before you came."

Travis stared at Rayo with piercing eyes, his insides ablaze with discontent. Night was probably better. He knew that, but he didn't like taking orders from anybody, especially when it came to Paco. He knew Rayo wanted his daughters back as much as he did, but Travis could get them. He was sure of it. He had the skills, the experience, and a sense of burning determination, motivation as he had never had in his life. If Rayo would just point him in the direction, he would kill Paco and get the girls back.

Rayo turned and rode off, leaving a man with Travis and Chase as a wall of water began to fall. Travis bowed his head away from the stinging deluge of rain. Below his horse, the ground transformed from dust to mud. The sky flashed and the air boomed as the ground turned to a red liquid.

Chapter 26

Travis squatted restlessly, antsy in the damp cave. He had been watching the fire for hours, the minutes slipping by, the mesmerizing flames jumping, the wood popping and sizzling, almost intoxicating. A coolness from the rain pervaded the night. Travis shook the sleep out of one of his feet as he looked outside at the darkness. He removed his watch from his pocket and scooted closer to the fire to check the time. It was eleven o'clock. On the hard rock floor, behind him, Chase slept on a blanket, gently snoring.

Rayo entered the cave with his four men.

Travis reached over and shook Chase's leg until he came to.

Rayo walked over and tossed two wet pieces of wood on the fire. "We go in soon. They're in three houses close together—stone walls, thatch roofs—probably eight bandits and the girls. No shots until we're inside. We'll stab the guards." Rayo grabbed a long spear from one of his men. It was made of thick, black iron, but had a sharp, shiny tip. He held up the long rod as if he were about to throw it. "When we kill the guards, we go in all buildings. Kill all the guerrillas. It will take us an hour to sneak up there." Rayo removed his pistol from his holster and checked to make sure it was loaded. "We go now."

It was an hour-long ride in the darkness, the horses slipping and sliding in the mud. Most of the ride was downhill until the group broke free of the mountains, onto an open plain. Travis could see little, only noticing the terrain had flattened. Even after an hour in the night air, he saw no farther than a few feet up the trail. Beyond that there was only blackness, not even the outlines of the mountains in the distance. Finally, he saw a light, only a yellow speck a couple of hundred yards up the trail.

Rayo stopped and dismounted, tying his horse to some sage. There were only the sounds of creaking leather, sabers rattling in their sheaths, spurs jingling, and the rustling of brush.

Travis felt as sick as he had ever felt before. He was not worried for his own safety; he had already prepared himself to die right here if need be. But he worried that Paco would kill Mercedes, something he had no control over. It would take the full repertoire of his wits to get her. He felt his mind focus, his movements become precise.

"We move up the side of this road. This old hacienda has a gate," Rayo whispered, appearing to point up the road, only the whites of his eyes visible. "The gates are the only way in. We'll sneak up there. If there's a guard, we'll stab him and then go in."

Travis turned to the darkness, then to Chase, only a dark figure. He turned back to Rayo, but the old Mexican had already disappeared into the night. He swung his leg over his horse. "We'll sneak up there and jump that wall. Won't bother with those guards. Follow me."

Travis then scurried off the road about twenty paces into the sage. He started walking toward the light, his only guide. It took the two Rangers only a minute or two to arrive at the hacienda's fence. They saw the light hanging outside a gate. It illuminated the entrance and nothing more. Travis saw no movement, no guards, no Rayo or his men. Travis hunched low and crept forward until he felt the rough adobe wall of the fence. He pulled Chase to him, grabbing his hands and clasping them together. He stepped into Chase's hands, and his partner stood, shoving him up. Travis swung a leg over the top of the fence and reached back down to pull Chase up.

The two Rangers quietly, slowly lowered their boots until they felt the ground. Travis looked around, his heart beating fast. His mind rapidly processed what little he saw: the faint images of the three buildings. The one in the center looked the largest. Travis removed his pistol from his holster and grabbed Chase by the arm, tugging on him. He led his partner to within a few feet of the largest building.

Chase pointed to the door; it was open. He motioned that he would creep forward and strike a match.

Travis tiptoed to the door behind Chase. He changed his pistol hand for a second to dry his sweaty palm on his pants, then quietly stepped across the threshold, not hearing a sound from inside. The scratching of the phosphorus broke the silence. The darkness suddenly turned yellow. As it did, two gunshots broke the silence from outside. Travis scanned the room, his vision sharp, his head turning quickly. He saw a blur of white in the corner: dresses. On a wooden bed, there were three more people: two bandits and a woman. The two bandits woke with heavy, sleepy, vexed eyes and looked at Travis and Chase. But both woke to find instant death as Travis put a shot in each man's head, the gun blasts echoing through the little house and the blood spraying the woman between them. Travis reached down on the floor and grabbed a candle that he handed to Chase.

Chase lit the candle, and the room brightened more as more gunshots came from outside.

Travis made a quick inspection of the little house. It had no more rooms. He turned to the corner. Both of Mercedes's sisters were on the floor. Travis quickly stepped to the bed. He grabbed both bandits by the hair, lifting their bloody heads. Neither was Paco or Grunji. He did not recognize the young mestiza girl still on the bed, now wearing terror on her face.

"Cut the girls loose and keep an eye on them,"

Travis mumbled softly, turning to Chase. Then he bolted out of the house. As he ran to the next door, he tripped on something and fell to the ground, his mouth tasting the wet dirt. He quickly regained his feet and entered to the next house. At the door, he lit another match and looked inside. The stone walls held nothing but an empty wood cot covered with a wool blanket. Travis reached down and felt the wool. It was still warm. He ran back outside, looking around frantically, but there was still just black. He looked at the third house. Its door glowed. He saw Rayo and two of his men entering. He dashed in that direction, arriving at the door in only seconds and panting heavily.

Inside the third house, Rayo and his two men stood, a candle lighting the room. Rayo's juniors held their pistols on Grunji and another woman, one of the two Paco had taken from the Casa del Dorado. Both were completely naked, their eyes roving. From the door, Travis watched Rayo hit Grunji over the head with the long spear, asking where his daughter and Paco were. Grunji stood still, barely breathing. In a fit, Rayo backhanded the woman so forcefully, she hit the wall and fell to the ground.

Chase arrived beside Travis with Mercedes's two sisters. Travis slowly walked inside, Chase and the girls behind him, his blood boiling. Grunji looked at Travis, his last look. Without ceremony, Travis raised his pistol and shot the bandit in the face. He then holstered the gun, tightened his fist, and punched Rayo in the mouth, expending every inch of his strength.

The old, gray-haired Mexican fell to the ground.

Travis looked at Chase, who had Rayo's subordinates in his sights. He then grabbed Rayo's long spear off the floor, raised it high, and with an roar chopped down at the two soldiers' arms, knocking the pistols from their hands. Travis, his face bulging and red with fury, bent over and grabbed Rayo by his flashy jacket and shook him a few times. He threw the frail man to the floor and grabbed his pistol, putting it to Rayo's chest. "He's gone, took Mercedes with him. We've got your two youngest daughters. Gone because of that fucked-up plan of yours. Can't track him till daylight. I've about had all the Mexican incompetence I can stand. Go over there and look at the thousands of unburied bones in the valley if you don't know how fucked up you are. If you would have let me come over here this afternoon, all these bandits would be dead, and you'd have your daughters back, all of them. Paco does not care about them; it's me he wants." Travis dropped his pistol and stood, his head dizzy, seeing stars.

Chase stepped forward, putting his hand calmly on Travis's chest. "He can't go far. He'll be easy to track on this wet ground. And like you said, it's you he wants. He'll get his wish tomorrow."

Travis, his heart beating slower, his mind returning to normal, reached over and grabbed the spear. He casually laid it on Rayo's chest. "If you promise to behave, I'll take you with us. If you don't, I'm going kill you."

"We need to get these girls back to safety," Chase said. "And two of Rayo's men are dead."

Travis walked over to the girls, their long, straight hair covering their faces. He was still so mad, he felt no pity. He looked at Rayo, getting up from the floor. He had shamed him in front of his daughters—daughters that the old man had just risked his life for. He felt a tad contrite and looked at Rayo's two men. "Your two can take the girls back. We'll go kill Paco tomorrow."

Rayo nodded an affirmative.

"All of us will leave at first light," Chase said.

Chapter 27

All morning long and into the afternoon, they rode, Travis leading, following Paco's trail. It was easy to spot on the still-wet ground, and Paco was making no attempt to cover his way. In fact, they had crossed two streams, and the bandit had made no attempt to use either to cover his tracks. Travis looked ahead; the ground was lowering but becoming harsher. The hills were getting smaller and more broken. There were more and more jagged outcroppings and less and less smooth earth. As Travis cantered along, he kept seeing Paco in his mind, ducking out from behind one of the tall rocks, emptying his pistol at the three men, his evil laugh echoing off the hard stones.

Chase pulled abreast of Travis. He removed his hat, ran his hands over his head, and took a drink from his canteen, gulping the water as it splashed over his chin and down onto his shirt. "What you thinking?" Chase asked.

"Not much," Travis said. "Whoever that was following us yesterday, is still on our tail. I saw them descending that tall ridge 'bout two miles back."

"Probably nothing," Chase said.

Travis looked at Rayo and his puckered lip. The Mexican had been riding quietly all morning.

Travis still felt bad about the previous night. He had always liked the jefe. And he had spent many an hour thinking about the old man. Why had he robbed him of his daughter? *Maybe it was his son,* Travis thought, thinking of that morning on the Texas coast. He looked at Rayo. "We'll get him today."

"He's close," Rayo said with no emotion. As with Travis, it was apparent that only one thing mattered to the old man now. "These hills play out in about five miles. Then the land opens up, flat for two days' ride."

"I hope so," Chase said, looking at their surroundings with the lazy alertness he was known for. "Because I'm heading back to camp tomorrow. Got to catch a ship to Vera Cruz."

"Hell, he may be watching us now," Travis said, looking ahead at the bleak land, fit only for bats, spiders, and scorpions.

"Don't think so," Chase answered. "I've been watching pretty good. We've had a good sun at our backs all morning."

Travis bit his lip. He looked at Chase. "You think you can handle Paco if you run into him by yourself?"

"Shoot," Chase said. "If it had been me back on that ditch bank in Texas, we wouldn't be here right now."

"Why don't you branch off? If we find him, one of us will have a reserve coming in that he doesn't know about." Travis took a drink from his canteen.

"I'll do that." Chase grinned. "Even if he gets you, I'll kill him before I go."

Travis looked at the morass of rocks ahead, a brown, uneven expanse of earth, and drove his heels into his horse's flanks, leaving Chase on the trail. He and Rayo rode on for about twenty minutes until the path squeezed through a tight arroyo. Travis stopped, studying the gap in the hills for a few moments. Not seeing anything, he cautiously rode into the arroyo, squinting his eyes. The sun, now halfway down the western sky, exacerbated the intense glare off the bright brown rocks. In the arroyo, the spiky stones and horses cast long, dark shadows. Then, some movement caught Travis's eye. He looked up to a high ledge, a quarter mile distant.

Paco was standing, legs spread, waiving his hat. "Here I am," the bandit yelled, taking three steps to reach down and pick up a body. "Here she is. Come get her."

Travis's and Rayo's horses sidestepped quickly, as if they were spooked. Travis narrowed his eyes. He could see Mercedes twisting, struggling, swinging her bound hands in despair. Everything inside him squirmed as the faint echo of her voice fell down the hill. Travis trotted forward behind some rocks and Paco disappeared. He scanned the hill, trying to find a route up. He

307

didn't see an easy one. *Paco must have come up from the back side*, he thought. Overhead, he studied a steep but climbable slant, about two hundred feet to the summit. At the top, where he had seen Paco, the rocks contorted and turned in every direction—a labyrinth of outcroppings and crevices.

Travis pulled back on his reins and looked at Rayo. "We're going to have to climb up there."

"I can climb up there. I grew up climbing these hills," Rayo said.

Travis dismounted and hobbled his horse. He then started to move up the hill, around the boulders, slowly ascending. He stopped twice in the shade of the rocks to drink from his canteen before continuing the climb. Finally, after twenty minutes of work, he paused in a deep cut, fighting for breath. He found a good flat spot and sat, resting. He removed his canteen and finished his water as Rayo crawled up beside him, just as winded.

Travis took two quick breaths, then leaned his head against the rock. "I think we might even be above him. Down below this big rock. Soon as we catch our breaths. We'll skirt around it. See if we can see him."

Rayo also gulped his water and gave a nod. "I'm ready now."

Travis secured his footing, leaning against a vertical piece of granite. He led Rayo along a dangerous strip of dirt; any slip would send either man cascading down two hundred feet. In just a minute, the ground got more level, the footing better. Travis looked at a house-sized boulder. He motioned that he would circle around to the left.

Rayo, without answering, walked out of sight around the right side of the boulder. Travis crawled forward on his hands and knees until the rocks opened up, a large area of the mountain now in his view. He searched forward, moving only his eyes. He almost did not believe what he saw. Paco was squatting behind a boulder, fifty yards ahead. Travis froze and held his breath. He lifted his pistol and rested his elbows on the ground. His mind was calm, his vision focused. He saw only Paco. He slowly pulled back on the gun's hammer with his thumb, trying not to produce any noise. Then he covered Paco's ribs with his sights and squeezed the trigger. The shot rang out. The pistol bucked. Paco squealed and fell to his knees, grasping at his left leg with his good arm. Travis put his sights on the bandit again, but Paco quickly grabbed Mercedes and disappeared behind some rocks.

Travis heard some movement somewhere behind him. He wheeled around. It was Rayo, crawling up beside him.

"You get him?"

"Got him in the leg. He got in behind those rocks. Bastard's got nine lives. I'll give him that.

Stay here. I'm going up there to finish him off."

Travis got to his feet and dashed into the opening, ducking behind a large rock. He peered around it, pistol at the ready. He looked ahead until he located a little draw where surely he could see where Paco had fled. He came to his feet and ran forward, half expecting to hear some shots as he dived into the draw. All was quiet. He gathered himself and looked around—no Paco. Shaking his head, he ran to the rocks where he had last seen Paco. There, he found a pool of blood and two sets of tracks, one dragging the other.

The silence broke. Mercedes's harsh voice filtered through the boulders. "Shoot him! Shoot him now!"

Travis turned around. He saw Rayo standing, his pistol drawn. Then he heard a shot. There was a moment's pause, followed by a second blast.

Rayo fell to his knees out of sight.

Travis ran forward, stopping and resting against a rock wall. He wiped some sweat from his eyes. As he did, he heard the shuffle of rocks behind him, then an excruciating sound: a metallic click. He turned his head to see Paco, silhouetted against the sun only a few feet away, only a brown mask surrounded by hair. The bandit's pistol was pointed at Travis's head.

Travis exhaled a long breath as he relaxed his tense muscles and stared at death; his thoughts and vision raced into a haze. It couldn't be. His soul sank, his blood got cold, as if he were dying before the impact of the bullet. He looked down at his pistol, a lifetime away, at his hip. Paco's pistol was steady, only gently rocking with his hard breath.

Travis squinted his eyes and locked them on Paco, trying to distract him, coax him into a chest shot. Maybe he would get a round off before he slipped away into eternity.

As Travis calculated, ready to jerk his pistol, a sharp noise rang out, a gunshot, and Paco careened over sideways, falling to the ground. Travis looked straight into the sun, and his chest collapsed as he pushed out all his air. He stood in a dumb state of nothingness. He reached and felt his face in disbelief. Was he hallucinating? Was this the afterlife? He looked over to where the gunshot had come from. Mercedes stood, her hands still bound, holding her father's still-smoking gun. She dropped the gun and fell to her knees. Travis slid down the rock wall and rolled over onto his hands and knees. He caught his breath for a few moments before standing.

He slowly walked over to Mercedes and lifted her unresponsive body up off the ground. Pulling her close, he held her tight. She put her bound arms around his neck, squeezing him. He felt her shoulders and soft, feminine legs quiver. He heard her crying beneath her hair. Over her shoulder, the Mexican sky was big, blue, and

311

spotless, like a huge dome over the land, broken only by the sun, hanging atop the western sierra. In the still of the afternoon, no wind spoke in the rocks and trees. Travis pressed Mercedes against his chest in a firm hug and brushed her hair gently. "It's going to be all right. He's gone."

Travis looked down at Paco. Dead, stretched out on the ground, he didn't look that daunting or scary. His lips had already started to turn gray. Mercedes sniffled and removed her head from Travis's shoulder. She looked down at her father, then Paco. She bent over and spat on the bandit, her dry mouth's shortage of saliva having little impact, then kicked him twice in the ribs. Travis almost laughed, a sad chuckle, and wiped her wet eyes.

She put her arms back around Travis's neck. "You're taking me with you now, for sure. I'm not going to let you ride off for the sunset this time."

"Don't worry. That's what I had planned." Travis backed up from Mercedes. He untied the ropes around her wrists and looked down at Rayo, sprawled out on the ground. Travis reached down and removed the old man's belt, looping it around one of his arms. "I'll drag him down. We'll find a nice place to bury him—somewhere you can come to visit him in the future."

Chapter 28

Travis flopped Rayo's dusty body over the back of his horse, setting him properly for what he thought might be several hours of riding out of the hills. He looked up at the sky and turned to Mercedes, who was out of sight, twenty paces away, sitting in the cool shade of a large rock outcropping, cleaning her face from his canteen. Travis cocked his head and yelled, "There's still four or five hours of light remaining. We need to get going. You can pretty up later."

"What?" Mercedes yelled back.

As Travis reached over to remove a piece of rope from his saddle, he heard some jingling behind him. He casually looked over his shoulder, thinking Chase had arrived. But suddenly, out of nowhere, he saw two men—and a long pistol muzzle—in his face. He locked up, and his skin instantly got sweaty and cool. The bright sun stood just over the men's heads, and he saw only their silhouettes atop their horses. Then he felt the cold steel of the pistol barrel touch his cheek. Straining and squinting his eyes, he slowly, quietly sidestepped a few paces, the pistol staying to his face, until he got at an angle where he could see the men.

"You want take him in for desertion?" a voice sounded from the sun and behind the pistol.

"I say we just kill him here. Not worried about that other stuff," another voice said, laughing.

Travis looked at the shadowy figures, cautiously putting his hand above his eyes and maneuvering his palm until he saw the two men. One was Chester, who leaned over in his saddle to an even better angle so Travis would see his sick grin and big white teeth. The other was a volunteer. Travis recognized him from that day at the hacienda—the rapist he had faced down in the hall. Chester moved back over his saddle and sat casually, no weapon drawn, leaning over his horse's neck, his forearms resting on his pommel.

"I thought he was tough," the volunteer said.

"Pretty easy to find. Just had to follow Chase out of camp," Chester said. He paused and looked away. "What do we have here?"

Travis felt his throat get thick as he slowly turned his head. Mercedes had come out from behind the rocks. She now stood, in her dirty dress, canteen in her hand, her big eyes flabbergasted. Travis watched the color drain from her face.

"This must be his greaser woman . . . the one he's been looking for," Chester said. "After you kill him, maybe you'd like to finish that business Lieutenant Ross interrupted you from, ah, Tuff."

Travis felt himself shake in fear and rage. He

noticed it. It was a first. He could never remember shaking before. His teeth gnashed uncontrollably. His eyes watered from the sun and still thwarted his attempts to see Chester's face. Just as his fury became uncontrollable and he was about to lunge at Chester in a final, desperate dance with death, the quiet of the arroyo was suddenly punctured with a bang. The pistol fell from Travis's face as the man behind it heaved over to the side, falling from his horse.

Travis jerked his pistol from its holster and tried to draw a bead on Chester, who had spurred his horse and galloped forward. But Travis's vision was still gone from staring into the sun. Almost blind, Travis saw only a red blur. He dived to the ground in the shade as a second shot filled his ears. "Run, Mercedes! Get out of here!" Travis yelled, a little sight returning. "Is that you, Chase?"

Another shot rang out. "Yes."

Travis heard a horse heave and blow. He stood and looked at Chester, getting up from his dying horse and turning to face him, only twenty paces away. Chester pulled his pistol. In the scarlet haze of Travis's vision, the Ranger looked as if he moved in slow motion, the pistol slowly moving up. Travis covered Chester's torso with his pistol barrel and jerked back on the trigger, never feeling the recoil. He heard the bullet smash into flesh. Chester fell backward, dropping his pistol, just as Travis looked into the hostile barrel.

Travis dropped his own pistol, his ears ringing, his vision still dubious. He looked around at the two dead soldiers, then at Rayo. Death surrounded him. He heard more sounds: boots hitting the ground. He didn't turn to look. "I hope that's you, Chase."

"It is."

Travis turned to Mercedes. She had not moved a step during the shoot-out. He felt Chase's hand on his numb shoulder.

"I'm guessing you killed Paco?" Chase walked over to Travis's horse to look at Rayo.

"He got Rayo. Had me in his sights. She killed him." Travis nodded to Mercedes. He walked over to his own horse and climbed into the saddle.

Chase looked up at him, then looked at the sun. He paused a minute. "I need to get going—back to camp. Looks like we had a big shoot-out. Killed Paco and Grunji. Left you for dead in the care of some Mexicans. Couple of guerrillas must have gotten these two while they were out on patrol." Chase looked at Mercedes, now sitting on horseback beside Travis. "Where you two going?"

"Probably Durango. She's got a ranch there. Maybe I'll stay a while."

"Don Ross de Rayo del Durango, huh?" Chase smiled.

"Kind of like the sound of that," Travis professed, turning and grinning at Mercedes. He extended his hand to Chase. "After you get to Mexico City, come see me. I might need a ranch boss by then."

"Will do."

"Do me one more favor before you get on that boat. Get word to her sisters where we're at."

"I'll take care of all that." Chase reared back his hand and slapped Travis's horse, sending him on his way.

AUTHOR'S NOTE

The Mexican War was the first American war fought outside the United States. It would rage on for another year before General Winfield Scott and his army would eventually subdue the Mexican capital and the Americans would force the Treaty of Guadalupe Hidalgo on the Mexican nation.

This treaty ceded to the United States all of the states of Arizona, California, Nevada, New Mexico, Texas, and Utah, as well as portions of Colorado, Kansas, Oklahoma, and Wyoming. It fulfilled America's dream of Manifest Destiny, to rule the North American continent, and marked the beginning of America's climb to world power.

Out of this war came the soldiers and tactics that led to the incalculable slaughter in the Civil War twenty years later. Among the soldiers who gained their fame on the Mexican landscape were William Tecumseh Sherman, Stonewall Jackson, George Meade, Franklin Pierce, Ulysses S. Grant, Robert E. Lee, and Jefferson Davis.

And what of Mexico? Unlike America, the war was a tragedy for Mexico that it would not rise from. The country counted thousands of dead, half its territory lost, and many of its cities destroyed. For most of the next eighty years, the bountiful land would smolder in almost continual war, poverty, and dictatorship. The war, known to the Mexicans as the American Intervention, provoked a profound resentment for the colossus of the north that still resonates into the twenty-first century.

Center Point Publishing
600 Brooks Road • PO Box 1
Thorndike ME 04986-0001 USA

(207) 568-3717

US & Canada:
1 800 929-9108
www.centerpointlargeprint.com